PRAISE FOR C

Mystery and magic combine in this charming tale of murder and mayhem.

— KIRKUS REVIEWS ON *THE GRIM STEEPER*

A compelling debut with a mature amateur sleuth, a solid supporting cast, and a cat to rival Miranda James's Diesel. For readers who enjoy the paranormal elements in Juliet Blackwell's and Bree Baker's cozies.

— LIBRARY JOURNAL STARRED REVIEW OF *STEEPED TO DEATH*

A fantastic series debut, this twisty mystery has all the cozy goodness – baked goods, enchanted tea blends, a bookstore, a fat orange cat, a charming small town full of quirky characters, and a witchy heroine who's funny, smart, and strong . Just my cup of tea!

— BAILEY CATES, *NEW YORK TIMES* BESTSELLING AUTHOR

A story that will fit you to a "tea" from page one, Gretchen Rue has crafted a cozy that will warm your heart, keep you reading late into the night, and leave you wishing for a little magic of your own. Don't miss this one!

— PAIGE SHELTON, *NEW YORK TIMES* BESTSELLING AUTHOR

"[A] charming, magical cozy."

— - BOOKLIST ON *DEATH BY A THOUSAND SIPS*

EARL GRAVE TEA
A WITCHES' BREW NOVEL

GRETCHEN RUE

Copyright © September 16, 2025 by Ashley MacLennan

Cover art by Adrian DKC

Hardcover ISBN 978-1-939291-47-9

Paperback ISBN 978-1-939291-48-6

All rights reserved.

No part of this book may be reproduced in any form or by any electronic or mechanical means, including information storage and retrieval systems, without written permission from the author, except for the use of brief quotations in a book review.

For Amanda T, who very politely informed me that if Raven Creek were real, it would be a desert, and not rainy, and who graciously accepted, "I guess the weather there is magic, too," as an explanation. Here's to magical rainy deserts.

CHAPTER ONE

"By the pricking of my thumbs, something wicked this way comes."

I glanced up from where I was crouched behind the counter of my tea shop-slash-bookstore, The Earl's Study, to focus on my full-time salesperson, Imogen Prater. I'd been doing an inventory of my loose-leaf teas to see what needed to be restocked and which seasonal summer teas I could further discount to make room for fall and winter blends.

Imogen was staring out the front window, and while it was hard to see her expression from my position on the floor, her stiff demeanor told me I wasn't going to like what she was looking at.

Imogen didn't usually bust out the Shakespeare quotes on a whim.

The bell over our front door jangled, and I got to my feet, cursing my late-thirties knees and joints for slowly starting to turn on me. The moment I was standing, I wished I had stayed on the floor.

The unmistakable bright red hair of Raven Creek's resident busybody—and my self-declared nemesis—Dierdre Miller was standing in our foyer, shaking her umbrella off just outside the door.

Raven Creek was nestled deep in the heart of Washington state, a good drive from both Seattle and any other nearby settlement. Aside from the small city of Barneswood about twenty minutes away, our closest neighbor was an old mining ghost town.

That made our little town one of those places where everyone knew everyone, at least by sight, and Dierdre Miller made it her business to know everyone's gossip as well.

About a month ago, her nephew Dylan had finally had the grand opening of his artisanal soap and candle shop At Wick's End just two doors down from The Earl's Study, and unfortunately that meant Dierdre was showing up a lot more frequently as she ostensibly passed by on her way to pay him a visit.

From all my encounters with Dylan—which had been admittedly scant—he seemed like a nice enough guy. He was in his late twenties, and was polite and friendly whenever he came around, though he did seem incredibly shy.

It had to be hard transitioning his totally online business into a brick and mortar one, and I wondered sometimes if his nervous energy would be an issue when it came to making sales.

The Earl's Study had been undergoing the opposite transition over the previous year, as we tried to adapt to the changing times and get our books and tea available online. I was forever grateful to my full-time online retail employee, Daphne, for handling that aspect of the store, because she was an absolute whiz with online formats and social media. I swear she had single-handedly doubled our monthly sales. I made sure her pay reflected her efforts.

Dierdre dropped her damp umbrella into the umbrella stand at the door and flashed a smile at us, though it was about as friendly as the toothy grin of a moray eel.

"Ladies, how are you both this morning?" She wore a bright red raincoat that clashed horribly with her hair, and her mascara had smudged under her eyes. Normally I might tell someone about their melting makeup, but Dierdre wasn't exactly my favorite person in the world. She'd figure it out eventually.

"Morning, Dierdre," I said to keep Imogen from saying what she was really feeling, because it probably would have been along the lines of *fine until you walked in*.

Right now, Dierdre was being too smiley. Too nice.

She wanted something.

"Can I get you a cup of tea?" I asked, hoping she would decline. It was, however, definitely cup of tea weather. The calendar page had just flipped to October the previous week, and our almost too-warm September weather had vanished right along with it.

I was a huge fan of fall, but the change had felt more abrupt than usual this year. Leaves were now changing at a steady clip, and as soon as the rain let up, Imogen, Daphne and I would get to work on the exterior Halloween display for the shop.

Raven Creek was *obsessed* with holidays. It was one of the big draws that brought tourists out of their way to visit us, despite our remote location. The holidays were never subtle here, and that, combined with our town's mishmash of incongruous European architecture, made Raven Creek an idyllic spot to visit any time of the year.

Dierdre made a face at my offer of tea, then shook her

head. "No thank you, Phoebe, though I'm sure you've whipped up something lovely for the season."

There were several good reasons why Dierdre was hesitant to eat or drink in my shop, so I didn't hold the unintentional grimace against her.

When I'd first arrived in town after the death of my beloved Aunt Eudora, having been left her house, her business, and her chubby orange tabby cat named Bob, I had thought that was the extent of the curveballs she had posthumously thrown at me.

As it turned out, she had one more.

Not only was I now a cat mom, but I was also a witch. It was something I was still adjusting to a year after finding out the truth, and sometimes when I worked magic it went a little... wrong. Dierdre had been at the receiving end of one of my first efforts to combine witchcraft and baking, and while I don't think she really understood what had happened, she had been a little on edge in my shop ever since.

Unfortunately, that hadn't stopped her from visiting us three times this week already. Except this time, she definitely looked to be a woman on a mission. She also looked eager for us to ask why she was here, something I didn't particularly want to indulge her in.

"Did you want us to order a book for you?" Imogen asked.

Bob, who had been dozing on one of the armchairs in the bookstore half of the shop, had come meandering into the foyer. Often, he would rub up against newly arrived customers by way of greeting, but he took one look at Dierdre and hissed.

I covered my mouth to stifle a laugh.

I guess I couldn't force all my staff to be polite.

Dierdre shot Bob an unfriendly look, which did nothing to boost my warmth in seeing her here. I hadn't been a cat person before I inherited Bob, but I'd quickly come to realize that I trusted his opinion more than that of most humans I knew.

Bob just fundamentally understood when people were no good and wasn't afraid to be vocal about it.

Still, Dierdre wasn't evil; she was just mean, so I gently shooed Bob back into the bookstore, where he returned to his armchair. In the spot beside him, our daily regular Mr. Loughery was snoozing with a copy of a Patricia Cornwell book propped open on his stomach. A cup of Irish Breakfast tea was growing cold beside him.

I'd much rather be in there with them than out here, but alas, my luck wasn't that good, and I hadn't yet found a spell that could block Dierdre from coming into the store.

Dierdre straightened herself primly and seemed ready to get to the point of why she'd come. "As you know," she began as if reading from a rehearsed speech. "Raven Creek is well known for our Halloween festivities. And as a member of the Town Council, it falls on me to make sure we are constantly finding new and innovative ways to draw tourists in for these major holiday events."

Imogen and I just stared at her, not sure if she needed us to interact with her, or simply listen to the speech like a good little audience. We both opted for the latter, though I gamely gave my head a quick nod to prove that we were paying attention. Maybe it would hurry her along.

"I'm incredibly pleased to announce that I... we have outdone ourselves entirely this year." She clapped her hands together delightedly, causing Mr. Loughery to awaken with a start in the other room, letting out a small *oof* of surprise.

It was Imogen's turn to fight back laughter this time.

Dierdre did her best to ignore us, which for some reason only made me want to laugh more. I could sense a fit of the giggles was on the cusp of overtaking both Imogen and me and hoped that Dierdre would be gone before the unladylike snort laughing began.

Dierdre chugged along, unstoppable. "I'm thrilled to say that Raven Creek has landed a very rare performance from the Seattle-based improv troupe Something Wicked, and they'll be doing a one night only showing of both Edgar Allen Poe's 'The Raven' and a stage adaptation of Agatha Christie's *And Then There Were None*."

I had anticipated Dierdre's news would be a bit of a letdown, but this was anything but. When I'd lived in Seattle, my ex-husband Blaine and I had season tickets to the theater where Something Wicked performed. Their shows were high-energy, compelling, and often incredibly funny spins on old classics. Several actors from the troupe had gone on to become big Hollywood stars, and sometimes they would pop up for performances with no notice, making it an exciting gamble to know you could see an Oscar-winner or A-list comedienne in your performance of an improv spin on *Hamlet* on any given night.

"Dierdre, that's incredible. How did you manage that?" I wasn't above giving her credit where credit was due. Something Wicked rarely travelled for engagements, and coming to a small town like Raven Creek would be a huge coup for the community.

"Well, as it turns out, Dylan was dating one of the cast members when he was living in Seattle, and they remained quite close. He was able to pull some strings." Apparently,

Dierdre *could* give other people credit, as long as it doubled as an opportunity for her to brag about her beloved nephew.

I wasn't going to complain.

"Are they the ones who did a performance of *As You Like It* while dressed as inflatable T-Rexes?" Imogen asked.

I nodded eagerly. "I got to see that performance; it was incredible." Reviews had been mixed as to whether it was genius or an abomination against the Bard, but I had been wheezing so hard from laughing I had to give it to the performers. It had been unforgettable.

"That, of course, brings me to why I'm here." Dierdre needed the attention back on her. "For starters, we are hoping you will display a sign prominently in your store's window."

"Absolutely. We'll put a few up around the store."

Dierdre rifled through her large purse and handed me a few papers, which were miraculously pristine, given that they'd been in her bag.

She waited, and I wasn't exactly sure what she wanted from me next, so I put the papers down on the counter and met her expectant gaze. "Was there something else?" I asked.

"Yes, well... You see, while the Something Wicked crew will be performing 'The Raven,' it's going to be up to locals to fill the roles for *And Then There Were None*. So, I'm counting on the staff of The Earl's Study to turn out for auditions. Even if you don't think you want to participate, we don't want to seem like we're poor sports, do we?"

She handed me another paper, this one with audition details for later that week, and a place online to download the audition scene. I glanced over at Imogen, who I expected to be making some kind of face, but instead she grabbed the paper out of my hand and was immediately absorbed in the details.

"I don't think anyone wants to see me act, Dierdre," I said.

"And while I'm sure that's true, Phoebe, I expect to see you there all the same."

CHAPTER TWO

Dierdre left, back into the rain, taking her scathing last words with her, and once she was gone, Mr. Loughery toddled out of the bookstore, carrying his mug of tea, and joined us at the counter.

"Did I hear that old Nosy Nancy say there were going to be acting auditions?"

Imogen handed him the paper. "According to this, they're casting all genders, ages, and races, so you and I both have a chance, Norman." She beamed at him.

"I'll be the age, you be the beauty," he said with a smirk, and for the first time since I'd met her, I saw Imogen blush. Mr. Loughery was too smooth. We had to find him a lady friend, lest his championship flirting skills go to waste.

"Let's make a deal," Imogen said. "If you agree to audition, I'll agree to audition."

Mr. Loughery mulled this over before giving a decisive nod and extending his hand for a shake. "Miss Imogen, you've got yourself a deal."

They shook on it, then turned and looked at me expectantly. I held my hands up as if to push their eager gazes away from me. "I wasn't kidding; no one wants to see me act. I auditioned *once* for *Fiddler on the Roof* in high school, and they banished me to set design for the rest of the time I was there."

"That's a musical, though," Imogen protested. "Just because you can't sing doesn't mean you can't act."

"One: ouch. Two: I promise you, for my own mental well-being, this is something I'm just going to have to sit out."

Imogen and Mr. Loughery were inflexible. They stood side-by-side, Imogen's arms crossed, and Mr. Loughery's brow cocked, and between the two of them, I was having a hard time coming up with a good excuse. I mean, there was no harm in auditioning—except maybe to my ego when I got rejected.

Bob sauntered into the room and sat where he could see me, then let out a long *mreeowwwww* noise, as if he just wanted to participate.

I threw my hands up in the air, then grabbed Mr. Loughery's empty mug from his hand before offering up a handshake to the both of them. They high fived each other.

"But when I get laughed out of the auditions, you two are responsible for the emotional damage, just know that."

Imogen held a hand over her heart. "I promise to bring ice cream and give you a pillow to scream into, but honestly, Phoebe, no one is going to laugh at you."

"Well, that remains to be seen." I topped up Mr. Loughery's Irish Breakfast and handed the mug back to him. It was one of our Earl's Study branded mugs that he'd insisted on buying and asked to keep behind the counter for him.

Ever since Mr. Loughery's wife died, he'd been a staple in the bookshop, something that pre-dated even my ownership. He came in almost every morning, sat down with his tea and whatever mystery series he was working his way through, and stayed well into the afternoon. About half of that time was spent napping, but just having him around was a soothing presence. It also meant our staff were very rarely actually alone in the place.

When I'd started to bring Bob into work with me, I'd worried people might not like to see a cat wandering around, but I'd been a hundred percent wrong to be concerned. For one, he had formed a fast friendship with Mr. Loughery, and the two tended to nap at the same time in their side-by-side chairs.

The other bonus of having Bob around was it got people enthusiastic about having their own cats, which had inspired me to open Bob's Place, a four-unit adoption center that let me take cats from the nearby Barneswood Humane Society and give them an opportunity to find new homes. It had been a slow start, but since we'd opened the adoption center in July, we'd had eighteen cats find homes —including one to my own home—and we had moved from having only two cats at a time up to four.

We tried to bring in cats who got stressed out by the shelter environment, or were long-term residents, with the hope that a change of scenery would help them meet the right owners.

And thanks to Raven Creek being such a tourist stop, we had adopted out cats to many people just passing through town. We had a handful from Seattle, one from Portland, and one as far away as Texas. Our success story corkboard was starting to fill up not just with photos, but with postcards from our cats' new hometowns as well.

Mr. Loughery and Bob returned to the bookstore, where they both paused outside the cat condos to say hello to our newest arrivals. There was a tabby cat named Junior, a tortoiseshell named Ginny, a white and orange cat named Mr. Greeves, and a shy but stunning long-haired white cat named Duchess. I didn't think she was going to last long, but apparently, she'd been at the Humane Society almost a year, so her quiet personality must have been making prospective adopters nervous.

The new cat I'd adopted over the summer—Coco—was a super shy girl, who still sometimes ran from the room when she heard me coming. But she did sleep with me at night and would let me pet her while we all sat on the couch, so we were making some slow but sure progress as a family.

Really, it had been Bob who picked Coco, not me, but there had been no question about letting someone else have her when I realized how besotted my chubby cat was with her.

Once Mr. Loughery and Bob had finished their rounds, they both went back to their respective chairs, and Mr. Loughery sneakily passed Bob a few treats. While we did have a sign posted that insisted Bob did *not* need any snacks, we let Mr. Loughery get away with it.

A moment later I heard a shriek outside the shop and my attention pivoted to the large front window of the bookstore. The sound hadn't been one of fear, but it was definitely the kind of noise that grabbed my attention.

Someone paused in front of the shop with their camera out, seemingly unaware they were being soaked in the rain, and I briefly wondered if they were stopping to photograph Bob, which happened a *lot*. But no, Bob was sitting next to Norman, and both were staring out the window.

The girl taking photos moved out of the way, and then three people bustled down the sidewalk. One was a tall, leggy blonde with purposeful steps, and the two people with her appeared to be trailing a step behind. One held an umbrella, and the other was carrying a tray of drinks in the signature pink cups of the Sugarplum Fairy bakery next door.

As we watched the crew move down the sidewalk, the few pedestrians outside all seemed to stop and stare, making me wonder what was so special. Apparently, we were about to find out because the trio stopped at the shop door and soon the bell jingled to announce their presence inside.

I returned to the main foyer of the store and then stopped dead in my tracks, immediately understanding what all the fuss had been about.

Naomi Novak was standing in my bookstore.

Naomi was one of the highest-paid comedic actresses in Hollywood, and easily the biggest success story out of Something Wicked. She'd appeared in some of the shows I'd seen in Seattle, so I liked to brag that I'd been a fan before she made it big.

She was more stunning in person than on screen, and more gorgeous up close than when I'd seen her doing live theatre. She looked like a cross between Cameron Diaz and Florence Pugh, all radiant smiles, and perfect teeth.

She was one of the biggest actresses in the world, and she was standing in my bookshop.

I exchanged a quick glance with Imogen, who was trying to play it cool, but her wide-eyed expression told me that even *she* was a little impressed by the company.

Naomi looked as if she was about to say something when the ring of a phone interrupted her. She shot an unimpressed look at one of the people lurking behind her—the one with the purse—and the assistant quickly answered the ringing phone.

Naomi mouthed a friendly *sorry* in our direction as the flustered assistant passed the phone over to her. Naomi moved into the bookstore for a little more privacy, then the assistant who had been carrying the umbrella came up. "Do you have the new Brandon Sanderson?"

Given Sanderson's output, this was almost akin to asking if we had the new James Patterson, but there was a new edition of the fantasy author's bestselling series that had come out the previous week, so I assumed this would be the title they were looking for. I grabbed one of the bulky tomes off our new release shelf and took it over to the till.

The umbrella assistant beckoned over the purse assistant, and the purse assistant pulled out a wallet and handed over some cash to pay for the book. "Oh, and one of those tote bags. Ms. Novak loves to support small bookstores."

I dutifully rang up one of our totes and put the book inside.

Naomi Novak herself emerged a moment later, looking so radiant and put together it was hard to imagine she had just come in from the rain. "So sorry, that was unbelievably rude of me. You have such a sweet store in here."

"Thank you," I replied, not trusting myself to say anything else.

She approached the counter where our featured teas were sitting and picked up the tin of Trick or Treat tea. She paused before she opened the lid.

"There're no nuts in this, are there? I'm allergic."

I shook my head. "Totally nut free, but don't open the Nutty Buddy beside it... uh... obviously."

She smiled, that megawatt smile I'd seen in a million movie trailers. "Thanks." After sniffing the tea, she put the tin back and headed towards the door. The person who had been carrying her umbrella got it ready.

"Hope to stop in again," Naomi said cheerfully. "And maybe I'll see all of you at the auditions."

Of course, Naomi had gotten her start with Something Wicked, so that explained why she was here. But still, when Dierdre said Something Wicked was coming, I don't think I'd ever expected its biggest former member would be included in that. Shouldn't she be off making a green-screen summer blockbuster with James Cameron?

We all watched her go with stunned expressions, as if we could barely believe she'd been there. Less than a minute after she'd left, a small, bald man came through the door, his gaze darting around.

"Was she just in here?"

I didn't bother pretending I didn't know what he was talking about. "Yeah."

"What did she buy?"

It was a weird question, but I supposed there was no harm in answering. I could see he had a cup from Amy's in his hands already, so I suspected he was just trying to re-create Naomi's day. It was... strange... but hopefully harmless.

"The new Brandon Sanderson." I pointed to the new release wall.

He wasted no time at all darting over and grabbing a copy, bringing it up to the counter. As I rang him up, he continued to cast glances over his shoulder out the windows, like he was trying to see where she was going next. I didn't recognize him as a local, but we always had our fair share of tourists here. He was probably just caught up in the excitement of seeing someone so famous in our little town.

After he paid, he darted out the door in the direction Naomi had gone. I gave my head a shake and went back to work.

The morning soon gave way to lunch, and while lunch was usually one of our busiest times of day, today the foot traffic had been decidedly slow thanks to the rain outside. Normally that might have bothered me, but rain wasn't doing anything to dampen our online sales, so Imogen and I used the quiet lunch hour to enjoy some tasty sourdough —cinnamon raisin—and go through our inventory to find the books in stock people wanted to order, or to place orders for the items we didn't have.

Plus, we were still riding the unexpected high of seeing Naomi Novak in our store.

At one, Daphne came in to start her shift and, seeing all the new spaces on the walls, she headed down to the basement to bring up a few new boxes of used stock.

Earlier in the year I'd been lucky enough to win an auction of books from an estate sale, and we'd added thousands of titles to our inventory. The issue was they were all a mixed bag of titles and authors, so we didn't add any of them to the website or store shelves until we catalogued them. It was a time-intensive process and one of the things Daphne seemed to love doing.

She grabbed a barcode scanner and laptop and plopped herself on the floor outside the office with the books beside her. With her AirPods in, she was now on a planet of her own. Periodically I'd see her curly blonde hair start to bob and the soft sound of her singing Harry Styles lyrics would fill the store.

I never told her she sang out loud because I thought it

might embarrass her, but over the summer I'd seen her singing with a local cover band and she was a divine singer, her tone reminiscent of Stevie Nicks or Pat Benatar, a little gravelly, but full of emotion.

She didn't really talk about singing as a passion, but she was very good at it.

Periodically as she worked, she would stop to take a photo of an interesting or funny book cover on her phone to then share to social media. Under Daphne's efforts, we now had *three* bustling social media profiles going. There was the shop's presence; there was one for the cat adoptions; and Bob had his very own profile called @bobthebookstorecat, and he was probably three times more popular than any of the others.

Daphne's expert management of our social media empire was part of the reason I'd been able to afford to give her full-time hours. And had managed to give both her and Imogen well-deserved raises.

She certainly made it worthwhile, and she was a delight to have around. Customers loved her.

During a break in the rain, Mr. Loughery put on his paperboy cap and returned his mug to the front counter, while shrugging on an old tweed jacket. "I think I'll take my chances, ladies. See you tomorrow."

"Say hi to Frodo for us," I said. His tuxedo cat Frodo was our first non-official adoption success story, and what had inspired me to open the cat condos in the first place.

Mr. Loughery grinned and gave us one last wave before heading out into the misty afternoon. It was so dark from the rain clouds overhead that it might as well have been evening already. Not long after Mr. Loughery left, a huge clap of thunder rattled the windows with an astonishing *boom*.

The three of us all looked outside, and Bob scurried under his chair, wide eyes peering out towards the large front window. Imogen went to the door to get a better look; I think we were half expecting to see a car crash. "He made it to his car okay," she announced.

From behind the counter I sighed, both from relief and from the frustration of the day. "Ladies, I think I'm going to call it early. We don't need three of us here, and Bob looks ready to climb the walls. You think you guys can handle the rest of the afternoon? Feel free to close early if it stays like this."

Imogen glanced around the completely empty shop. "Yeah, I think we can manage it."

From her place by the office, Daphne smirked. "It's pretty busy. I'm not sure."

"I thought we were a bookstore, not an amateur comedy club," I countered. "Bunch of jokesters in here." I loaded an extremely puffy and stressed Bob into his little bubble-domed carrier, and exited through the back where my car was parked.

I actually had an ulterior motive for wanting to leave early, one I wasn't willing to discuss with the girls thanks to its witchy implications.

Over the summer, I'd been bedevilled by my magic powers acting up all on their own. As the result of a spell cast by two much stronger witches than me, I had an opportunity to share a bit of a spiritual one-on-one with my dead aunt. My friend, Honey, had insisted this was just a version of my aunt who lived in my memory, but some of the things Eudora had said when I was in my disembodied state made me think it was really her.

Aside from a much-needed pep talk on how to fix my glitching magic, she'd also said something else.

Something that made me think she'd left something for me in the house.

It wouldn't be the first time she'd made me play hide-and-seek. When I first moved into Lane End House, I'd ended up locating a secret stash of property deeds in an old family album. Those deeds meant I owned almost all the buildings on Main Street, something that only a scant handful of people knew.

I didn't want my friends and neighbors to know I was their landlord. My property management company took care of all that, and we kept the rent as low as humanly possible, while funnelling any extra proceeds into a town improvement fund.

That was part of the deal with how Eudora had been allowed to buy the properties so cheaply from their original owner, and I kept things status quo.

But in my dream state, she had told me the deeds weren't the only thing she'd hidden for me in the house, and that when I found the other surprise, I would know.

I'd spent *months* so far looking through the house, and while I'd managed to organize several of the spare bedrooms, I still hadn't found the hidden secret.

Now all I had left was the attic, and I was a woman on a mission.

Today was going to be the day I discovered my Aunt Eudora's secret.

CHAPTER THREE

As soon as we arrived home and I released Bob from his carrier, he made a beeline for the living room and wriggled his chubby butt underneath the couch. I knew my furry companion pretty well after the last year we'd spent together and figured he had probably torn a hole in the lining under the couch to make himself a little hidey hole in the coiled interior.

I *also* felt confident that he had shown Coco his secret hiding spot, because I'd often see her skulking in and out of the living room when she was trying to avoid being perceived.

Right now, there was no sign of the small calico cat, so I was willing to guess the two of them were curled up inside together, keeping each other safe from the storm.

As if on cue with my thoughts, lightning illuminated the room and was followed shortly thereafter by a loud *boom* of thunder that I could feel in the floorboards. The storm was close.

Since it wasn't uncommon for us to lose power during big storms thanks to our remote location, I put off my mission to explore the attic long enough to get the house prepared in case I'd be spending my evening in the dark. I started a fire in the big fireplace that opened into both a large sitting room and also the kitchen.

When Bob wasn't being a literal scaredy cat, the hearth by the kitchen side of the fireplace was his favorite place to spend time. Since getting Coco, I'd added a bed for her next to his, and when I would sometimes wander into the kitchen to find them both wedged together in one bed, I couldn't stop myself from stopping to take a few photos. The cuteness levels were on overload.

I'd worried that getting a second cat would upset the dynamic Bob and I had, but it hadn't seemed to have a huge impact. He did like to spend time with Coco, but that was time he might normally have spent napping, so our quality moments together weren't lessened.

And Bob was a real mama's boy, so he was inclined to want to be with me above all other options. I was glad he still wanted to go to the shop with me every day. I gave him the choice, of course, by setting his carrier out by the door in the morning. Every day he pawed at it, waiting to be let in.

I think I'd have been heartbroken if he'd decided he would rather not come.

In an ideal world, I would have loved to bring Coco along, too, but I didn't think she was ever going to warm to being a bookstore cat. People scared her, noises scared her, and it was probably best for both of us that she stayed home where she felt secure and protected.

She didn't seem to mind being left alone during the day. It was probably a nice break from Bob loving on her whenever they were together. The poor cat had never been better groomed in her life.

After the fire was lit and the warm glow started to fill the kitchen, I made myself a cup of my new fall tea blend. I'd mixed chocolate peppermint with cinnamon and cloves, giving the tea a vibe of the way late fall felt before shifting into winter. I wasn't sure I'd perfected the recipe yet—I was still new to making my own teas, that had been Eudora's area of expertise—but I knew I was close to this one being ready to sell.

With my tea in hand and a battery-operated lantern at my side in case the power went out while I was upstairs, I headed to the attic. Lane End House, the old Victorian house I'd inherited from Eudora was large enough I might hazard to call it a mansion, but I didn't know the definition. What I knew was that it had a metric ton of unused bedroom, it took forever to vacuum, and the attic was actually kind of cool.

Instead of being tucked away behind a pull-down ladder, the attic in Lane End House had a narrow staircase leading up to it, and I suspected the space might once have been quarters for service staff. There were several bedroom-sized rooms, and a common area space between them, as well as a tiny kitchenette with functional running water. There wasn't a bathroom on the attic level; otherwise, it could have been its own self-contained apartment.

Not that I was thinking of renting out. I had enough property to worry about on Main Street without taking on tenants at the house.

And the truth was, after being married, I sort of liked living alone.

Or as alone as I could be with a permanent orange shadow.

The faint sound of *click-clack* on the hardwood floors

told me two things: Bob had followed me upstairs, and two, I needed to trim his claws.

That was decidedly not our favorite activity; neither of us enjoyed the process, but it was a necessary evil if I wanted to keep him from sharpening his murder mittens on every nearby chair or drape.

I let him go up the steps ahead of me as I opened the door for him, and we entered into the musty-smelling attic together. On a day when it *wasn't* pouring rain, I would really need to open up the windows here to let in some much-needed fresh air.

Bob made a huffy sneezing sound, then meowed at me once before wandering off to explore and see if there were any toys or blankets he might be able to claim as his own. So far in this exploration, we'd found almost as much stuff for Bob as we had found things I needed to offload at a local antique store.

Once I *finally* figured out what Eudora had hidden for me to find, I would ask someone to come in and appraise the items, then find a place to sell anything I didn't want to keep.

Eudora had so many things, I don't think she expected me to hang on to every one of them. At some point, the house had to become mine.

The attic was especially dark thanks to the grim weather outside. Whenever lightning flashed, I could see the outlines of cardboard boxes and plastic tote bins in every direction I looked.

There was a very good reason I'd left the attic for last.

"Oh boy," I muttered under my breath as I navigated around some boxes to get to the light switch. There was only one light in the main area, and it was dimmed by a very pretty Tiffany-style cover, so the room still felt pretty dark.

I kept the lantern by my side, not wanting to have to stumble through the minefield of boxes to find it if the power did happen to go out. The air in the attic was cooler than down on the main floor, but not downright cold. Still, I was grateful to be wearing a sweater.

"Where should we start, buddy?" I asked Bob, surveying the landscape around me. My mission this afternoon was twofold. One, try to find whatever mystery item Eudora had left for me. And two, create some kind of system so I'd know what was up here.

That latter part was probably going to take me longer than one afternoon of work, but I was hoping I could use the four former tiny bedrooms as storage zones, which might help me streamline the various seasonal decorations and other assorted antique goodies she'd collected over the years.

A lot of the stuff up here, I suspected, pre-dated even Eudora's time as the house's owner, and probably went back through several generations of the Black family, my father's ancestors.

I was only Phoebe Winchester by marriage, and I'd kept the name because changing all my legal documents again sounded like an expensive annoyance. No matter how I felt about the man who I'd taken the name from—my ex-husband, Blaine—I didn't actually dislike the name itself.

I'd lost a lot of things in the divorce: my home, my friends, the life I'd thought I would be living for the rest of my earthly years. But things have a funny way of working out exactly as they're meant to. If Blaine hadn't cheated on me with a waitress, I likely never would have moved to

Raven Creek. I wouldn't be living the gorgeous, idyllic life I lived now, and that would be a real tragedy.

Of course, being surrounded by a veritable box fort didn't feel like much of a blessing at the moment.

I heard delicate tip-tapping up the stairs and saw Bob's ears perk up. A moment later Coco appeared, her demeanor cautious, bordering on anxious. She spotted me and seemed to briefly consider dashing back down the stairs until Bob approached her and gave her a generous grooming on her face. This relaxed the younger cat enough that she hopped up onto a nearby box overflowing with old blankets and started to make biscuits until she was comfortable enough to lay down.

I let out a breath I hadn't realized I was holding.

Maybe this was going to be a good afternoon after all.

CHAPTER FOUR

Five hours later, I was coated in dust and waiting by my front door for the pizza delivery guy to arrive. I was no closer to uncovering Eudora's secrets, but I *had* uncovered about twelve boxes of vintage magazines from the fifties and sixties, all in premium condition.

I had sorted through multiple boxes of clothing that likely went back two or three generations and had divided them into piles for regular thrift disposal and for more high-end antique or online reselling.

Maybe it might be worth it for me to enlist Daphne to help me set myself up on eBay. She was such a whiz with these things I could probably pay her by the hour to help me photograph and post a lot of items rather than deal with an agent or reseller.

But that did sound like an awful lot of work, even with assistance, so I put a pin in the idea to see how I felt later.

Every time I opened a new box, I'd hope to see personal letters, journals, a blinking sign that said Phoebe, *this is what you're looking for*, but so far it was just tons and tons of *stuff*. I was surprised the house was still standing under the weight of so much accumulated personal debris from my family.

And now here I was, the curator of the museum of our lives.

I didn't know whether my dad or my brother Sam would want anything, but I figured if I stumbled across any items that might tickle their fancy, I would set them aside. I'd been here a year and neither of them had asked for anything to this point, so I doubted there were any items in the house they were dying to get their hands on.

I had a lofty ambition of inviting Sam and my parents to Raven Creek for Christmas, so it gave me a deadline for getting everything cleaned up. I had plenty of room for my family to stay comfortably, and it would be our first time getting together since my divorce, and I really wanted to show them I was doing okay.

Selfishly, I also kind of wanted to introduce them to the new people in my life, and more specifically to Rich Lofting.

Rich was a private investigator who lived over the bookstore. We'd grown up playing together during the summers I had spent here with Aunt Eudora, and we'd fallen back into each other's orbits since I'd moved back.

The last few months, our will-they-or-won't-they romantic entanglement had become a lot more *they will,* and we were tip-toeing our way to being a—gasp!—couple. We still hadn't had any conversations about our status, which felt like too high school of a discussion for two divorcees in their late thirties, but we spent an awful lot of our spare time together smooching and watching old movies, so I had a feeling he wouldn't be opposed to being considered my boyfriend.

A knock on the door drew my attention, and I opened it to collect my piping hot pizzas from the delivery driver, giving him a big tip since the weather was starting to feel extra frigid outside.

My favorite local pizzas were in the nearby town of Barneswood, but a new pizza place had opened in Raven Creek about a month earlier, and the convenience was too much to resist.

I had to be up early to get back to the shop, but I still wanted to put in at least another hour or two in the attic before calling it a night. Coco was still up there, fast asleep on the blanket box, though Bob had followed me downstairs. I took my pizza and a glass of rosé up to the attic level and propped one hand on my hip while I surveyed the space again.

"How did it get *messier*?" I asked the empty room.

It is a truth universally acknowledged that a space in want of a good tidying must get infinitely messier before it actually looks good. We were definitely in the disaster phase right now.

I set the pizza down on a stack of boxes and ate a slice. Pepperoni and sausage with banana peppers. Yummmm. It actually gave me a great idea for a savory sourdough loaf I'd like to try. I was betting the flavor combo would be a hit, especially if I topped with burrata and a little red pesto.

My stomach rumbled even though I was already in the process of feeding it.

Outside, the storm raged on, with bright lightning periodically filling the one small window before the house rattled with thunder. At least I wasn't seeing any unexpected leaks anywhere, which was absolutely a blessing in a house this old. I'd had to do my fair share of repairs on the place already, since Eudora hadn't been physically well enough to do them before she passed, but I didn't even want to imagine what it would cost me to get the roof redone.

I put that horrific thought out of my mind, not wanting to accidentally manifest anything, or have my magic go haywire in an unexpected way. I'd recently learned that stress and magic were terrible bedfellows, and while I'd solved my wonky magic problems, there was no saying what might happen in the future. I didn't feel like tempting fate.

I was about halfway through both the pizza and a large box of baby clothes when a *clonk* sound filled the house and the lights went off. The sound of silence that follows a power outage was always strange to me. You rarely paid attention to the day-to-day noises of your house like the furnace or fans or the buzz of lightbulbs and refrigerators until you could no longer hear them.

Lane End House was quiet as a tomb, with only the sound of rain pattering overhead and the rumble of thunder. I wove my way through the boxes by feel until I got to the window and looked outside, where it appeared the power was out as far as the eye could see.

Super.

If the whole town was out, it meant something had gone wrong at the main power... thingy... and we might be out of power for hours. I rarely used the fireplace in my bedroom, but this was shaping up to be a good night to do it.

My phone buzzed, still getting data even if it wasn't getting Wi-Fi. A text from Rich brought a smile to my face.

You in the dark?

Constantly, I replied. *But at present, also literally.*

He sent back a laughing emoji because we were both

elder millennials, and Gen Z could not convince us to change our ways this late in the game.

You and the kitten crew okay? Got everything you need to stay warm?

I knew he didn't mean it in any kind of double entendre way, yet my cheeks still flushed and I was tempted to write back something a little cheeky. But the truth was, I was pretty tired, and inviting Rich over wasn't going to be in the cards tonight, no matter how well-intentioned the offer was.

We're okay. Got the fires going. Are you *okay?* I realized he was all alone above the shop, and he didn't have the nice option of just throwing some logs on to keep the place warm.

I'm totally comfy at the moment, and I have a propane heater if things get too cool, but don't worry, if I start freezing to death I'll knock on your door.

Is that a threat or a promise?

He sent back a winky emoji and a devil emoji, and my heart did a little flip-flop. Who said you needed romantic sonnets to woo a lady?

Sleep tight, he wrote.

You too, don't freeze; I want to keep you around in thawed form.

I'll do my best.

I slipped the phone back into my pocket, smiling like a lunatic, when I noticed something on the floor. At first, I thought it must be a reflection from some light outside, until I remembered there *was* no light outside. Bob seemed to notice it too, because he was sitting beside the place on the floor, his orange tail swishing and his attention entirely focused on the wooden floorboards.

Because something under those floorboards was glowing.

It was subtle, a white-blue light bleeding out through the fine lines of the flooring, something you likely wouldn't notice unless it was pitch black, and it had also been buried under several boxes for the last however long.

My heart raced.

"What is it, bud?" I asked the cat, as if he might actually be able to answer me. He simply looked up, his eyes glowing in the dark in that eerie way cat eyes do, and he seemed to ask me, *do I look like an expert to you?*

"Yeah, fair enough. Never hurts to ask though."

I sat down on the floor about a foot away from the light, and ran my fingers over the wood, testing the seams. As I checked them, the board felt noticeably loose beneath my hands, as if it wasn't even hammered in, just resting in place. I found one of the ends and used my fingernails to pry it up, letting it lift easily. Once it was gone, the light was substantially brighter, filling the room around me with a faint glow, but enough light to see the shapes of Bob, Coco, and the surrounding boxes.

I set the floorboard down beside me and peered into the space beneath, more curious than concerned about a glowing thing in my floorboards.

That just seemed par for the course in this house.

The light was emanating from a small wooden box that was set in the area under the floors, and on top of it there was a yellowed white envelope. I pulled out the envelope first, and in Eudora's distinctive scrawl, she'd written *Phoebe* on it.

The box itself was light but sturdy, and made no sounds when I tilted it from side to side. When I tried to open the lid, I found it wouldn't budge, and there was no obvious spot to put a key.

As soon as I touched it, it stopped glowing. It was suddenly just a box, and I was in the dark holding it.

I fumbled around for my lantern, careful to avoid the open hole in the floor, and once I had the light on, I double-checked the space where I'd found the box to make sure I wasn't missing anything important.

You know, like a key.

The space was empty, so I replaced the board and collected the box and letter before making my way downstairs, the half-empty pizza box balanced on my other hand. The wine glass would need to wait until I retrieved it tomorrow.

Coco had decided she was all napped out, and she and Bob raced downstairs, as if there might be a limit on how much food was in their dishes and they'd need to fight for it. I put the pizza in the dark fridge, hoping we got power back before anything in my freezer spoiled, and stoked the fire in the main fireplace before heading back to my room to start one there.

The air in the bedroom had started to chill despite all the heat from the main level, and I knew I'd be glad for the fire tonight. Even Coco, who rarely slept in my bed, was in the room with us, because who could deny that an October power outage was perfect snuggle weather?

I set my lantern on the nightstand to illuminate the room as much as possible, then started a fire in the small fireplace. About a month earlier, when the days started to cool down in September, I'd had someone come in to clean and safety check all the fireplaces, even the ones I rarely used. In a house the size of Lane End House there were several bedrooms with fireplaces, and even best efforts couldn't always keep animals or tree debris out of chimneys. The peace of mind I had knowing the fireplace would work made the cost of that visit feel very worth it right now.

Once the fire was crackling and the room had a nice cozy glow to it, I changed into my fleecy pajamas and crawled into bed with the cats. Toasty warm, I finally picked up the letter Eudora had written me, though my eyes kept darting back to the mysterious box.

She was right about one thing: I certainly knew I'd found what I was looking for.

But what it *was* was a lot less clear.

The envelope the letter was in felt almost brittle under my fingertips, making me wonder how long it had been under the floorboards. I tore it open, expecting to find a key inside, but instead it was just a letter and an old quarter. Odd.

The letter should give me something to go on though, surely.

My dearest Phoebe,

Look at you, you clever girl, you found it. Now, if everything has gone to plan, I hope you aren't an old woman by now and just discovering this late in life, because that might mean I've hidden it a bit too well.

Knowing you, and knowing me, though, I'm sure by now I've found a way to set you on the hunt. I'm sure you've figured out there are plenty of wonderful secrets hidden in this old house, and I'm going to help you find them. Along the way, I'm hoping you'll be able to solve a problem.

But don't let me get too far ahead of myself. You have the box, and that's the final clue, but to open the box, you'll need to find all the rest. They might be right under your nose, but some might require a little digging.

Let the quarter take you for a ride, and you'll find the next question to answer.

Much love, my beautiful girl.

Eudora

I stared at the letter, reading and rereading it. I held it up to the lantern to see if there might be sneaky hidden text, but there was none. It was so simple, and yet it told me nothing at all. Worst of all, it seemed that rather than coming to the end of my mission to find Eudora's hidden secret for me; I was only at the beginning.

I set the box and the letter on the mantel of the fireplace and added some more wood to keep me warm through the night.

I fell asleep with the old quarter in my hand, wondering what on earth any of it could possibly mean.

Knowing Eudora, it was sure to be one heck of an interesting journey.

CHAPTER FIVE

The next two days were too busy between work and Rich for me to spend much time unravelling the riddle left for me by Eudora. Instead, I'd been forced to learn lines for a play I didn't want to be in and had closed the store for the afternoon so my staff—and grudgingly myself—could audition for the big Halloween program.

I had slept fitfully the night before the auditions, haunted by dreams of opening my mouth and singing "Matchmaker" from *Fiddler* horribly off key every time I tried to say one of the play lines. At the end, I was being laughed off stage by every person in town. I'd woken in a cold sweat, and started to worry it might have been a premonition rather than a dream.

I was still edgy when we arrived at the community center where auditions were being held.

Honey Westcott, one of my closest friends, and a natural witch with a gift for dream magic, was one of the last people I expected to see in the audition queue, but I was grateful beyond words for her presence. She was exactly who I needed right then.

"Honey!" I shouted excitedly, leaving Imogen, Daphne, and Mr. Loughery in line and jogging up to my friend. She had recently cut her blonde-dyed Afro back, and it was currently styled in a cute platinum pixie. Her brown skin was practically glowing, even in the terrible fluorescent lighting of the community center, where we'd all convened.

"Hey doll, what's up?" She kissed both my cheeks in greeting.

"How's your mom doing?" Honey's mother, Karma, had visited over the summer and helped me unravel my magic malfunctions, but she'd also just been a general delight to get to know.

"Oh, she's wonderful, usual Karma, trying to extend the garden season as long as she can. How's your *maaaaaan*?" She drew the last word out to great lengths, beaming mischievously at me.

My cheeks flushed. I was going to protest that he wasn't my "man," but at this point that seemed like a losing argument. "He's good. We're taking it slow, but not snail's pace slow anymore."

"Girl, I don't know what you're waiting for — like an invitation from the Queen or something? Jump in with both feet. You two are obviously crazy about each other."

"Okay, okay. Consider me jumping, I swear."

"Excellent. Now, do you want to explain what the heck you're doing here? Don't take this the wrong way, but you're the last person I ever expected to see auditioning for a play."

My head bobbed along in stern agreement. "I have no desire to be here whatsoever, but I made a deal with Imogen and Mr. Loughery that I'd audition, and that got Daphne excited to audition, so now I can't back out. It's going to be awful."

Honey chuckled. "The things you do for your staff." She leaned out of the line and waved to everyone, which was when I noticed that Amy Beaudry had joined our little motley crew. Amy ran the Sugarplum Fairy bakeshop, right next to The Earl's Study, and made the most out-of-this-world baked goods and coffees. I'd probably added a good five pounds to my waistline since moving here thanks to Amy's tarts and chocolate hazelnut lattes, and I wasn't complaining.

Now that I was talking to Honey and the stress of my morning had melted away, I felt silly even thinking that my dream could have been a premonition. Sometimes a dream was just a dream. Even the bad ones.

I opted not to bother Honey with my dream nonsense and just gave her two quick kisses on the cheek and told her to break a leg before returning to my group.

"I think everyone in town is here," Amy announced, craning her neck to try to get a look down the long row.

She was right; the line stretched far behind us, right out of the community center and into the parking lot, and we couldn't even see the actual waiting room yet. Raven Creek wasn't a big town, but apparently it was enthusiastic about theatre. I suspected we probably had a few folks here from Barneswood as well, the allure of working with Something Wicked too much to resist.

I could hear snippets of our scene dialog coming up and down the line, which for some reason had me paranoid I was going to forget it, even though we were allowed to bring the script in with us for auditions.

And why did I care, honestly? I wasn't going to get in; this was all just for a fun team-building activity for the shop.

With Amy standing next to me, I bumped my shoulder

into hers. "You didn't bring Leo with you?" I asked teasingly. I shouldn't have gotten on her case when I'd only recently been similarly hounded by Honey, but Amy had it coming. She'd done her fair share of pestering me about Rich.

Leo had been the third musketeer of my childhood friendship with Rich. He'd always been the quiet one of the three of us, and growing up that hadn't changed. As an adult, he was a huge bear of a man, but still as quiet and protective of his friends as ever.

Over the summer I'd noticed a flirtation building between him and Amy, which was a relief because I'd worried I might have given him some flirty vibes before Rich and I finally figured ourselves out, and I was glad to see he wasn't holding a torch for me.

He and Amy were a perfect match, even if she was short and he was super tall and broad. Their personalities balanced each other in such a wonderful way I was surprised I hadn't considered them as a possible pairing before. Amy was a few years older than he was, but at this point in our lives that didn't matter one bit.

While they weren't officially dating yet, they had certainly been spending a lot of time together. Leo, who ran Lansing's, the local grocery store, was about as busy as Amy, so I knew their spare time was limited, but they certainly seemed to be getting cozy.

She batted me away, but the smirk on her lips was undeniable. "Honestly, Phoebe. Can you *imagine* Leo at an event like this?"

I *could* imagine it, and it would have been delightful, but I also knew why he hadn't come. He was so quiet and shy I doubted anyone running the auditions would be able to hear a single word he said.

I heard a murmur of excited voices from behind us getting louder like a wave. We all turned together to look behind us, and a gasp rippled through the crowd as none other than Naomi Novak walked through the door, and when she smiled everyone in the line started to applaud.

I felt like I was ahead of the game knowing she was in town and expecting she was going to be here thanks to her visit to the store, but it still felt surreal to see her standing in our community center.

She waved to everyone and stopped for selfies, and I recognized a few of the other members of the troupe behind her, popular in the theatre crowd but certainly not the household name Naomi Novak was.

And then, to my absolute horror, I recognized someone else in the group coming through the doors.

He was tall and handsome. His dark red hair had grown out since I'd last seen him, so the curl pattern was more obvious. He wore an impeccable outfit of tailored slacks, a stylish wool peacoat, and a rich green sweater that brought out the green in his hazel eyes.

I knew that, because I'd bought the sweater for him for that exact reason three Christmases ago.

"*Blaine?*" I said, not realizing how loud my voice was.

Everyone stopped what they were doing to stare at me.

Including my ex-husband.

CHAPTER SIX

Now I *knew* this was a nightmare, and all I needed to do was wake up.

There was no other explanation, because in the real world, I wouldn't have a famous actress judging my acting chops, nor would my ex-husband be here inexplicably.

Here, of all places.

But I didn't wake up, even after pinching my own arm.

And Naomi and Blaine kept staring at me, and then she was looking at him, big blue eyes searching for an explanation. I watched in absolute horror as he reached out and gave her hand a squeeze, lifting it to his lips for a kiss. It was a gesture so loving, so intimate, I realized with a harsh sting he'd never done anything like that for me.

"Blaine, what's going on?" she asked, trying to keep her voice low. Unfortunately, the line had gone dead silent at my outburst, so you could have heard a pin drop in the hallway.

Why was America's Sweetheart, the woman *Us Weekly* once called "Reese Witherspoon's next Reese Witherspoon," looking at *my* ex-husband like that?

Why did she even know his name?

I couldn't tear my eyes away from them, the logic centers of my brain understanding something that my emotional cortex simply wouldn't allow for, so I was just coming up confused.

"Phoebe?" Blaine said, as if it should be odd that I was here despite this being the town where I lived.

Understanding seemed to settle over Naomi's face, her mouth forming a little *o* and her eyes going wide.

"Ohhhh, you're *that* Phoebe," she said. As far as I could tell, she didn't remember meeting me only yesterday.

Instead, I was *That* Phoebe.

Oh my God, what had he told her about me? Was I being discussed at tables with other A-list celebs? This was getting worse and worse by the second.

Naomi smiled at me, a wide, beaming, camera-ready smile, and then she wrapped her arms around me in a tight hug before I even knew what was happening. "Gosh, it's nice to meet you. Blaine has told me so many nice things about you."

If the shoes were on the other feet, I can't say I would have had very nice things to say about him. I had to wonder if she knew why we'd split up.

Wait, did this mean...

"Blaine, are you dating Naomi Novak?" I squeaked out, still wrapped in her embrace.

"Dating?" she giggled. "Oh, honey, no."

For a moment I almost let myself breathe; the sense of relief was so palpable. That was until the moment she flashed an enormous diamond ring in my face. "We're engaged."

I gawked at the ring, then at my blushing ex, who was not currently willing to meet my eye. The ring was huge, absolutely massive, and definitely worth a heck of a lot more than he'd been willing to spend on mine.

It also didn't escape me that we'd been divorced just over a year, the ink on our documents drying only days before I'd arrived in Raven Creek. He was *engaged*? I was barely ready to call Rich my boyfriend; we were both so gun-shy after our mutual divorces.

Blaine, meanwhile, was marrying an actress.

A beautiful, friendly, wealthy, famous actress.

I had a million questions, like how had they met, how long had they been dating, what had happened to the waitress, and what on earth did Naomi see in him, but only one question came out of my mouth.

"What are you *doing* here?"

His blush deepened, something that had always stood out on his pale Irish complexion. "Nene decided at the last minute she wanted to participate in the Halloween show this year since she had a break between movies, and we decided to surprise everyone during auditions. Phoebe, I honestly didn't even make the connection. I think I thought you moved to Leavenworth."

I gave him an incredulous look, not believing for one second he'd mixed up the towns that badly, but he *did* seem surprised to see me. Perhaps it was being at a theatre audition that had been shocking to him. That would be fair.

Also... *Nene*?

They were getting married and had cutesy nicknames.

I wasn't jealous. I knew what the bitter tang of jealousy tasted like, and I had *long ago* stopped being wrapped up in the romantic memory of my ex. But it still rankled that he was getting married again so fast, as if our near decade together had been meaningless to him.

Jealousy and anger were two very different things.

Of course, I wasn't sure I'd have felt exactly this bad if it was some normal woman who had shown up on his arm, instead of one of *People* magazines most beautiful people in the world.

"Oh," I said. Because I am very articulate.

"Phoebs, is that your ex?" Imogen whispered.

I nodded, then realized I was being aggressively rude considering how nice Naomi had been to me. "Everyone, this is Blaine, my, uh... my former husband? Blaine, this is Daphne, Imogen, Amy, and Norman." I nodded to each of my friends in turn. "Daphne and Imogen work for me at my aunt's shop, Amy owns the shop next door, and Norman is our favorite regular."

Mr. Loughery blushed. "She's just being nice. I have to go so often to give them an excuse to keep Irish Breakfast tea in stock."

Blaine nodded disinterestedly, and I knew him well enough to know he wasn't even trying to remember their names. He had always been terrible at remembering people, and at some point in his life had decided not to bother making the effort if he didn't think that knowing them would benefit him.

He had called my brother Shawn instead of Sam for at least the first few months we dated until he decided I might be worth staying with and learned my family's names finally.

There had been so many red flags with him I'd gleefully ignored until it was much too late. I wondered how many Naomi was missing.

"Baby, we should get into the theater," Naomi urged.

I'd almost forgotten about the little entourage behind Naomi with the rest of the troupe—all of them looking peeved at the delay—and the ever-building line behind us.

"It was nice to meet you, Phoebe, Daphne, Imogen, Amy, and Norman." She smiled at each of my friends, repeating their names clearly.

When she left, Daphne flopped against my arm and let out a little squeal. "*Phoebe*, you didn't tell us you knew Naomi Novak."

"Phoebe *doesn't* know Naomi Novak," Imogen clarified. "But her ex seems to know her very well."

"And here you thought you had won the post-divorce rebound," Amy said, elbowing me lightly.

"Hey, I'm going to tell Rich you said that. And I think I still *did* win, because he might have landed Naomi Novak, but now *she* has to marry my cheating ex. I almost feel sorry for her."

Imogen snorted. "Yeah, I also feel just awful for the beautiful rich woman who can go cry into her pile of Golden Globes."

I gave her a look, and she raised her hands in surrender. "I'll say this much," she added. "Rich is definitely an upgrade from that guy."

"*That* we can agree on."

CHAPTER SEVEN

As much as I wanted to completely bail on the auditions—and I doubted any of my friends would hold it against me—a deal *was* a deal. At least I hadn't been counting on getting in, because I suspected now there was no way that was remotely possible, with Blaine's new fiancée being one of the people deciding.

I'm sure she would be perfectly lovely to my face and then toss my name in a trash can the moment I walked out the door.

I would probably do the same thing.

But my friends had made a commitment to be here, and I was going to stay to support them, no matter how awkward the whole situation was shaping up to be.

The line moved at a snail's pace, not too surprising given the length of the performance we'd been asked to prepare, and the amount of people waiting to perform it. The parts available to locals were incredibly limited, and it had been made very clear that no one was going to walk away with a leading role, but still, people were so eager to participate.

When news about Naomi Novak's appearance spread, the line behind us grew so long that eventually Dierdre had to go out and tell people past a certain point that they simply would not be able to participate due to time constraints.

Normally I wouldn't envy anyone with that particular job, but I got the feeling Dierdre might actually enjoy disappointing people, so she was probably the best-suited person to do it.

Indeed, after she went out to cut off the line, she returned beaming, her whole day having been made. She was also having the time of her life barking out directions at us, telling us where to stand, where to move, not to talk, not to use our phones, and a million other things that didn't really matter but made her feel important.

By the time we got to the head of the line, my stomach was rumbling, and my patience was wearing thin. Honey had already had her audition and was now hanging out with our group until we went in. She was cagey on details, and when I asked her how she thought she did, she just gave a little half-shrug.

I think a different witch from Honey might have used charm spells to help give herself a leg up—I myself might have considered it if I were a stronger witch—but not Honey. I knew she wouldn't use her magic that way, so the shrug was more about the mystery of the process than about anything she'd done to get accepted.

When our crew got up to the front of the line, there was some general bickering over who would go first, namely because none of us wanted to be the first lamb to the slaughter, and finally it was Imogen who gave us all a stern look for being wusses and went through the doors.

It felt like she was gone for ages when she walked back through, her cheeks flushed red. It was obvious she was furious.

"Immy, what's wrong?" Daphne asked, squeezing Imogen's shoulder.

I'm glad it was Daphne who went to her first, because it was basically impossible to have a rage-fuelled outburst when such a sweet human was speaking to you. Imogen looked like she might want to give it a try anyway but decided instead to take a few deep breaths.

She squared her shoulders like she was ready to go into battle, then looked right at me and said, "Your ex found someone he absolutely deserves."

I blinked a few times, trying to process what she was saying. I initially thought she was insulting me by saying Blaine had traded up, but the tone of her voice and the dripping disdain on the word *deserves* told me this was more about Naomi than it was about me.

"Oh, Imogen, was she awful?"

"She kept cutting me off, and I don't think I've ever had someone be *that* rude just because I ad libbed a line. I thought since they were an improv troupe, they might appreciate it. Apparently *not*." Tears glistened in her eyes. This was the first time I'd ever seen Imogen even close to crying, and my blood *boiled*.

Honey let out a little sigh. "I was kind of hoping I'd misinterpreted what she was saying to me, but I think you might have just confirmed my suspicions. She was awful to me too, just super passive-aggressive." She shook her head. "I'm sorry, Imogen."

"And she did it in a way you can't even call her out on it, just all smiles the whole time," Imogen said, her hands balled into fists at her side. "I'm sorry, guys, please don't let me rain on your parade."

"Well, I'm not sure I want to audition at all anymore," Amy said sternly. "Why on earth would I want to act alongside people who act like that?"

"It was really just Naomi," Honey said with another sigh. "The guys from Something Wicked were so lovely and gave great feedback; one of them laughed at my line delivery, which felt like a win. But for some reason, she was just *itching* for a reason to dismiss me."

Imogen nodded. "Agreed, everyone else was so nice. I don't know what her deal is; maybe she's that rude to everyone, like she thinks she's hazing us or something. All I know is, I hope I never lay eyes on her again."

The door opened and two of the other members of the troupe emerged. I wasn't sure if they'd heard us talking about the auditions or not, but one of them definitely looked a little abashed.

"Hey folks, we're going to take a quick ten-minute break. We just need to stretch our legs, and then we'll be right back to the auditions. You guys are killing it so far." One of them seemed to take a moment to look right at Imogen when he said this, but I wasn't sure it did much for her mood.

I waited for Naomi to emerge, ready to tell her that her taste in performers was as clouded as her taste in men, but she simply never came out. After a few moments, I decided she must still be in the auditorium, and I might never get a better chance to approach her alone.

It didn't seem like anyone in line was likely to stop me, so I opened the auditorium door and, despite Daphne saying, "Phoebe, *don't*," I slipped inside. The room was silent, and I could see where the troupe had set up amid the seats to watch as people took the stage to audition.

A door at the back of the stage opened, and my heart leapt into my throat because I only just realized I hadn't really planned what I was going to say to Naomi. Kill her with kindness? Get right to the heart of it? I guess I'd see when she emerged.

But it wasn't Naomi who came out onto the stage, but Blaine.

I stopped dead in my tracks, my brain still unable to compute his presence here.

"Phoebe?" He paused, arching a brow. "I think they're taking a break from auditions for a bit."

"I know. I actually came to have a word with Naomi."

Blaine glanced over his shoulder to the door he'd just come through, then back to me. "She's busy right now. She's in the green room." He looked down at his feet before adding. "She won't even let me in."

I wasn't about to let him dissuade me, because if I waited until later, I would change my mind and chicken out, and the fact was, someone needed to defend my friends, and tell Naomi she had to get her head on right. I was willing to bet she'd let me in if I mentioned telling Honey and Imogen's story to a gossip blog.

They would never want me to do that, I was sure, but the threat of doing something was often as powerful as actually following through.

"Well, I can't imagine why she wouldn't want to talk to *you*," I replied, my tone a little more vicious than I had intended.

It had been a long time since Blaine and I were happily married, and long enough since the divorce that there were times I didn't think about him for weeks in a row. He wasn't a deciding factor in my life anymore, yet having him stand in my town, among my friends, with his hot actress fiancée, for some reason it was bringing up all my old animosity towards him.

"I probably deserved that," he said, sitting down on the edge of the stage.

He looked good, which probably only made me angrier. He'd lost some weight around his midsection, and it looked like he'd been working out. His clothes were nicer, too, making him look like a more polished version of the man I used to know.

"You deserve a lot worse than that. I can't believe you'd show up here." I crossed my arms tightly over my chest. "It wasn't enough that you got Seattle and all our friends, but now you want to show up here?"

"Phoebe, you're being so dramatic." He rolled his eyes and lolled his head back to sigh. "I already told you, I forgot this was where you moved."

"Probably because you never bothered to listen to anything I said."

"That's not true."

I waved my hands in front of my face before I attempted to get another barb in. This was all so stupid and pointless. Fighting with him hadn't done us any good when we were married, and it wouldn't do me any good now that we were divorced.

"I didn't come here to fight with you. I came to say something to your girlfriend. And if she won't let me in, I'll just say it to her through a door." I mounted the stairs and ignored any protest he made.

Blaine wasn't a very confrontational person; he never had been. So, I wasn't surprised when he just stayed on stage as I headed through the door and into a long, dark hallway with Halloween decorations stacked almost up to the ceiling filling the corridor, as well as boxes marked *1920s Costumes*, likely meant for the production of the play.

One of the rooms had a hastily printed sign on the door that read *Green Room*. I rapped lightly. No answer.

I took a deep breath to steel myself, then knocked again. "Naomi?"

Again, she didn't answer. Maybe she was taking a power nap. Or perhaps she really wasn't interested in talking to anyone, as Blaine had intimated.

Too bad.

"Naomi, it's Phoebe Winchester. Look, I know we don't know each other, but I'm hoping you'll listen to me for just a moment. I spoke with two of my friends, and they suggested you may have been a little rude in some of the auditions today, and that's really just not the way we do things around here. That's obviously not a story you want getting out. I think..." My voice drifted off.

Was she really not going to say anything? No disagreements or shouts at me to leave her alone?

That didn't seem possible.

I knocked again, louder this time. "Naomi, are you listening to me?"

When no reply came, I checked the handle and was surprised to see that it wasn't locked.

I pushed open the green room door and found the space inside to be dimly lit with only a single lamp sitting on the desk. A coffee cup was sitting on the dressing table, with an open bag of makeup next to it, and the chair was askew, like someone had stood up in a hurry.

Then my eyes drifted down, and I realized that it wasn't because someone had stood up.

It was because they had fallen down.

Naomi lay in a heap on the floor, a mascara wand near her outstretched hand, her cell phone clutched to her chest. I ran across the room and kneeled beside her, pressing my fingertips to her throat to find a pulse.

But just looking into her glassy, sightless eyes, I knew I wouldn't find anything.

Naomi Novak was dead.

CHAPTER EIGHT

The following hour flew by in a blur. Before I knew it, I was sitting outside the community center on the front steps, an itchy blanket draped over my shoulders as I looked at the knees of Detectives Patsy Miller and Kwan Kim.

Someone at some point had handed me a coffee.

"Where do you guys get these blankets?" I asked, looking down into my coffee. "They're awful."

"We'll take your complaint into consideration with our distributor, Ms. Winchester," Detective Martin said, her voice betraying no humor, but when I looked up at her, I could see a glint of laughter in her eyes.

This was hardly the first time I'd crossed paths with Detective Miller, and only recently, she and Detective Kim had made something of a confession to me: my aunt Eudora had sometimes used her magic skills to help them solve crimes.

That made my aunt seem much more badass in retrospect—and she was already a phenomenally badass lady—

but it also meant that following their revelation I got the feeling they were expecting me to pick up the torch.

The only issue there was: Eudora was a gifted witch who had known how to use her powers since she hit puberty, whereas I was a witchy late bloomer who sometimes made things float unintentionally and had a rare ability to stop time whenever my animal brain thought we were in danger.

None of those skills were going to be much use to me in pointing them in the direction of answers to what had happened to Naomi Novak.

As a matter of fact, despite the presence of the detectives, there hadn't been anything at the scene to indicate Naomi had met with foul play. She appeared to have dropped out of her chair quite suddenly while doing her makeup, something that easily could have occurred if she'd experienced and sudden heart attack or stroke.

She was a young, seemingly vital woman, but that didn't mean she didn't have health issues we didn't know about.

"Can you just walk us through it all again?" Detective Kim asked, pushing his sunglasses up on his head to reveal his warm brown eyes. He was incredibly handsome and had a youthful quality to him, even though I knew he was the same age as Rich and me. They had worked together at the Barneswood Police Department before Rich left to become a PI.

Think of the devil...

Rich Lofting wound his way through the amassed crowd, and once he caught sight of me, he was like a homing pigeon coming in to land. He barely acknowledged his former colleagues as he came next to me, hands touching my face, shoulders, arms as his eyes scoured over me for any sign of injury.

"Are you okay?" he asked.

If Detective Kim was handsome, Rich Lofting was devastating. His eyes were the colour of whiskey in sunlight, or rich clover honey. His dark hair had natural waves, and if he let it grow just an inch or so longer, it would form lovely, unruly curls. I knew that because as children he'd frequently let it grow almost to his shoulders, and the photos I'd found recently reminded me of how cute he'd looked.

He was wearing jeans and a deep purple sweater that was somehow the perfect color for him, even though I wasn't sure I'd ever seen him wear it before.

"She's fine," Patsy answered for me. "I think just a little shaken up."

I sipped my coffee and was relieved to discover it wasn't the toxic sludge that was served at the police station. It had likely come from the instant machine in the community center canteen, so it wasn't much better, but drinking the police station coffee was like drinking motor oil.

Motor oil and dirt.

Motor oil and dirt filtered through an old gym sock.

It was the worst coffee on the planet.

"She was just going to walk us through what happened, so I suppose your timing is impeccable," Kim said, a little teasing smile on the corner of his mouth. Rich had worked with these two for such a long time it was impossible for them to be too serious with each other, which helped lighten the mood significantly.

"I wanted to go talk to Naomi about the auditions. Before I went in to see her, I bumped into my ex-husband, Blaine Winchester."

I darted a quick glance over at Rich to see how he would react to this tidbit, and while he didn't say anything, I felt a little jerk of surprise go through him and his eyebrow raised just a fraction of an inch.

I squeezed his hand.

"How long have you and Mr. Winchester been divorced?" Kim asked.

While it was his name, too, I made a little face at *Mr. Winchester*. I hated being reminded of how I'd gotten my current name.

"It was a year at the end of August, not long before I moved to Raven Creek."

"What did you two discuss?"

"Nothing valuable. We argued a little, mostly over nothing, which is a good reminder of why we're not married anymore, and then he mentioned to me Naomi hadn't answered her door for him."

"Why did you think she'd answer for you?" Patsy asked.

I shrugged. "I thought maybe if someone brought to her attention that she had some hopefully unconscious biases about the people auditioning, she might be able to course correct herself. I thought she might listen to me, but it ended up not mattering. When she didn't answer, I checked the door and found her on the floor. I checked her for a pulse, but she was already gone."

"And did you notice any signs of a struggle in the room?" Kim asked, his little notebook poised and ready.

"The chair had been pushed back, but not over. Things were kind of messy, but more like someone had hastily put their stuff on the dresser, not like someone had rifled through it." I shook my head. "It kind of just looked like she keeled over. I didn't see any wounds on her, no blood or anything."

"Did you see anyone else in the vicinity besides your ex?" Patsy had her thumb hooked in her belt loop, looking effortlessly casual with her close-cropped black afro and intense dark eyes.

"The rest of the troupe had gone to lunch, but they were all sharing the same green room based on the bags and stuff inside. But there wasn't anyone else in the room with her, or anyone in the hall."

"Who was the last person to audition before they called for the break?" Kim asked.

"Imogen Prater. She works for me."

Patsy gave me a look to let me know she obviously knew who Imogen was. It was a small town. I had no doubt they were familiar with just about everyone by name.

She exchanged a quick look with Kim, then back to me. "What was your opinion of Miss Novak?" she asked.

"Me personally? I only met her for about two minutes. She seemed nice enough at the time, but after what Imogen and Honey told me about their auditions, I wouldn't say I had a very high opinion of her."

"And the fact that she was engaged to your ex-husband?"

I let out a quick snort of humorless laughter. "Better her than me."

Rich rubbed my arm supportively.

"No jealousy?" Kim asked.

That made me laugh for real. "No. I don't miss my ex, detectives. She's welcome to him. It stung a little that he was able to propose to someone so soon after we ended things while I wasted time before starting something new." I gave Rich a quick look, and he smiled. "And sure, it's weird to see your ex with an A-lister. But no. I wasn't jealous."

I briefly wondered if, despite everything they knew

about me, they were wondering if I might have done something to Naomi.

Patsy must have read my mind, because she said, "We're just making sure we cover all our bases, Phoebe. It's not personal, just doing our jobs." She and Kim both smiled at me in a way that put me at ease. They gave a quick nod to Rich and then headed off to do more questioning.

Still, it stung that the questions needed to be asked, even in a professional capacity. Patsy and Kwan knew me well enough by now to know I wouldn't be involved in this... if there was even something to be involved in.

I was inexplicably furious with Blaine.

While none of this was likely his fault, and he had just tragically lost his new fiancée, part of my brain couldn't help but wonder if none of this would have happened if he just hadn't come here.

"Are you really okay?" Rich asked, pushing a long strand of dark brown hair behind my ear. I looked at him, and my animosity melted away.

"Yeah, sorry, it was just a bit of a shock, that's all."

"I should hope it would be a shock to find a body. The day that starts to feel normal, you might have a problem." He gave me a soft smile.

"I could just become a PI if that happens," I teased. Rich had shared the reason for leaving his job with the police, and I didn't think he'd mind my using it to lighten the mood slightly. It wasn't a *happy* story, but it had also led him to make an important life choice.

And that choice was a big part of what had brought us together.

"Oh, heaven help us the day Phoebe Winchester decides to become a PI. You're entirely too nosy for your own good as it is."

"*Rude*," I chastised.

"It's only rude if it's not true."

I snorted. "Shows what you know. Getting called on your actual shortcomings is much worse than getting called out on imagined ones. I'm not nosy, am I? Do people think I'm nosy?" I glanced around to see if anyone was actively saying it within earshot, but people were huddled together in small groups having hushed conversations about Naomi's sudden death.

No one was interested in me.

Rich laughed and pressed a gentle kiss on my forehead. "Nosy was the wrong word. I'm sorry. Curious. As curious as that chunky cat of yours."

"He's on a diet," I said, feeling bad for Bob. He *was* a little portly, but I pretended no one else noticed.

"You and Bob are both perfect just as you are, Phoebe, don't worry. And don't worry about Patsy and Kwan. They didn't mean anything by the questions; they just had to check all the boxes. If they find out something happened to Naomi later, they need to know they were as thorough as possible at the crime scene."

"I know." I set my cup down, unable to stomach more of the coffee, even though it wasn't the worst. "Do you think something *did* happen to her?"

"I just got here, Phoebs. You tell me."

I thought about Naomi and the way I'd found her lying on the floor, phone clutched in her hand. What was it about that that bothered me so much? Was she trying to call for help? Or had something she'd seen on the phone been what set off the episode that killed her?

There were no easy answers, just more and more questions.

"I wish I knew," I said. "But I have a funny feeling this isn't going to be as cut and dry as the police would like."

CHAPTER NINE

I'd only been home for an hour when there was a knock on my front door.

I knew it couldn't be Rich, since he'd left about twenty minutes earlier with a promise to bring by dinner for the both of us tonight when he finished doing a little paperwork. Apparently, even when you were self-employed, there were annoying business-related things that needed doing.

Though I suppose I knew that myself from running the shop.

Sometimes I forgot that The Earl's Study was *my* store. Most days it felt like I was just keeping the ship afloat for Eudora, and she'd come waltzing back in one morning to pick up where she left off.

I opened my front door and found Honey standing on the porch, a bottle of wine in one hand and a large smoky quartz in the other. Until that moment, I had totally forgotten I'd invited her over. The excitement of the day's events made everything that had happened in the hours beforehand seem like a distant dream.

"Honey, come on in! I'm so sorry, I forgot I'd invited you."

She held the wine bottle to her heart. "Ouch, you sure know how to make a girl feel special." But there was no malice in her tone. "How are you doing? It can't have been fun to be the one to find her like that."

I took the wine bottle from her, still not sure if the large crystal was for me or not. "I can safely say I could use a little of this. It was a huge shock. She'd seemed fine before the auditions started. I don't know if she had any conditions or anything, but it sure looked like it happened quite suddenly."

We went into the kitchen, and Honey started scanning shelves and countertops with her eyes before nodding at the mantle over the fireplace and setting the gray crystal down. Bob, who had been nestled happily in his bed, blinked up at her with a confused expression that likely matched my own.

"Smoky quartz helps ward off negative energy. After today, I thought you could use a little metaphysical booster shot."

Honey had incredible magical abilities, but she'd also been raised by a Wiccan mother, so she was both a witch in the *real* magic sense, and also a witch in the *magickal* sense, where she used herbal tinctures and crystals in everyday aspects of her life. I was never sure which side of her witchy heritage she was using to help me, but I would never say no; she was too good at what she did for me to question any of it.

"Thank you."

Bob squinted at the large rock before tucking his nose under his tail and returning to Nap Town. Coco had vanished the moment I'd answered the door. She had started to accept Rich's presence and would come out if she heard his voice, but everyone else she still treated like a terrifying stranger.

Pet parenting guides assured me this was normal, and some shy cats just needed more time to work up to accepting visitors. I had begun to understand that Coco might never be enthusiastic about guests the way Bob was, and was just grateful she had started to warm up to me.

Honey put a bundle of dried sage on the mantel next to the quartz. "I grew that all myself," she told me. "Make sure you go through the house and smudge when I leave; it'll get rid of any bad energy hanging around."

I narrowed my eyes at her. "Honey, is there a reason you're especially concerned about bad energy hanging around me?"

She smiled, but I couldn't read any deeper meaning in it. "Just let me take care of my friend the best way I know how, okay?"

It didn't exactly answer my question, but if Honey thought I needed some wards against bad energy, I wasn't going to reject them. She knew more about all of this than I did.

"Now that that's all taken care of, what was it you wanted to show me?"

I had all but forgotten the reason I'd wanted to bring her over. The excitement of the audition and with Naomi's sudden death had left me feeling topsy-turvy, and there wasn't much room in my head for other things. Poor Eudora's mystery had been pushed by the wayside.

Thankfully she was no longer on this mortal plane, so I didn't think her riddles had a deadline attached to them.

"You remember how I said I spoke to Eudora when you and your mom put me in that magical trance?" I led her into my formal dining room, which was now officially just storage for all the things I was trying to get rid of.

For a while it had just had a few banker's boxes, now the place was crammed with boxes and totes and stacks of paper everywhere. It was beginning to overwhelm me every time I came into the room, and I was almost embarrassed to show it to Honey.

She didn't say anything as we walked in, but I could sense her taking in the piles of semi-organized clutter.

"Does this have something to do with what you saw in your vision?" Honey asked. She owned a new-age shop in town that was its own kind of joyous chaos, so I knew it wasn't the amount of stuff that was setting off her alarm bells; it was just that it was so obviously *stressful* stuff.

"When I spoke to her, or... when she thought things into my head I guess, she said she'd left something for me to find."

"Oh, Phoebs... I told you that wasn't really Eudora; that was a reflection of your memories of her."

I shook my head and set the box in front of her on the table. "It wasn't just a memory, though. It was really her. And I found that under the floorboards in the attic this week."

Honey's brows creased, and she picked up the box, turning it around in her hands, her fingers searching for any seams or latches. "How does it open?" she asked.

"I don't know. There's a letter. And a coin?" I showed her the old coin and then let her read Eudora's letter. When she was finished, she was smirking, which was surprising.

"She's sending you on a scavenger hunt," Honey said with a laugh.

I picked up the letter again. "*Let the quarter take you for a ride.* What does that even mean?"

"A lot of old kids' rides used to be coin-operated. Like the little horses or airplanes in malls that would rock back and forth. Maybe it's something like that."

"Do you know of any of those around here? I think Lansing's might have had one back in the nineties." I could dimly recall an old spaceship my brother Sam had been obsessed with. But I'd been almost everywhere in town since moving back, and I couldn't think of a single place with coin-operated rides.

Honey read the letter over my shoulder. "Maybe it means something more abstract, but I can't think of anything right now. Do you mind if I take a picture of the letter? I love riddles, and it might have some doublespeak clues in it."

"Knock yourself out," I said, putting the letter on the table so she could snap a photo on her phone.

As she was framing up the shot, Bob jumped up onto the table and plopped his butt down right on the paper, then fixed us both with a stern look and declared, "*Mreeoooow.*"

"Oh, don't you dare," I scolded. "You've been fed, and treat o'clock isn't for another couple of hours."

At the pronouncement of the word *treat*, Coco suddenly appeared in the doorway, her ears and eyes alert. When she saw I still had company, she gave me a cross, betrayed look, and disappeared once again.

Just my luck that the only English word she'd learned summoned her like a Ouija board calling to a spirit from the great beyond, but she was just as hard to pin down.

"Do you happen to know any spells to improve cat friendliness?" I asked.

Honey smiled as she scratched Bob behind his ears, and he purred loudly. "Maybe you should ask the resident expert."

She wasn't talking about the riddles anymore, but her offhand comment had given me an incredibly goofy idea.

"Honey, you're a genius."

CHAPTER TEN

Bob liked to be held like a baby.

I stood in the front entrance looking at the grand staircase and the two main rooms leading off it, and gently bounced the big furry lump in my arms like I might soothe a child to sleep. He purred like he was having the best time in the world, his green eyes squinting, a tiny dollop of drool on his lips.

His paws made little biscuits on my forearm.

"Okay pal. You were here when Eudora hid that box; I'd bet my life on it. So, you can tell me what her first clue means."

The purring continued, and he made a small *ekekek* sound, almost like he was trying to talk back. His eyes were now almost entirely closed, and I feared I had perhaps made him a little *too* comfortable to complete our task.

If this wasn't the craziest idea I'd ever had to begin with.

Beside me, Honey didn't say anything, so her opinion of my sanity was still up in the air.

I peppered Bob's forehead with a half dozen kisses and

then gently set him down on the floor. For a moment he stared at me as if asking *Is cuddle time over*, before sitting back on his haunches and slow blinked first at me, then at Honey. It was like watching a toddler slowly wake up, except my toddler was furry, round, and slept seventeen hours a day.

"Come on, Bob. I know you can do this." I held out the quarter and the box, which Honey had been holding for me, and he sniffed them both.

After a long, languorous yawn, I felt almost certain this idea had been a bust. Until his ears perked up and he sniffed the air around him, like he'd just sensed an open tin of food somewhere.

"*Merow?*" Bob asked, though it wasn't clear what his question was.

"Yeah, buddy, you got this," I encouraged.

Bob stood up, tail high, and headed in the direction of the kitchen, further making me wonder if this new enthusiasm was just about getting fed. But as Honey and I trailed him into the kitchen, he bypassed the food dishes on the floor completely and made a beeline for the basement door, which he pawed at before giving me a meaningful look and a plaintive *meow*.

"The basement?"

This whole thing had shades of *What's that Lassie, Timmy fell in the well?* But I trusted my cat, and I knew he was smarter than any non-animal lover would give him credit for. If Bob thought there was something in the basement, there was something in the basement.

I switched on the light from the kitchen and opened up the door, where Bob raced down faster than I'd ever seen him move unless food was involved. Honey and I shared a quick glance, and if she was thinking this was nuts, I appreciated her not saying so to my face.

The basement of Lane End House was not your typical basement, if there was such a thing. Most basements in the area were concrete slabs squares. Some were even just glorified dirt crawl spaces. While Eudora's basement had once been the concrete slab variety, she had breathed new life into it by turning it into a storage space for all her teas.

Of course, the humid, rainy weather of the Pacific Northwest meant that I was running a dehumidifier twenty-four seven to stave off dampness in the air that might threaten the tea, but it was ultimately a pretty perfect place to mix delicious blends and keep the overstock we didn't have room for at The Earl's Study.

It was also where Eudora had kept her plethora of seasonal decorations, because she—like the entire town— took holidays *very* seriously. I hadn't even begun to plumb the depths of everything she had, but it was clear she had been prepared for every possible holiday she might need to kit out the house and shop for.

When Honey and I reached the basement floor, it wasn't immediately obvious where Bob had disappeared to. Normally his general orange roundness stood out in a room, but this was a very busy space, and I couldn't tell where he'd gotten himself to.

"Bob?" I said, then gave Honey a little shrug. She was still holding the box I'd found under the floorboards, while I clutched the letter and quarter in my hand.

"*Mreow*," trilled Bob from the back of the room.

I still couldn't see him, hidden as he was behind stacks of boxes and things I'd added since I moved, like overstock for mugs and tote bags from The Earl's Study.

I moved a few things out of the way, following his little

voice, until something emerged from behind all of the Halloween storage bins I'd pulled out a week earlier.

Bob sat perched atop the saddle of the old carousel horse that had been down here since I'd moved in—and likely decades before that. He looked for all the world like he was ready to take an afternoon horseback ride. His orange tail flicked back and forth, and he squinted his eyes at me with a few slow blinks for good measure.

Cats can't smile, *per se*, but I swear he was beaming with pride in that moment.

I had never known how Eudora came to have the carousel horse, or *why* she had it stashed down here so long, and the longer I'd lived in the house the less I noticed its presence in the basement.

Now, as Bob licked his front paws to clean his whiskers, I wondered if the gorgeous old antique was more than just a fun piece of kitsch my aunt had found in her travels.

What if it were something magical?

The horse had seen better days. It was obvious just by looking at it that it had spent most of its life outdoors—as most carousel horses do—and its paint was sun-bleached and peeling. Still, the animal maintained an undeniable aura of majesty. The horse had once been a rich plum color, its mane painted silver, and the saddle a combination of lilac, teal, and burnt orange, with silver and gold accents. The colors were all still there, though pastel, muted versions of their former glory.

There were rings at the horse's mouth where reins had surely once gone, though the straps had been lost long ago. The stirrups for the saddle still remained, though. The horse's head was lifted slightly, as if it was about to toss its beautiful mane in the wind.

I could picture small children clamoring to pick this specific mount for their ride.

Bob curled up on the saddle, a rather precarious position, but he seemed to be managing it fine. I swear, cats can make themselves comfortable just about anywhere.

"That's incredible," Honey said, her voice barely above a whisper. "Has that always been down here?"

Well, I guess that answered any questions I had about whether or not Eudora had used the horse for seasonal décor of some kind. "It's been here as long as I've been here, and no idea how long she had it before then."

"I think that might have been from the original fairground carousel that used to be here in the forties," Honey said, approaching the horse with reverence and brushing her fingers over its wooden mane.

"There was a fairground here?" If that was the case, it had been long gone before I started paying my aunt summer visits as a kid.

"It was where the Lansing's parking lot is now, just down the road. It was a small place, with only a few rides, but it ran from the early forties up until 1980. They had to shut it down because the cost of upkeep on the old rides was going to be more than they could ever make operating it."

"How on earth do you know all that?" I asked.

Honey wasn't a Raven's Creek lifer, she'd moved here in her early twenties to open her New Age shop. Her family's roots didn't go all the way back the way mine did, but I also felt like new blood here. Even after a year, there was still only one person in Raven's Creek newer than me, and that was Dierdre's nephew Dylan.

"I was looking up old historical records of my shop not long after I rented it. I like to know if places have good or bad history; it can really impact the vibes, and while I was doing that, I found an old map of town that showed the fairgrounds. I wanted to know more. You'd be amazed what you can dig up at the library." She gave me a faint smile, as if she knew how strange her research hobby sounded.

"That's very cool. I wonder if they'd have pictures of the carousel from back in the day."

Honey, now encouraged by my interest, nodded enthusiastically. "They do! That's why I thought it looked so familiar. I wonder how she ended up with it."

"Knowing Eudora, she probably just pointed at it and said, *That's coming home with me* and no one argued with her." I could practically imagine my aunt with an early eighties perm, telling the crew who dismantled the fairground to drop the horse off at her house. She had a commanding presence; I doubted anyone would have blinked twice.

But what did the horse have to do with my mission? Bob had clearly led us here with a purpose, but a carousel horse wasn't a coin-operated ride outside a shopping center. As far as I knew, there was nowhere to put a quarter into one.

"Can you help me check this thing to see if there's somewhere the quarter goes?" I asked, setting the letter down on top of a nearby tote.

Honey put the wooden box down on top of it, and we scoured the horse from top to bottom, looking at every crease and dent to see if it might be a place where a coin could fit.

No luck.

I let out a little sigh of frustration. I guess it had been too much to hope that my cat might be the secret key to this little magical scavenger hunt.

My cat.

My cat. Who was currently blocking a good chunk of saddle real estate.

I gently lifted Bob from the saddle, and though he made a little grunt of protest, he went without a fight. Once I'd placed him on the ground, he made a trilling noise and pawed at the horse's leg.

There on the saddle was the tiniest slot at the base of the pommel. I gave Honey another loaded look, and we both barely dared to breathe.

"This better work," I whispered. "Because once I put it in there, I don't think there's any way for me to get it back without taking the whole darned horse apart."

"Only one way to find out," she said, nudging me with her shoulder.

I took a deep breath and dropped the quarter into the slot.

CHAPTER ELEVEN

I expected to hear the hollow sound of the quarter tumbling into the horse's empty belly, telling me this whole experiment had been a fool's errand. Instead, there was a soft *click* sound, followed by a whirring that was almost too quiet to hear.

The horse started to glow the same faint blue as the box had, though it was hard to tell in the brightly lit basement. Bob noticed it well enough, as his tail puffed up and he darted back to the top of the stairs to observe us from a safe distance.

I wasn't sure if that was a bad sign, or simply evidence that he was sometimes a literal scaredy cat. Nevertheless, Honey and I took a few steps back from the horse as the sound of whirring became something more like moving gears, and motes of dust started shaking off the old wooden object as it apparently vibrated.

I couldn't take my eyes off it, the shimmer of light, the strange noises. Obviously, I'd found the right home for the quarter, but what was I about to discover, and was it something that might have been better left alone?

Finally, after a few achingly long seconds, the horse went still, and a soft *pop* noise sounded as the saddle apparently clicked open from an unseen hinge. Whether that was a real hinge or a magical one was a question for another day.

Together, Honey and I inched forward until I was close enough to lift the saddle. Inside the horse's belly, the blue light continued to glow, and while there was no sign of the quarter, there was another letter, and next to it an old-fashioned key. I'd seen many similar keys around Lane End House. In fact, it bore a striking resemblance to the front door key.

I hesitated a moment before reaching inside, as if worried this might somehow be a trap. But ultimately, that was very silly. My aunt had loved me as much as she might have loved her own daughter. She'd left me this house, her business, and entrusted me to care for Bob. There was no way she would have set a trap for me.

A trick perhaps, but nothing dangerous or malicious.

Putting my hand into the belly of the beast, I withdrew the letter first, then the key. I was surprised by how cold the key was, though perhaps I shouldn't have been considering it was October in Washington and it had been in my basement for heaven only knew how long.

Honey collected the box and the first letter, while I took the new letter and key, and we headed back upstairs where the light was better and the atmosphere just a little less mysterious.

We didn't go far, taking everything to my small kitchen table. Before we indulged in my aunt's scavenger hunt anymore, I desperately needed a cup of tea, because I could feel a faint trembling trying to overtake my body and wanted something to calm my nerves.

Honey had told me once, beyond question, that ghosts did not exist. There was no way for my aunt to reach out to me beyond the grave. Yet, when Honey and her mother had helped me fix an issue I was having with my magical abilities acting up, I'd found myself in a spiritual plane where Eudora had clearly been present. Honey tried to tell me this was just an echo, something out of my memory.

Yet that so-called echo had hinted there was something to find in the house.

And now I was looking at a variety of clues on my kitchen table.

Was Eudora still out there somewhere? Watching over me in some capacity. Not for the first time, I wished she were. I had so many questions for her, so much I longed to know. She was my only tie to my family's witchy bloodline, and I was still so new to this whole magic thing. I wished I'd been able to learn my witch skills directly from her, rather than fumbling around in the dark learning them by accident.

I put Eudora's old kettle down on the stove and turned on the range. Once that was heating, I collected two mugs —dainty teacups wouldn't do at the moment—and put a heaping bag of my shop's newest Earl Grey blend in. It was a combination of a classic Earl Grey tea base with black tea and bergamot, but we'd added lavender flowers and lemon verbena, as well as vanilla sugar, to give it a floral and citrus aftertaste that was to die for. It was also the precise level of comforting and calming that I needed right now.

I added the nearly boiling water to the cups and put one down in front of Honey and the other in front of me, with a spare plate between us to put the tea bags on after they were done steeping.

Honey and I both took our seats and stared at the

objects on the table while plumes of cozy steam unfurled from our mugs.

"Maybe the key opens the box?" Honey suggested.

I didn't want to point out the obvious, that the box had no keyhole, because who even knew if that mattered considering we were dealing with magic, here.

I took the key in my hand, my fingers jerking slightly because it was still so cold, and held it up to the side of the box. I tried angling it like I would if there *were* a keyhole, and then I resorted to trying to tap it or press it along each unblemished side of the box.

Nothing.

Well, that would have been much too easy, wouldn't it?

I glanced around for Bob, wondering if he might have a suggestion for this one, but he had vanished, likely cozying up to Coco in the living room. Lucky for him that this puzzle wasn't going to give him any sleepless nights.

"I guess we'll see what Eudora had to say for herself with this one." I grabbed the unopened envelope and gently ripped it open, and inside was a letter that looked nearly identical to the first in its age and texture, confirming they were likely all written at the same time.

I wasn't much for reading out loud, so I read it myself before passing it over to Honey.

Dear Phoebe,

Congrats, my darling girl, you figured out the first clue! I never had a single doubt. I hope you didn't think that they were going to get easier from here, because what is a challenge if it isn't challenging? I'm certain you might think me a little cruel for making you jump through all these hoops, but give an old woman her pleasures. Do you remember how you used to love playing hide and seek in the house when you were younger and making me come looking for you? Think of this as my *hide and seek for you. I'll be waiting when you find where the key fits.*

Much love,

Eudora

After Honey had finished reading it, she glanced up from the letter, clearly as lost as I was.

"Not really much to go on in terms of clues, is it?" she asked.

I shook my head glumly.

"She thought the first clue was easy!" I said with a sigh. "I needed my cat to solve that one for me."

Honey smiled and put the letter down between us, then sipped her tea with a satisfied look on her face. I did the same and had to admit the taste was exactly what I needed to bring me back down to earth.

"I guess you could just try every keyhole in the house," Honey suggested.

I leaned back in my chair and groaned. "I was afraid you were going to suggest that."

Before I could try to wrangle her into my efforts, my phone started to buzz in my back pocket, startling me. I pulled it out and saw that Detective Patsy Martin was calling me.

Though I knew perfectly well that Patsy wouldn't think me a suspect in Naomi Novak's murder, there was still something immediately anxiety-inducing about having a homicide detective call you.

"Hi Detective Martin," I said, trying to keep my nerves out of my voice.

"Phoebe, I think at this point it's probably all right for you to call me Patsy."

I paused. "You know, I'm not sure if I can."

She laughed.

"Well, I'm hoping you might be able to meet me down at the police station. I have a few more questions for you about what happened and was hoping to chat with you about... other things." The way her voice drifted suggested these were things she didn't want to hash out over the phone, which likely meant *magical* things, but also could have meant something else.

And why was she making me come to the station instead of visiting me here?

I had been certain she didn't think I was a suspect, but now I wasn't so sure.

"Um, sure. Of course. I can be there in about fifteen minutes if that works?"

Honey quirked a curious brow at me but didn't say anything.

"Sure thing, see you then."

Detective Martin hung up, leaving me with all sorts of fun new worries. I gave Honey a quick look and said, "Looks like you're off the hook for further scavenger hunting. I need to go talk to the police."

Honey finished off her tea and reached across the table to squeeze my hand. "I don't envy your afternoon plans one bit."

CHAPTER TWELVE

I hadn't killed anyone, but that didn't mean I didn't feel guilty walking into the Raven Creek police station.

The place was usually quiet, with crime not exactly being a huge part of the lifestyle in our cozy little town. But as soon as I'd pulled into the parking lot, I knew this wasn't going to be a regular visit.

The lot was crammed with news vans, and camera crews were set up facing the front entrance. There were stations I recognized like CNN, TMZ, FOX News and more, plus a half dozen regional outlets, and the editor-in-chief and head reporter of our town's own newspaper, the *Raven Creek Gazette*.

I actually admired Winnie York for squaring off shoulder-to-shoulder with the big boys of broadcasting. I didn't know Winnie personally, but often wondered if she ever slept, because there were very few stories in our town—no matter how small they might seem—that the *Gazette* didn't put into print.

She didn't miss much, that Winnie.

Winnie was in her mid-forties and had once been a

reporter for the *Boston Globe*, which explained her devotion to the printed word, not to mention her nose for a story.

She'd inherited the *Gazette* from her grandfather, and like me, had come to Raven Creek for a fresh start. That had been almost ten years earlier in her case, and her fresh start had looked a lot different from mine. She had curly red hair that she had never learned to tame and certainly helped make her easy to spot in a crowd.

Unfortunately, she was also very capable of picking out others.

"Phoebe Winchester?" she said when she spotted me approaching the building. She didn't miss a beat, slipping immediately into investigation mode. "You're the one who found Naomi's body, aren't you? Do you want to make a statement?"

Her questions caught the attention of a few of the other reporters standing nearby, men and women from the bigger outlets. One of the CNN reporters, whose face I recognized but couldn't place to a name, flipped through some notes she had in front of her. "Did you say Winchester? Isn't that the name of Naomi's new fiancé?"

"Blaine Winchester," offered up the TMZ reporter, like they knew the information off the top of their head. Actually, considering they were a celebrity gossip channel, they probably did.

This was a terrible mistake. I should have asked Patsy to meet me *literally* anywhere else.

"You have a connection to the dead woman's fiancé?" Winnie asked, her tone affronted, as if we were friends and she couldn't believe I'd kept this from her.

"No comment," I muttered meekly, feeling stupid the moment the words were out of my mouth.

"Who's she?" someone asked as I bumped my way through the throng.

"Naomi's fiancé's wife?" Someone guessed a little too close to the truth.

"Woah, she was engaged to a married man?" another reporter asked.

It took every ounce of restraint in my body not to correct them. I knew that saying anything would only do more harm than good. And these were journalists, so surely they'd do their due diligence and fact check things before going to air with some wild tale about Blaine cheating on me with Naomi Novak.

He'd cheated on me, yes. But not with an A-lister.

He'd had to work his way up to that.

I bit my cheek, trying to chase off the unkind thoughts flooding my mind. Obviously, I was still mad at Blaine, but I had to remind myself that his fiancée was dead. Whatever animosity still lingered between the two of us, I knew he had to be hurting right now.

I didn't say anything even as the crowd volleyed questions at me, and soon enough I was safely inside the police station, where Patsy was waiting for me in the lobby.

"I'm sorry, Phoebe, I wasn't thinking."

I shook my head, trying to rattle loose all the invasive and hostile questions I'd just had to endure in my short walk through the parking lot. "It's okay, but I think I might take the back way out later if you don't mind."

"I'd offer to send you home with one of the officers, but I think the sight of you in a squad car might send those vultures into a whole new frenzy."

"Ugh, no thank you. You know, I always thought paparazzi were shady for following celebrities around, but I can honestly say I never thought I'd be at the receiving end of all those personal questions. I hated it."

"Were they asking you about Blaine?" Patsy asked as she guided me into the privacy of the main office area of the police station, where there were several desks set up. Detective Kwan Kim was at his usual place across from Patsy and raised his hand in a friendly wave.

That, coupled with his warm smile, immediately set me at ease. Okay, I obviously wasn't in trouble. So why then go to all the effort of making me come down here?

I realized I'd left Patsy's question unanswered. "Yeah, Winnie said my name, and it didn't take long for them to make the Winchester connection. They were *very* interested by the sounds of it, but they were also making all the wrong assumptions." I let out a sigh.

"You might want to warn your staff," Detective Kim prompted. "Now that they know your name, it's not going to take any time at all for them to figure out where you work. With Winnie in the mix, she'll already know. They'll probably show up wanting to talk to you."

I let out a long groan, realizing he might be right. I thought I'd gotten through the worst of it by escaping the crowd outside, but until Naomi's case was closed, Raven Creek was going to be a hotbed for news and tabloid reporters alike, and I wasn't naïve enough to think they wouldn't come sniffing around to ask me more questions.

I fired off a quick text to Daphne and Imogen to tell them to be on their toes when I wasn't around, and that "no comment" was all they needed to say.

Imogen replied almost immediately by saying, *I can think of a few more choice words I can share with them if they show up*.

Normally, I'd caution her not to be confrontational, but

in this scenario I felt she was more than welcome to say whatever she wanted to these people. I didn't want to make friends with the reporters, and they weren't customers, so I just sent the thumbs-up emoji as a response.

Daphne replied with the face-melting emoji, which I was about a decade too old to properly translate.

"Thanks," I said to Detective Kim.

Patsy pulled out a chair and put it between their two desks. We were the only people in the entire building, which seemed odd, given how high-profile Naomi's death was. Had they called in backup from Barneswood? If so, where were they?

Or had Patsy and Kwan cleared the station for another reason?

They seemed to be sensing my unease, because Kwan shot a quick look to Patsy and raised a brow, as if to ask, *do you want to tell her or should I?*

"Guys, come on, let's not with the cloak and dagger and asking each other eyeball questions. I'm here. What can I do to help?"

Patsy cleared her throat. "Well, as you recall, a few months ago after that break-in at your house, we overlooked a few details on our official report."

By *break-in* they meant *attempted murder*, and by *details* they meant that I'd used magic to pin my attacker to the ceiling. Something I hadn't even known I was capable of until that moment, and not a skill I'd tried to practice in the interim. "Yeeeessss," I replied slowly, not sure I liked where we were going.

"And we told you then that before she passed, Eudora had sometimes used her magical skills to help us on cases. Just from time to time."

I raised an eyebrow at them, suddenly realizing exactly where this was going.

"You want me to help you figure out what happened to Naomi? With... magic?" I had no idea what tricks Eudora had up her sleeves to help them in the past, but there was a vast ocean of difference between my aunt's witchy skills and my own. For starters, she'd had years to hone her gifts, and I'd only known about mine for a little over twelve months.

I wasn't *good* at being a witch. I had graduated from disastrous to passable, but I was still learning new things every day, and solving mysteries with a wave of my wand wasn't a skill I had in my back pocket.

To be honest, I didn't even know if that was a skill *any* witch had in her back pocket. For starters, no one I know— however small the sample size—used a wand.

Was I supposed to be using a wand?

"Of course I want to help you guys, but I'm not sure I can be your new Eudora," I admitted. "She was a lot better at... everything." My heart clenched a little. "Plus, isn't a doctor a better bet for figuring out how Naomi died?

Between the scavenger hunt at my house, and now the police asking for me to step into my aunt's shoes in a new and unexpected way, I was feeling Eudora's absence in a fresh way. Not painful exactly, but it certainly felt new again. Like she had just been in the room a moment ago, and stepped out, as opposed to having been dead for over a year.

She cast a long shadow, even from beyond the grave.

Maybe she can help you, a little voice in the back of my head nagged.

Help me *how*, though? Honey was right about one thing: ghosts weren't real, at least not in the way old stories and modern horror movies might lead us to believe. Eudora wasn't some see-through spectre floating through my house and popping out of closets at me.

Yet I knew deep in my bones she was still in that house in some capacity. One I just didn't know how to reach yet.

"Look," Patsy said, breaking up the silence. "We won't pretend to understand what the full scope of your powers are. We know there was plenty Eudora kept from us, and I want you to know we respect that, and we respect your boundaries of not wanting to tell us."

I shook my head and had to laugh, though I knew this wasn't a particularly funny moment. "I don't think you understand. Eudora had a lifetime to hone her power. I've only been doing this for a year. What you guys saw me do? That was an accident brought on by a pretty high-stress situation. Most of my best magic seems to crop up in high-stress situations. It's not as..." I searched for the right word. "Not as refined as hers was." *Refined* felt less scary than admitting to them I had little to no control over my skills half the time.

Which I suppose was an improvement over the beginning, when I had *no* control over them.

"We were hoping for your help on two fronts, actually. No magic necessary... unless you think it will help, of course."

It was far more likely that my magic would hinder the investigation rather than help it, but I just nodded.

"First, we were wondering if you might have an opportunity to speak with Blaine. I know that's something of an awkward thing to ask you," Patsy admitted sheepishly. "But he won't talk to us until his lawyer shows up, and given your history with him, we thought there might be a chance he would say something unguarded to you."

I snorted, causing both detectives to look surprised. "Blaine and I aren't exactly besties. I don't know how many friendly divorces there have been in history, but ours wasn't one of them."

Patsy nodded. "Be that as it may, you are the only familiar face to him in this town aside from Naomi's crew. He might find... comfort in talking to you."

I made a little face. "I can try, but I can't guarantee anything. I can barely stand to be in the same room as him, and he knows it. He might think it's a bit peculiar that I'm being friendly." Blaine wasn't a stupid guy.

Well, I suppose he'd been very stupid about a lot of things, but he was also observant. If I were going to get him to talk, I couldn't be too nice to him.

"All we ask is that you try; it would help us a lot."

I had questions about this. Why did they want to talk to Blaine so badly? And why was a lawyer involved at all? Naomi had died, which was very sad, but surely Blaine could tell them about any medical issues she had without a lawyer being involved.

"What's the second thing?" I glanced between the two of them.

Patsy opened the drawer next to her and pulled out a medium-sized plastic evidence bag. Inside was a cup.

"We found this cup beside Naomi's body. We're testing the contents, but we wanted to see if you recognized it."

Again, I was confused. What did this have to do with her heart attack or stroke, or whatever had happened to her?

"What's the deal with the cup?" I asked, finally voicing some of my confusion.

Patsy and Kwan exchanged a quick glance, then seemed to agree on something between them.

"Phoebe, we don't believe Naomi died from natural causes. We have good reason to believe that she was poisoned. Intentionally."

"You think Naomi Novak was *murdered*?" I said, my mouth practically hanging open.

Then, my attention returned to the cup. At first, I was worried Patsy was implying the cup had come from The Earl's Study, but ours were teal blue with a distinctive logo featuring a cat dozing on an open book with a steaming mug beside him. This was a plain brown cup.

Unfortunately, I did recognize it, because before she'd switched out her branding I had received one of those brown paper cups every single morning.

I swallowed a lump in my throat.

"Yeah. That's Amy's. From the Sugarplum Fairy."

CHAPTER THIRTEEN

After I confirmed a few parts of my statement with Patsy and Kwan, they let me leave through the back door and made me promise to check in with them if I learned anything from Blaine.

But Blaine was the last person on my mind right now.

I could see the reporters were still milling around the front of the building, and decided there was no way I would be able to get to my car without being pestered. Thankfully, despite the chill in the air, it was a lovely evening.

I sent Rich a quick text telling him I was running an errand, but I'd be back at my place in an hour. I didn't want him to show up with dinner and me not to be there. Our relationship was new, and I didn't want to prove myself to be a thoughtless girlfriend so early on.

This conversation was one that could certainly wait until another time, but my feet were already moving in the direction of Amy's house, and I couldn't think of a single reason to turn away other than being a chicken.

I *knew* Amy hadn't done anything to hurt Naomi. The very idea of it was ludicrous. Amy was the sweetest, gentlest woman I knew and would rather open the door to shoo a fly out rather than swatting it. Which typically resulted in creating a bigger problem, but that was just the sort of person Amy was.

The notion of her doing something to poison Naomi's drink was insane. I was still reeling from that revelation. Naomi had been *poisoned*? Who could want to kill America's Sweetheart? It was inconceivable. But the evidence remained. That had been Amy's cup, and Amy had likely been the person to make the drink inside of it, since she currently worked as a one-woman show.

It didn't look good, and I wanted to be the one to break the news to Amy rather than letting the police do it. Detectives Martin and Kim were good people, but they weren't always warm and cuddly, and if Amy was going to find out she was a suspect in a famous actress's murder, she needed someone warm and fuzzy to tell her.

Amy lived on Gaiety Road, a block that seemed to have been designed purely to delight anyone who happened to walk or drive down it. Every house on the block had a quarter-acre lot, and each house was designed to resemble an English country cottage. They had sloping roofs—with shingles, not thatch—and robust gardens that seemed to have color in them the whole year round.

Even though it was almost Halloween, Amy's yard was lush with greenery, her roses were still in bloom, and the walkway was lined with cheerful pansies. She, like everyone else in town, was in the Halloween spirit, and I counted no fewer than eighteen pumpkins adorning her porch and front walk. Some were carved with jolly, toothless smiles, while others remained whole and purely decorative. She had white ones, and some that were such a dark green they looked black.

Little ghosts fluttered in the trees, and on a large oak in the front yard she had the figure of a witch splattered up against the trunk, as if she had flown into it by accident.

I stared at the flattened witch and raised an eyebrow, wondering if I should be offended.

Of course, I didn't ride around on brooms, but if I did, there was a chance I'd be so bad at it I might end up looking just like that piece of seasonal décor, so perhaps I could let it go.

In Amy's flower beds there were miniature skeletons pretending to pull up flowers, and she had fake plastic grave markers smattered around the entire front lawn with terribly punny names on them. I.M. Dunn, Barry DeLyve, Noah Scape, Bea Fraid. I shook my head as each got worse than the last.

Amy clearly *loved* Halloween.

I looked at her lovely, whimsical yard, and I felt profoundly guilty for coming here to tell her such bad news.

Making my way up to the door, I practiced what I was going to say in my head, but no matter how many different ways I tried to structure the news, my imagination still just showed me Amy bursting into tears.

I steeled myself and rang her doorbell.

She answered a moment later, wearing a black and orange apron that said *Bone Appetite* on it, and she had flour dappling her cheeks and forehead. She smelled of cinnamon and sugar, as usual.

"Amy, are you baking during your downtime?"

She grinned at me and wiped her hands on an orange and white tea towel before draping it over her shoulder. "How do you think I come up with new recipes? I don't have time to experiment at the shop, so I do it when I'm home. It's a good thing I love baking."

She opened her door wider and ushered me inside, where the house smelled of pumpkin spice and everything nice. I took in a deep breath and just let the seasonal aromas waft over me.

"You're just in time. I have a cranberry pumpkin loaf coming out of the oven, and I'm about to put in some rosemary, apricot, white chocolate cookies that I'm test-running for my Christmas menu."

My mouth was watering, but that just reminded me there was business to get down to before she was able to distract me with sweet treats. "Amy, I've got some news. Do you mind sitting down for a second?"

We were in the kitchen, and while I expected it to be a disaster of baking supplies, the counter was neat and tidy, with several trays of perfectly proportioned cookies ready and waiting to go into the oven. Other treats were laid out on cooling racks, but it was clear Amy was a meticulous clean as you go chef.

Amy pulled a tray of mini loaves from the oven and set it down on top of the stove, then placed a tray of cookies in to replace it.

"That sounds serious, Phoebe. Is everything okay?"

I took a deep breath to prepare myself, then just went for it. "Amy, do you remember serving Naomi the morning of the auditions?"

Amy laughed, setting her oven mitts down. "Remember? Well, it's not something I'd be likely to forget. Not a lot of Oscar-nominated actresses walk into my shop on a regular basis."

I forced a smile and continued. "Did you recently run out of your branded cups?"

"I did! And what a terrible week for them to be back-ordered, too. I just imagined it. Naomi Novak posting a picture of *my* famous pumpkin pie latte, and it's in a boring brown cup with my name nowhere on it! Talk about tragic." She seemed to realize what she'd said and bit her lip. "Oh. I mean, you know... before that whole thing happened."

"Oh, I know, hon. I get it. But... um..." I glanced around the kitchen, which was a lovely French country inspired space filled with warm light and a shocking number of goose ornaments. "Do you know how Naomi died?"

Amy shook her head, obviously uneasy about the direction this conversation was going.

"She was poisoned."

We stared at each other for a long moment, and I saw her expression shift from confusion to realization to horror. I knew the precise moment she understood what my questions were getting at.

"Oh no," she said, pulling up a nearby stool and slumping into it. "This isn't good. This is very, very bad." She was wringing the tea towel in her hands, and while I suspected she would take the news hard, there was something about the way she'd said *this is very, very bad* that made me wonder if she had more reasons for thinking that than just being upset about the implication.

"There's no way you're going to get in any trouble, Amy. Everyone in town knows you could never hurt anyone."

She darted a quick glance at me, then looked back down at the counter, her cheeks flushing deep red. "I forget sometimes you aren't from around here. You're just such a part of the town now..."

"Okay?"

"Well, you see, the thing is, that's not exactly true."

"What isn't?"

"That I wouldn't hurt anyone."

I stared across the counter at her, not sure what she was trying to say.

A tear slid down her cheek, and she refused to look up at me.

"Phoebe, if the detectives start looking at me as a suspect, they're going to find out I have a criminal record."

My mouth hung open in a very unladylike manner, but I couldn't manage to make it close again. "What are you talking about? What did you do?"

She swiped away her tears and then looked right at me.

"I tried to kill someone."

CHAPTER FOURTEEN

It was a good thing my jaw was already slack, because of all the things Amy could have said to me in that moment, her having a criminal record for attempted homicide wasn't anywhere near my top ten list of possibilities.

"What are you talking about?" I guess my voice had inched towards hysterical, because Amy seemed to come out of the stupor she'd been in and shook her head vigorously.

"Oh, my goodness, I realize how that sounded. I'm sorry." She waved her hands in front of her as if her previous words were smoke, and she was trying to clear them away. "I could have said that so much better."

"So... you *didn't* try to kill anyone?"

She laughed, though it was humorless. "No. Though I almost wish they'd been right. And it doesn't matter; my arrest record is still there even though all the charges were ultimately dropped."

"What happened?"

Her oven timer beeped, and she hopped off the stool to take her cookies out of the oven and put another batch in. I couldn't decide if this was just a natural motion for her, so easy to complete under duress, or if she wasn't actually all that worried about being a potential murder suspect.

When she got back to her stool, though, I could see I was mistaken; her features were drawn, and there was obvious stress weighing on her now that hadn't been there before.

Amy was in her forties, petite, plump, and her blonde hair always perfectly in place even when it was pulled back for the kitchen. She reminded me often of Sookie from *Gilmore Girls*, though less klutzy. Seeing her usually bubbly persona dimmed like this made me wonder if I'd done the right thing by coming here to break the news.

"I don't really talk about this much. It's not the kind of story you want to lead with when you're making new friends. But you *have* been a good friend to me, Phoebe." She reached across the table and took my hand, giving it a firm squeeze.

"Of course," I replied. "You were the first person here to be nice to me. I think I would have run screaming back to Seattle after one night if I hadn't met you."

She gave me a smile that briefly wrinkled the corners of her eyes before letting out a long sigh, bracing herself for whatever story she was about to tell me.

"My family has lived here my whole life. I actually spent the first few years of my life in the apartment over my shop —my parents' shop then—and we moved a few blocks away after my brother and sister were born." She must have seen the quizzical expression on my face because she added, "Twins. That little apartment was fine for one kid, but for three, they needed something bigger."

She picked up one of her oven mitts and started plucking at a loose piece of thread.

"I loved my siblings, but being six years older than them, we weren't exactly close. We were never at the same school at the same time, and because they were twins, they were often off in their own little world. They could practically read each other's minds, and it could be so frustrating trying to have a conversation with them or do anything with them because sometimes they'd just look at each other and start laughing at you and you weren't in on the joke. Pests." Amy smiled mostly to herself, and I could hear the genuine warmth in her voice when she spoke about her siblings. She'd mentioned a brother and sister in passing over the year we'd been friends, but I'd never met them, and she didn't often say much about them.

To be fair, though, I didn't spend a lot of time talking about my brother, Sam, either. As adults, we just sort of all became our own people. It didn't make us love them any less, though.

Amy very obviously thought the world of her siblings, but I wasn't sure what her story had to do with her having a criminal record.

"One summer, I was home for a break from college. I was already through culinary school, but I was taking a business management course to prepare myself to take over the bakery one day. My sister, Caroline, was in high school, and she'd started dating this real piece of work. His name was Trent."

The T-sound at the beginning and end of his name sounded like it had been sharpened coming off her tongue. I didn't need to ask what Amy felt about Trent, and I was starting to see where her darker history might be taking shape in this story.

"Anyway, I didn't want to meddle too much in Caro's life. She was sixteen and thought she knew everything, but worse than that, she thought she was in love. Trent was her sun and moon, and nothing me or anyone else in the family said was going to change her mind. It didn't matter that he was rude to our parents, that he was a known thief in town —he was actually banned from Lansing's—and he was a future burnout. She just saw a good-looking boy with a fast car, and for some reason that blinded her to common sense."

Amy set down the oven mitt before she could pull out all the stitches and gave me a look. "Did you date anyone like that? I know I didn't, but I barely dated at all in high school."

"I didn't, but I did marry a pretty useless excuse for a husband." It felt weird to be talking about Blaine like that knowing he was in the same town as me even as I said it. Like I was worried he might hear me or something.

Amy laughed, putting me more at ease.

"Anyway, I talked to my parents about it, but even though they didn't like him any more than I did, we all agreed it was a live and learn situation for her. Eventually he was going to do or say something to make Caro realize what a weasel he was, and she would be heartbroken, but she would move on and hopefully learn not to invest herself in a guy like that again."

The oven timer beeped again, and Amy did another switcheroo with the trays. She started to put the cookies from her very first tray onto the cooling rack.

"We were wrong, though. We thought the worst thing he would do would be to break her heart. But instead, he broke her arm."

I gasped. "He *what?*"

Amy nodded solemnly, still putting the cookies onto the rack.

"We still don't know how it happened. Even now, Caro won't talk about it, but after we got back from the hospital, she said she was done with him and she didn't want to say anything else. She wouldn't press charges, but she also wasn't going to forgive him. My parents wanted to go to the police, but Caro insisted she didn't want to go through that, and we should just leave it alone. But, Phoebe, I couldn't leave it alone. He hurt my baby sister." Her voice was calm, but I could hear the hint of rage, even after all these years.

"I get it," I said. Sam and I might not be tight, but if someone ever did anything to hurt him, I would be there, and I would be merciless.

"I waited until everyone was out of the house, and I called him. I said Caro wanted him to come by for a chat, but our parents wouldn't let her talk to him, so she asked me to deliver the message. I think he must have been really worried about her potentially pressing charges, because he didn't ask any questions; he just said he'd be right over. When he showed up, I was ready. Before I get any further, I want you to know I never planned to actually hurt him. I was mad, that's true, and he deserved to be hurt for the pain he caused my sister, but I just wanted to scare him. I wanted to make sure he'd never go near her again."

I nodded and swallowed hard, not sure how dark this story was about to get.

"I'd been to culinary school, right? So, I had a really nice set of knives. Anyway, maybe I was being a bit dramatic, but when he came over, I was sharpening my knives at the kitchen table. Such a silly villain move to choose, but I wanted him spooked, and it worked. I told him he was going to leave Caro alone, that he was going to forget her name from the moment he left our house. He wouldn't call, he wouldn't show up, he would never speak to her again."

I took a deep breath, waiting to see where this was going to end up.

"It worked. The problem was, I guess I forgot that even though he was a punk, even though everyone knew he was bad news, I didn't factor in that he was still only sixteen and had parents. Parents who apparently had no idea what their son was really like. He went home to his parents and said I threatened him at knifepoint to stay away from my sister." Amy actually laughed then. "I never went anywhere near him, and of course he neglected to tell them about whatever had happened that left Caro with a broken arm. They went to the police and tried to file attempted murder charges, and when that didn't work, it was uttering threats. After we finally got our chance to tell my side of the story, they dropped the charges and I was allowed to go, but I did have to attend like six months of anger management classes. Trent never did speak to my sister again, though."

She put two cookies on a plate and set it down in front of me.

"Anyway, it's long in the past, but I don't like to talk about it, and it's not going to be fun to have to explain why *attempted murder* comes up next to my name in the police files."

I took a bite of the cookie to give myself time to come up with an appropriate response. The sudden burst of flavor completely sidetracked my train of thought. The cookies were dense but chewy, and the mixture of apricot, fresh rosemary, and creamy white chocolate were a Christmas cookie combo I'd never imagined but was somehow everything I'd ever dreamed.

"Oh, my goodness, these are incredible."

Amy flushed. "Thank you. I do a version with cranberries, too. Those are a bit more obviously festive, but something about this version just hits the spot. I love making them this time of year."

"I can see why." I put the half-eaten cookie back on my plate before I could gorge myself on them any further. "And look, I'm glad you told me the truth. I know it can't be easy to dig up all the skeletons in your closet, but now we can be prepared."

"We?" she asked.

I reached across the island to squeeze her hand and could see tears starting to form in her eyes, which she hastily swiped away with the back of her sleeve.

"Yes, we. Because I know precisely how to make sure no one thinks you're guilty of anything."

"Oh?" She quirked up an eyebrow and leaned closer as if I was about to share a secret with her.

"Yes. We're going to figure out who *did* kill Naomi Novak."

CHAPTER FIFTEEN

I was glad I'd had the foresight to text Rich before going to see Amy, because I was definitely running much later than I'd hoped to be by the time I jogged up the steps to my old Victorian home and made my way inside.

The lights on the main floor were on when I'd come up the walkway, so I knew Rich was already there. It wasn't so much that I'd given him a key—way too soon for that!—but he did know where my spare was hidden. All the convenience of having a key, none of the relationship pressures of being given said key too soon.

I also had a key to his apartment, but that was a technicality because I was his landlord. I had to have a key.

Rich called out from the kitchen, "Welcome home. Your cats are driving me crazy."

I glanced at the clock in the entryway and let out a groan. I was about an hour behind schedule for feline dinner as well as human dinner. Upon hearing the front door close, both Bob and Coco came dashing out of the kitchen to sing me a sorry lament about how starved they were. Their tails were foisted high in the air, and they circled my ankles as if rubbing up against me might activate a genie who would provide them kibble.

"Okay, okay, hello, I love you, I'm sorry I'm late." I bent over and gave each of them a thorough rubdown. I was always amused by how much friendlier Coco became when there was food on the line.

She purred loudly and butted her tri-colored head into my hand, then went over to Bob and head-butted him as well just in case it might help move this along.

I chuckled at them and got my coat off, hanging it on a hook near the entry, then draping my purse strap over the staircase banister. The cats followed me into the kitchen, where Coco briefly lingered at the door out of Rich-based shyness before coming all the way in and pacing back and forth over the hearth.

"Sorry I'm late." Planted a quick kiss on Rich's cheek. He was busy at the stove cooking up something that smelled wonderful. "I thought you were just going to grab takeout."

"I was, but then I got inspired. So you're lucky, actually. Being late means you're right on time." He was sporting one of Eudora's old aprons with a frilly hem, and I had to admit it looked fairly adorable on him.

The kitchen was filled with the fresh scent of basil and tomatoes, making me smile. There was a bottle of wine on the table that hadn't been opened yet, with two glasses beside it.

"Let me feed these starved waifs and then I'll get us some wine."

"Sounds good. I thought about feeding them myself, but I know how cats can be. You might have fed them earlier, and they'd just lie to me to get more."

"I'd be offended on their behalf if that wasn't a very accurate description of Bob's feline con artist ways."

The cat in question meowed in indignation. That or he was still trying to communicate to me that he was dying of starvation, though this meow had sounded decidedly more offended than hungry.

Live with a cat long enough and you definitely learn to tell the difference.

I rinsed out their kibble dishes and filled them with dry food, then grabbed their wet food bowls out of the dishwasher and gave them each a little helping from a new tin. I topped the wet food with a little fish oil, something I was trying to help Coco with her slightly unsightly coat.

She'd been in a shelter a long time and had overgroomed herself in patches as a stress response. I was trying a bunch of different suggestions I'd seen online to help them get more out of their meals. I even had quail eggs in the fridge I'd asked Leo Lansing to order for me, but I hadn't tried them yet, because I was worried they'd either hate them, or love them so much I had to order them all the time.

I loved my cats; I just wasn't sure how far I wanted to take being a bougie cat mom.

With the cats settled in and wolfing down their dinner, I opened the wine Rich had brought along, the cork coming free with a satisfying *pop*. I poured us each a glass of the fruity-smelling red wine and then plopped down at the table to watch Rich cook.

He cracked some fresh pepper over the dish he was cooking, then opened the oven and pulled out a tray of garlic bread. The sudden scent of garlic that wafted out into the room made my mouth start watering.

"All right, you've been coy long enough," Rich said, taking off the oven mitts and putting them on the counter. "Spill the beans. Have you been arrested for murder yet?"

I almost snorted wine out my nose and ended up sputtering into my glass so badly he was forced to hand me a tea towel.

"Sorry, I didn't think you'd react like that," he chuckled.

"Well, how would you feel if I just walked around accusing *you* of murder on a whim?" My tone was playful, letting him know I didn't actually think he believed it.

"Hey now, there's a little precedent for you getting into trouble. I just wanted to make sure we weren't going to need to go on the lam anytime soon."

"On the lam," I chuckled. "No, we're not going on the lam. But I'm curious if you've heard anything?"

He waved a wooden spoon at me. "*Aha*, I knew it. You are digging into this. I knew you wouldn't be able to help yourself."

"Extenuating circumstances!" I argued. "I'm looking into it to help someone out."

Rich looked at the pot on the stove rather than at me when he asked, "Blaine?"

He wasn't looking, so he probably missed the way my nose wrinkled in distaste. So, I emphasized the expression by saying, "Ew, no," out loud.

Rich glanced at me with an eyebrow raised, and for a moment I could picture that exact same reaction on a much younger version of his face. We'd spent childhood summers together playing all over town, me, him, and Leo. I sometimes forgot that I'd known him as a child until moments like this, where I could see that boyish expression peeking out.

It made my heart melt.

Rich had grown up handsome, rugged, so different from who he'd been as a boy, but it was nice to see that Ricky was still in there sometimes.

"Though, the cops do want me to see if I can maybe worm a little information out of him. Since we have a history," I explained.

"The police asked you to interrogate your ex?" Rich made a face at me like he thought maybe I was fibbing or misrepresenting the truth. I made a face back that said he should trust me more than that.

"They *did*. You're all buddy-buddy with Detective Kim, so you can ask him yourself. They wanted me to use my witchy skills to solve the crime, but I had to disappoint them because the only things my witchy skills can do is turn off light switches when I'm too lazy to get out of bed, and very occasionally find things I thought I'd lost." This was underselling things a little. I could also stop time, but I hadn't yet learned how to activate that skill on my own, rather than it being a panic reaction to immediate danger.

He laughed at me. "Okay, I don't need to check with Kwan. I believe you. But you can't blame a guy for being dubious; you do sort of have a history of looking into these things on your own, you know."

My cheeks flushed, but then I pointed at him. "*Actually,* I have a history of looking into them with *you*." I waggled my brows at him and gave him my best innocent expression.

Rich turned off the stove and looked at me, barely able to keep a straight face. "What are you doing?"

"I'm using my finely tuned powers of seduction to manipulate you into helping me."

"Helping you grill your ex?"

This time he saw the expression on my face, and he wasn't able to restrain himself from snort-laughing at me. "Wow, if I'd had any concerns about there being lingering feelings between you and your ex, I would have been quickly disabused of that notion by the look on your face right now."

"There are *plenty* of lingering feelings I have about Blaine, but none of them are warm and fuzzy."

"Good to know."

I resisted the sudden strong urge to ask him about his own ex, but we never really talked about her, beyond my knowing that we were in pretty similar boats. I got the feeling that she was very out of sight, out of mind for Rich, and it would probably spoil our night if I mentioned her. For me, unfortunately, Blaine was in sight and on my mind.

My ex was many things: coward, cheat, stupid poopyhead—yes, I'm nine—but when I went through his very long list of flaws, there was nothing on that list that might lead me to think he was capable of murder.

I knew Blaine's playbook pretty well, and when he decided things were over, he was kind of the opposite of confrontational about it. He just moved on without letting you know, and then eventually you'd learn he was cheating on you and be devastated by how unexpected it was, meanwhile he kind of figured you knew it was over.

Or at least that was how it had gone for me. I wondered if the waitress he'd cheated on me with learned he'd moved on when she saw photos of Blaine and Naomi in *Us Weekly*.

Still, as terrible as he was, I had a hard time believing he was terrible enough to *kill*.

Unless...

Unless he wasn't the one who wanted to move on.

What if Naomi had made it clear she was going to end things, and Blaine had decided he'd rather kill her than let her leave him? I chewed on my thumbnail as I thought about that.

Rich served up our dinner, which was a thick and tasty

Italian sausage pasta sauce smothering some adorable noodles I didn't recognize.

"They're *caserecce*," he said, noticing me looking at the medium-length hollow noodle. "They're great with thick sauces because you get all that goodness on the inside and the outside."

I took a big bite and let the rich, delicious flavor lull me into a brief food coma. "Oh man, you can come cook for me anytime."

He laughed. "I'm glad you like it."

We ate for a bit, exchanging stories about our day that weren't related to murder, before heading over to the couch to enjoy a little mindless TV viewing. While Rich and I had been seeing each other only a few months, we also weren't exciting young twenty-somethings. We both worked a lot and fit in time to see each other where it made sense. Rich's job forced him to work a lot of evenings, so we tended to have to sneak in dinners or lunches wherever we could.

On a night like this, where we didn't have anything immediately demanding our attention, it was nice to just be able to be with each other but not have to *do* anything.

I was just about to toss a blanket over us and queue up our most recent Netflix obsession—a docuseries about Dallas Cowboy cheerleaders—when movement outside my living room window made me scramble to my feet.

"Did you see that?"

Rich was on his feet right behind me, heading directly to the window, so he must have seen the same thing I did. But I still wasn't even sure *what* I'd seen. There was a huge covered porch that wrapped around most of the house, so it was absolutely possible for someone to come up the front steps and look directly into the window. I rarely closed the curtains on the main floor of the house at night because Lane End House was on its own at the top of a hill and I had no immediate neighbors. Peeping Toms weren't really a concern in our town.

At least they never had been before.

"Stay here," Rich instructed, as if he had never met me before, and headed out the front door.

I was practically on his heels, though I did turn and look at Bob briefly, saying, "Don't you even think about sneaking outside, mister." He blinked at me, his approximation of an innocent face looking eerily similar to the one I'd given Rich earlier.

The cat was learning too much from me.

It was a little spooky.

I dashed outside after Rich, who had already disappeared around the corner of the house when I was having my chat with Bob. Suddenly my boldness in following him out here was dampened. What if someone had been lurking in the shadows waiting for us and they'd done something to Rich?

Rich was a strong guy, but someone taking him by surprise in the dark could still spell trouble, even for him. If I went around the corner, was I just setting myself up to walk into the same trap?

I heard scuffling sounds, followed by a grunt, and then someone swore.

"Rich, are you okay?" I picked up a flowerpot sitting on my little café table. The flowers in it were dead, having yielded to the changing seasons, but the pot itself had some good weight, and if I managed to aim it at someone's head, it might do some damage.

This, of course, overlooked the fact that I had almost zero coordination when it came to throwing, and only my participation in track and field had saved me from failing gym.

I could run.

Maybe that's what I should be doing now.

I rounded the corner and nearly dropped the pot.

Rich had a man by the collar of his jacket, and the man was squirming, trying to get away. He was holding onto a camera, and the flash kept popping off in bright explosions as he took pictures of seemingly nothing, perhaps trying to distract his would-be captor.

It took me a moment to process what I was seeing, but then the camera was what finally made it click. So to speak.

"Are you a *paparazzi*?" I gasped, barely able to comprehend why else a man with a camera would be standing outside my living room window.

Actually, with those parameters in mind, paparazzi was a best-case scenario.

The man continued to try wrestling free of Rich's hold, and had worked one arm out of a sleeve, but seemed unwilling to relinquish the camera.

"Rich, let him go," I said, setting the flowerpot down on the porch railing.

"He's trespassing. You should call the police," Rich said through gritted teeth.

"I'm not a pap," the man said, his voice high and shrill.

"Then I should *definitely* call the cops," I said.

"Nooo," the man wailed. "Please, I'm sorry."

"Rich," I said again, and this time he listened to me, letting go of our snooping intruder.

I half-expected the man to go flying off the porch and disappear into the night—which would have forced me to actually call the police—but instead he stood between Rich and me, panting like he'd gone three rounds with Mike Tyson.

Now that I could properly see him, I was surprised that I recognized him. He was a chubby guy in his early forties, balding and wearing thick black glasses. The fact I recognized him was almost shocking, because he was the dictionary definition of nondescript.

But I'd seen him around town since Naomi's arrival. He had come into The Earl's Study not long after she'd drifted through, and I was pretty sure I'd also seen him around the community center the day of the auditions. He wasn't a local, though, so why would he have been there?

With his jacket off, I could see he was wearing a T-shirt with an image of Naomi from her portrayal of Sue Storm in a *Fantastic Four* movie. There was only one reason someone would own a shirt from that movie—it had been panned by critics and audiences alike—and that was if he was a fan.

A super fan.

Possibly even a stalker?

"What are you doing here?" I asked, turning on my most annoyed parent voice. This was one I usually reserved for Bob when I found that one of my potted plants had been dug up.

It seemed to have more impact on this man than it did on my cat. Bob didn't care much for authority; the only power he bowed to was catnip.

"I saw you at the police station earlier. The reporters said you were the wife of Naomi's fiancée."

"*Ex*-wife," I emphasized. "And that doesn't explain why you're standing on my porch like a ghoul. Were you taking pictures of me?" I pointed to his camera.

"I thought if you were involved, they might be worth something."

I gritted my teeth, trying to remain calm, but I was getting ready to call the police on this guy after all.

"I'm not involved. The police had routine follow-up questions for me because I was the one who found her body."

"I m-mean," he stammered. "You have to admit it looks pretty bad, the ex-wife of Naomi's new fiancé being the one to find her dead."

"Does it look worse than standing outside someone's windows at night with a camera?" I asked as I pulled my phone out. I'd been willing to give this guy the benefit of the doubt that maybe he had some innocent reason for being out there, but it turned out he was just like the other vultures outside the police station.

Except he didn't have a press badge.

I dialled Patsy's number, and she replied almost immediately. "Already have something for me, Winchester?"

"I do, but it's probably not what you're hoping for." I quickly explained the situation, and Patsy said she would be over as quickly as she could, but in the meantime, she would send a uniformed officer by to help secure the man.

Though Naomi's number one fan was wriggling to get free and making noises of protest that he wasn't guilty of anything, Rich seemed to have him under control.

"You might as well make yourselves comfortable," I told both of them. "The police are on their way."

CHAPTER SIXTEEN

I liked Patsy Martin and Kwan Kim a lot, but that didn't mean it wasn't a bad sign to see them twice in one night. Generally speaking, things are going poorly if you're around the police that often, at least in a professional setting.

It made me think that perhaps I should make an effort to see the two of them more in a friendly capacity so I wouldn't dread the meetings as much.

But before I started planning dinner parties for our local detectives, both Rich and I needed to give our statements about our little intruder.

His name, which I heard him wailing to the uniformed officer who was handcuffing him, was Howie Steadman. Evidently, he was waiving his right to remain silent, because he was talking the arresting officer's ear off as he was ducked into the cruiser.

Patsy watched as the man pressed up against the rear passenger window, continuing to talk so much he was fogging up the glass.

"Times like this, I wish *Being Annoying* was a crime," she muttered.

"Well, trespassing still is," Rich said, his tone curt. He was a lot more annoyed about our intruder at this point than I was. I'd gone past annoyed a few minutes earlier and now I was just tired.

"Do you want to press charges, Phoebe?" Patsy asked.

I'd thought about this since they had arrived, and finally I shook my head. "No, I think this will probably scare him off from doing it again. He seems harmless, I think just maybe a bit too enthusiastic about Naomi."

Patsy nodded. "Unfortunately, I think we're going to start seeing more of that in the coming days. She was incredibly famous, and I think people are going to show up just to see where she died."

"That might put a damper on poor Dierdre's Halloween show."

Patsy snorted. "If you think things like unwanted guests, or even crime scene tape, are going to stop Dierdre from putting on her show, I don't think you know her very well. Last I heard, she's still planning to post the cast list tomorrow."

My immediate reaction was to say that not everyone had gotten a chance to audition, but I also didn't think anyone would be in the mood to go through that whole process again. I was just grateful I'd managed to avoid the humiliation.

I also wasn't feeling particularly vindictive. Howie shouldn't have been lurking on my porch, but he also didn't seem like a career criminal to me, especially given how quickly we'd caught him. I didn't want to be responsible for someone having a criminal record just because they were a bit too enthusiastic about their favorite actress.

Patsy nodded. "Well, we're going to let him think about it in the drunk tank overnight and give him a pretty clear reminder about the definitions of private versus public property. If you see him again, let us know."

"If he comes back again, I probably won't let Rich be so nice about it," I said, though I forced a smile, so everyone knew I was kidding.

Mostly.

Rich let out a sigh. I think he'd been hoping I'd crack down on the guy, but he probably understood why I didn't. Rich was a former detective himself before he'd retired from the force to become a private investigator. I think part of him still had the police mentality when it came to dealing with any crime.

I rubbed his back and pressed a kiss to his cheek, feeling the tension in his body start to melt away.

"Thanks for coming so quickly," I told the detectives.

"You barely needed us with this guy around." Kwan chuckled, giving Rich a punch to the shoulder.

"Yes, well, I'd rather keep him as a boyfriend than a bodyguard if you don't mind."

Rich looked over at me when I used the word *boyfriend*, and all the former frustration and anger had completely disappeared from his face. It was replaced by an expression so unexpectedly tender that my heart actually hurt to look at him. I felt my face getting hot.

"On that note, I think we'll call it a night," Patsy said, clearing her throat so Rich and I would stop making high school googly eyes at each other. Oh no, were we going to turn into that gross couple no one could stand to be around?

"I'll let you know if there's any other trouble," I said, then Rich and I headed back into the house.

We sat on the couch again, but neither of us was feeling like we could focus on which of the Cowboy rookies might make the new cheer class. As the girls fretted over whether their high kicks were good enough to perform "Thunderstruck," Rich paused the episode.

"Are you really okay?" he asked.

"Are *you*?" I countered.

"I'm sorry, I know I got a little fired up with that guy, but the idea of someone looking in your windows... threatening you. I just saw red."

While I didn't want to promote Rich getting angry on my behalf, there was a semi-primal part of my brain that found it the tiniest bit romantic he'd been willing to tackle a guy just to protect me.

Once, Blaine and I had been walking home from an evening at the theatre in Seattle when we'd been mugged. At the time I'd been too terrified to pay attention to what had happened; I'd just handed over my purse and a pair of nice diamond earrings I'd been wearing.

Only after the fact did I realize Blaine had hidden *behind* me as the two men pointed guns in our direction.

Perhaps *that* was when I should have known things weren't going to work out.

I squeezed Rich's hand. "Thank you. For looking out for me. It's not unappreciated. But don't put yourself in harm's way for me, okay?"

Rich snorted out a quick laugh. "I definitely wasn't in harm's way with him." Before I could argue, he went on. "I get it though; I hear what you're saying. I promise I will disengage my caveman brain."

"Thank you." I leaned in and gave him a grateful kiss. We'd played a will they or won't they game with each other for most of my first year in town, and it felt nice to be able to kiss him instead of just *thinking* about kissing him. I smiled against his lips.

He really was a very good kisser.

"You want a distraction?" I asked him.

He raised his eyebrows at me, and when I realized where his mind had gone, I swatted his arm. "No, not that. Hold on." I left the room and found the wooden box and key from Eudora where Honey and I had left them on the sitting room mantel.

"What's this?" he asked, shifting forward to the edge of his seat.

"It's a *mystery*," I enthusiastically emphasized the last word while thrusting the wooden box into his hands.

"The Mystery of the Wooden Box?" he asked, turning it over, scanning every surface for a latch, keyhole, or hinges. He's brows drew together in consternation when he came to the same conclusion Honey and I had early.

There was no logical way for the box to open.

"What on earth have you gotten yourself into this time, Nancy Drew?" He gently shook the box, but the contents gave no clues as to what was hiding within. Part of me wondered if the box might actually be empty, as that would feel like a very Eudora kind of trick to pull, but no, there had to be something inside. My heart told me this wasn't a wild-goose chase.

I explained what I'd learned so far, and about what Honey and I had discovered with the carousel horse earlier —had that really just been this afternoon?—then showed him the key we'd found inside the horse. He turned it over in his hands, holding it up to the light to see if there was an inscription in the metal.

There wasn't, but I was surprised it hadn't occurred to me to check that earlier. I was going to need to pay closer attention to Eudora's clues. She was just the type of person to leave something sneaky in plain sight like that. Rich was now scouring the letter, his brows knit together either because he was deep in concentration, or he needed reading glasses but was too cool to admit it.

"She talks about playing hide and seek in the house. The three of us used to play that game for hours."

I'd almost forgotten that Rich would have been present for some of the throwback memories Eudora teased. I'd wanted his help because he was a PI and unravelled clues professionally. Turned out he was doubly the right person to ask because he'd been in the house with me for much of my childhood.

"But I tried just about every lock in the house, and it didn't work on any of them."

"Phoebe, think about it. When we played hide and seek, where did we play?"

I gave him a confused look, but then suddenly it struck me. We would *start* in the house until our giggling and shrieking drove Eudora up a wall, and then she'd kick us out saying, "There's no better place in the world to hide than..."

"Outside," I whispered.

CHAPTER SEVENTEEN

I had been gung-ho to grab flashlights and head out that very night, but Rich was quick to point out that we'd have much better luck finding Eudora's clue—and not getting lost in the woods—if we waited until morning.

Unfortunately, as two adults with grown-up responsibilities, morning meant I needed to work, and work started dark and early, with me getting up before the sun was out.

I loved fall, but as the darkness started to take over—compounded by the ever-present Washington clouds—I started to yearn for a little extra sunshine in my life.

Thankfully, The Earl's Study had a ton of large windows, so while I worked, I was able to see sunlight, whenever there was sunlight to see. And since I owned the place, I could sneak out for fresh air whenever I started to feel a bit claustrophobic in our tiny kitchen.

But the bottom line was, we *might* get an hour after I finished work to look outside for the next clue, and if we weren't lucky, it would have to wait for the weekend. I was antsy to learn more about whatever Eudora was hiding, but I had to concede that I had gone almost forty years without knowing whatever this secret was, and I could last a few more days.

That didn't mean I wasn't thinking about potential hiding spots as Bob and I biked to work.

I'd left Rich sleeping upstairs since he didn't need to be up as early as I did, and I also liked the idea of him being in my house when I wasn't there. While it was *way* too soon to start thinking about things like him moving in, I could admit to myself there was a certain selfish delight in seeing the guy you had feelings for look like he was starting to feel at home in your house.

Heck, I had lived there a year, and I'd only *just* started to think of the place as mine instead of Eudora's.

I wondered what she would think of this little development.

Considering she'd asked Rich to watch out for me, I kind of felt like she had the tiniest involvement in getting us together. She'd always loved Rich, so I knew she would be over the moon that he and I were now together.

I smiled to myself as the cool autumn wind rustled my hair and turned my cheeks rosy. Soon enough I wouldn't be able to take my bike to work, at least for a few months, but I was enjoying it while it lasted.

Bob, on the other paw, was counting down until we could cruise in the warmth and comfort of a car. While I knew he didn't mind being outside—he would often follow me out onto the porch, and the cats had a new catio I'd installed at the back of the house—he didn't *love* to have wind blow around him in his little cat carrier.

"*Mreoooooow*," he yowled into the breeze.

"Oh, come on now," I said. "It's really not that bad." It *was* a little crisp, but not cold, and there wasn't a cloud to be seen, making it a perfect fall morning.

I took in the festive sights on my way down the hill towards Main Street. The old black lamps that looked like oil lamps but had been updated for modern fixtures, were all sporting flags that depicted jack-o'-lanterns, black cats, ghosts, bubbling cauldrons, and spiderwebs, with the words, *Raven Creek Wishes You a Haunted Halloween*. The town's beautification committee had also affixed plastic ravens to each post, making it appear as though a flock—or an unkindness—had moved into their namesake town.

The base of each post was bedecked with cornstalks and wrapped in orange and black ribbon. The result of this specific décor choice, I'd learned, was that the streets of Raven Creek were littered with corn detritus from Halloween through Christmas.

The town's flowerpots had all been filled with orange and yellow mums, which so far had held up brilliantly to a few near-freezing cold snaps. It gave Main Street a cheery, vibrant palette even on the darker grey days that were more frequent.

The shops of Main were all decorated, each more elaborate than the last. Leo—who was not big on decorating himself—had let the staff of Lansing's Grocery put bloody handprints up all over the front windows and have the signs partially torn down around the edges to make it look like a zombie apocalypse had run through the place. There had been a minor scandal about the decorations when they went up with a few pearl-clutching moms worried that the theme was too scary, but I'd seen dozens of kids posing for pictures outside, so I was pretty sure those fears hadn't amounted to much.

Amy's shop, the Sugarplum Fairy, had a cauldron set up in the front window with iridescent bubbles rising from the interior along with cupcakes and macarons. She'd rigged up the cauldron with LED lights that flickered in different colors, and every hour the whole thing would start to smoke. It was delightful.

On the opposite side of my shop was the Tanaka's plant shop, and they had built a life-size Audrey II from *Little Shop of Horrors* in the front of their window. While most of the displays were indoors—largely due to weather concerns—almost everyone had three or four pumpkins outside their entrances, and the whole town had decided on a front door skeleton theme to tie every shop together, so each shop had an articulated plastic skeleton outside somewhere. The Tanaka's was watering one of the mums. Amy's was sitting in one of her outdoor patio chairs holding a paper cup.

I did a double take.

Hadn't it been holding a paper cup yesterday?

Today the skeleton was just sitting with a scarf wrapped around its neck bones, but no cup to be seen.

It was possible it had blown away or someone had absconded with it, but it seemed like a silly thing to steal.

I wondered if perhaps someone had grabbed it so they could make a believable decoy of Naomi Novak's drink order…

Locking my bike up in front of the shop, I shook off the paranoia about missing paper cups and took a moment to enjoy the window my staff and I had put together. A huge spiderweb covered the entire main bookstore window, with carefully selected horror titles caught in the web, along with cheeky other references like James Patterson's *Along Came a Spider* and some Spider-Man graphic novels. We had also made use of the giant fuzzy spider Eudora had stashed in her basement. At first, I'd thought it was creepy, but now that I'd been looking at it for a week, and Daphne had started calling it Charlotte, it had kind of grown on me.

Not enough to keep it around once November first hit, but enough that I was no longer jumping out of my skin every time I walked into the bookstore half of the shop.

Our mandatory skeleton was leaning over an old metal library cart, where we put our super-discounted bargain books out every day. Books that were a little too damaged to go in with the regular used stock, but that were still perfectly readable as long as no one was too picky about dog-eared pages or broken spines.

I'd have to get the cart stocked up before we opened. The weather in Washington State meant it simply wasn't possible to leave the discounted books out overnight, even with a cover. The damp that seemed to cling to the fall air would have been too much for them to handle.

I unlocked the front door and let Bob out of his backpack. He sneezed at me, as if trying to pretend he'd caught a cold on the way here. Such a furry little drama queen.

He followed me into the bookstore where I started the fire in the sitting area—I needed to get it ready so Bob and Mr. Loughery would be comfortable all day—and once the flames caught the kindling, I grabbed the plastic tote of books that I'd fill up the cart outside with.

With my skeletal book cart loaded, I closed the front door and headed next door to the Sugarplum Fairy, where Amy would have my morning order of pastries ready to go.

Only the Sugarplum Fairy was closed.

Amy usually arrived unspeakably early to get the ovens warmed and things like her breads and other yeasted treats rising and baking, so they'd be ready for all the early birds. Her doors opened at six, and it was six-thirty now. The lights inside were off, and the front door was locked.

A pit formed in my stomach.

Before I let my imagination run wild on me, I returned to The Earl's Study and got my cell phone out of my purse, dialling Amy immediately. Anyone else I might feel bad about waking them, but if Amy wasn't here, then something might be wrong.

Her phone rang and rang, but after the fifth ring, her voicemail picked up. I left her a quick message, hoping I didn't sound too frantic, and then stood in the middle of my store unsure what to do next.

This could be something completely innocent. She might have overslept for the first time in her life, or perhaps she'd caught a seasonal flu. But if either of those were the case, then wasn't the right thing to do to go over to her house and make sure she was okay?

I couldn't just ignore it. Maybe there'd been a time in my life, when I lived in Seattle and barely knew the people I saw day-to-day, that I would brush off an absence or a closed shop door. But I *knew* Amy. She was the first friend I'd ever made in this town, and over the past year I'd come to grow accustomed to her habits because of how they interconnected with my own.

Glancing at my watch, I knew I had plenty of time to go to Amy's house and be back before my shop opened at eight. Our sourdough might be a bit behind schedule, but I was willing to accept that if it meant knowing my friend was okay.

"Bob, you're in charge until I get back," I shouted into the seating area.

A handful of our adoptable cats in the Cat Condos meowed in return. I'd need to make sure I fed them as soon as I got back.

Outside, I jumped on my bike and made the short ride

over to Amy's. Her little Mini Cooper—pink just like her shop—was parked outside. Amy tended to drive to work just because of the hours. We both had parking spaces behind the shop, and now I knew her car wasn't there.

I let my bike drop onto her lawn and ran up to the door, where I knocked as loud as I could to avoid disturbing her neighbors, but so that she could hear me even if she was in a deep sleep.

There was no response. I knocked again, and tried her phone, but to no avail. I wasn't even sure who else I could check with. Amy had been dating Leo for a few months, but I wasn't sure how serious that was, and didn't want to jump right to freaking him out too if this was all just a misunderstanding.

At a loss for what to do, I had no choice but to bike back to the store and promised myself I would come back at lunch to check again. In the meantime, I hand-wrote an *Out Sick* sign and taped it to Amy's front door, hoping it might help keep anyone else from freaking out that she was closed.

They'd probably freak out anyway, because Amy never closed.

I sent her a text and stared at my phone hoping to see the little typing bubbles pop up, but my message just said *Delivered* and not *Read*. I swallowed the pit of dread in my stomach and went through the rest of my morning routine. I fed the adoptable cats, who were all grateful, except for one of them, who swatted my hand when I took his dish away. Then, I made sure our signature Earl Grey tea shortbread cookies were in the oven and the sourdough loaves were ready to follow them in. Surprisingly, I wasn't behind schedule at all, even with my little detour.

I'd be by myself for the morning until Imogen arrived at

ten, which meant I still had several hours of nauseating worry ahead before I could find out what was going on with Amy.

Maybe I should text Rich. He was a PI after all, wasn't it his job to help find people?

My phone buzzed in my apron, and I let out a yelp of surprise.

Seeing Amy's name on the screen when I pulled it out, I felt like the weight of an elephant had been lifted off my chest.

Until I read the message.

At the police station. Not sure if I'm going to be allowed to leave.

CHAPTER EIGHTEEN

At the police station.

But Amy didn't say she'd been *arrested*. So that had to be a good thing, didn't it? The police could detain her briefly and ask her questions, but if she hadn't been arrested, then it was clear the only thing they had to go on was the cup.

Anyone could have gotten a cup from Amy's. She had dozens of customers a day. Naomi dying from a drink in one of Amy's cups didn't make Amy the killer.

I had to believe that Detectives Martin and Kim were smart enough to know that. To know Amy couldn't do this.

By the time Imogen came in at ten, it must have been obvious that I was a little stressed, because she took one look at me and said, "Someone needs a cup of Soothing Spearmint ASAP." She went to the office to hang up her coat then came back and stood across the counter from me, staring me down without saying a single word.

It took approximately three seconds for me to crack and tell her about Amy, and what the police must suspect.

"Amy?!" Imogen said, astonished. "Next thing you

know they'll be arresting the Lieberman's six-year-old daughter. I'd believe Lacey was capable of murder before I believed Amy was." She scoffed. "Unbelievable. I want to go down to the police station and ask them why they're wasting time on Amy while whoever really killed Naomi is still out there."

Evidently, the notion that Naomi had been murdered was only surprising to me.

"Or we could just figure out who that is..." I said, almost to myself, but Imogen was too sharply focused today and heard me.

She arched a brow and pursed her lips, but then her expression shifted to something more thoughtful. "You know, if the police aren't going to bother looking at real suspects, you might be on to something."

The store was empty except for Mr. Loughery, and I thought he was deep in his usual morning nap until I heard his voice from the other room announce, "The first rule of solving a crime isn't to figure out the *who* it's figuring out the *why*."

Imogen and I exchanged glances before we both leaned over to look into the reading room. Norman was still sitting by the fire, but his book was now closed and sitting on the arm of his chair. Bob was curled up in the armchair beside his, and he did not look interested in solving a crime with us.

"Well, of course the *who* is the most important part," Imogen protested. "That literally solves the whole crime." She drifted over to the doorway leading into the bookstore, and I followed behind her. Mr. Loughery smiled, clearly pleased to have drawn in an audience.

"Of course, my dear. I didn't say it didn't matter. I just said that learning the *why* matters more. Once you know *why* someone was killed, it becomes much easier to figure out the *who*."

Imogen leaned against the doorjamb, crossing her arms over her chest. "All right, since you're our resident expert, tell me what the *why* is for Naomi Novak." Her tone was light, teasing; there was nothing mean in it at all, which was actually a rarity for Imogen, who could sometimes be a little brusque.

Obviously, we both cared a great deal about Norman. I suspect Imogen would have been more likely to come to blows with someone who said anything negative about him than she was to ever say anything cruel to the man himself.

"I've been thinking about that, actually," he said as he removed his paperboy cap and smoothed his thin white hair back from his forehead. "There are a number of options. I'll get the most obvious out of the way, since I don't think it's the correct one. Romantic jealousy." His gaze cut over to me, and Imogen's followed.

I let out a laugh. "Me? Because of Blaine? Absolutely not, she's welcome to him."

"Don't worry, I don't think that's what happened either," Norman chuckled. "But we're looking at the why, let's not forget that, so if we remove the *who*—you in this case—it does look like a pretty reasonable motive, you must admit."

"I don't like this game." I moved over to the cat condos and gave a little all-white male cat a scratch on the chin after he butted his head up against the bars demanding it. It was the same cat who had swatted me this morning, so perhaps this was his way of atoning for his bad attitude over breakfast.

All was forgiven.

"What else can you think of?" I asked, not wanting

Norman to think I was genuinely upset. Just a slightly bruised ego. I was also a little miffed about being an easy candidate for suspicion every time someone died. That got to a girl's head after a while.

"I think we can look at jealousy in general," Imogen suggested. "I noticed there was some tension between her and the other members of her acting group during the auditions, just little bickering things, but that might indicate there were other problems going on between them."

Norman snapped his fingers, pointing at Imogen. "Now you're thinking like a fictional detective," he declared enthusiastically.

Imogen, who never seemed capable of taking a compliment, flushed with what seemed like real pride.

"There's also a potential for relationship trouble," Norman said. "Not to speak ill of your former husband—"

"Oh no, go ahead. I've spoken plenty of ill about him in my day."

Norman gave me a smile that was part amused and part sympathetic. He and his now-deceased wife had been one of those couples that were damn near perfect, from what I'd learned. While everyone had their issues, Norman and his wife could have gone in the dictionary next to the entry for *perfect couple*.

My disaster of a marriage must have seemed very dismal by contrast.

It was.

I was happy, in retrospect, to be divorced.

Being divorced was how I'd ended up here.

"Well, Blaine Winchester certainly is a good suspect," Norman said, and I nodded my agreement, because on paper, he was.

Though, I simply couldn't imagine Blaine actually

killing anyone. But I suppose that's what everyone says when someone they know turns out to be a killer. *He always seemed like such a nice man.*

"Oh!" I stopped petting the cat and turned to look at the two humans in the room. Bob briefly lifted his head and looked at me expectantly. "What about her weirdo superfan?"

"You mean that guy who was in here the day she first stopped by the store and asked all the questions about what she bought?" Imogen wrinkled up her nose like she'd smelled something gross. "That guy gave me the creeps."

"That guy ended up at my house yesterday trying to take pictures of Rich and me through the living room window. He tried to say he thought I was involved because he'd seen me at the police station, but I don't think that was the whole story."

Imogen and Norman looked horrified. "He was at your *house*?" Imogen asked, her mouth hanging open in shock. "I hope you called the police."

I nodded. "We did, I'm not pressing charges, but I think maybe it's worth considering that the *why* might be good old-fashioned obsession. What if Howie, the stalker guy, was deluded, and Naomi's engagement to Blaine set him off?"

Norman, after recovering from my unexpected story, nodded along with my reasoning. "Yes, that's a very strong possibility, definitely one to consider."

Bob had decided this conversation was not worth waking up for and rolled himself into a ball, covering his face with both paws, which was so cute I wanted to scream.

I sat down on a little bench next to the cat condos, hugging a throw pillow that said *Cats are Purr-fect*. "It's great that we've got all these ideas, but how is any of it going to help us get Amy out of jail?"

"She hasn't been arrested, has she?" Norman asked.

I shook my head. "I don't think so; her message just said she was at the jail but didn't say she'd been arrested. Still, I think they can hold her for like forty-eight hours, can't they? Amy shouldn't be in a holding cell at all."

"I'm glad you think so," came a familiar voice from the doorway.

CHAPTER NINETEEN

I hadn't even heard the bell tinkle to announce someone entering, yet there was Amy, with Leo trailing behind her as if he was afraid to let her out of his sight.

"Oh, my goodness, *Amy*." I scrambled to my feet, accidentally dropping the throw pillow on Bob as I passed. He meowed solemnly until Norman lifted it off him.

I was already across the store, sweeping Amy into a big bear hug and squeezing her with every ounce of strength I could muster. Somehow, even fresh out of the police station, she smelled like butter and sugar.

She hugged me back for a long minute before whispering, "I can't breathe," in my ear.

I released her immediately but then grabbed her shoulders and held her at arm's length just to make sure she was really there, and not a wonderful-smelling figment of my imagination.

"They let you out?" I asked.

"Yeah, not long after I texted you, actually. Leo came to my rescue, along with the grocery store's lawyer. Vinny might not be a criminal attorney, but he does know how to throw enough legal jargon into a conversation to annoy the police into letting me leave. I'm going to owe him cinnamon buns for the rest of my life."

Amy took Leo's hand and squeezed it. "And you get whatever you want. A lifetime supply of chocolate babka."

Leo's cheeks—where they were visible under his beard—flushed red.

"I know what it's like. Didn't want you to go through that. Especially not overnight." Leo was not a man of many words, but when he used them, he made them count.

Looking at the glances they were exchanging, it was clear the connection between Amy and Leo was not casual at all. I was glad she had been able to connect with him, too, and kicked myself for thinking I shouldn't bother him earlier when I was worried about her.

I guided Amy into the bookstore and, in a rare moment of selflessness, Bob vacated his favorite chair to make room for her. He balanced this out by stretching himself to his full length against my leg and meowing at me until I picked him up and held him like a baby.

His purring was so loud it briefly drowned out any possible conversation. Amy smiled and shook her head. "I know I wasn't there long, but my goodness, it feels good to be anywhere else. Phoebe, thank you for putting that sign on my door; hopefully it can keep the wagging tongues to a minimum."

"Did you manage to avoid the rabid photographers?" I asked.

"Apparently, they need to sleep, too. I got pulled in very early this morning—I think the detectives wanted to get to me before I went to work to avoid a scene—which meant I got to skip over any cameras. Leo brought his delivery truck around the back to pick me up."

"What did they say to you?"

Imogen—who I hadn't noticed leaving the room—returned with a steaming mug of tea for Amy, which the blonde accepted gratefully, holding it in her palms like she needed something to warm her up.

"They asked me a lot of questions about my interactions with Naomi, and if I remembered what I'd sold her. Of course I did, you don't forget what you sell a celebrity." She made a noise of annoyance at the mere suggestion. "But that seemed to really throw them off, because I *know* I made Naomi a pumpkin spice latte. You know the one with the white chocolate mocha and the cinnamon-cardamom sprinkles on top?" Her eyes momentarily glittered as she thought about her fall speciality.

None of us had the heart to urge her back onto topic.

"Anyway, I remember it clearly because I asked her if she wanted whipped cream, thinking she might not since she's such a skinny thing and those actresses never eat anything fun. But she *insisted* on whipped cream. Said *That's the best part.*"

"Why would that confuse the police?" I asked.

"Because, apparently, the drink that poisoned Naomi wasn't a pumpkin spice latte. It was an apple cider."

She gave me a meaningful look, and suddenly I understood why. "Amy, you don't sell apple cider."

She smiled and sipped the tea Imogen had brought her. "No. No I don't."

Amy stayed only for a few more minutes before Leo insisted she needed to go get some rest. She was resistant, but they ultimately compromised that he would let her go into the bakery only long enough to make sure her doughs wouldn't spoil overnight, and then he was taking her home.

I marveled at Amy's dedication to her shop, then realized it was precisely because of that dedication that I'd even known anything was wrong today. I could also relate. In my past life, living in Seattle and working in an office, I hadn't felt *involved* in my work. I came in every day and did whatever was expected of me, but I'd never been in love with my job. I certainly wouldn't have thought twice about taking a fake sick day if it had been especially nice or I just wanted to stay in bed a bit longer.

In the year I'd been living in Raven Creek, I had never once called in sick. I'd been forced to stay home a few times by others—life-threatening injuries apparently make people insist you get some rest—but I hadn't had to call in for a cold, a flu, nothing.

I *loved* my job. Maybe it was because I was my own boss, maybe it was that my job involved spending my entire day surrounded by books and people who loved books, while I got to take breaks to bake and sell tea. None of that was a hardship. Coming to work every day was a genuine joy for me.

There were days my staff had to kick me out.

Right now, half of that staff was deep in conversation with Mr. Loughery in the bookstore.

"Are you guys still trying to figure out the motive?" I asked after I finished ringing up a customer who was buying several bags of our loose-leaf tea. She'd wanted each blend explained to her, even though the brewing instructions were all on the label. But I didn't mind nerding out about tea, and any opportunity to tell people not to oversteep was one I was going to jump on.

"We've moved past the motive stage. Imogen is helping

me look up members of Naomi's improv troupe on the Internet." I could actually hear the capital I on Internet in Mr. Loughery's intonation. He was pretty with it for an old fellow, but I also thought he was likely to spell out the h...t...t...p...slash...slash...w...w...w...dot at the beginning of website addresses. In fairness, my mother was considerably younger than Norman and I had trouble explaining the concept of a right click to her sometimes.

I'm sure Daphne found me to be just as exhausting when I made her repeat her comments about the TikTok algorithm, which sounded more like witchcraft to me than any spell I was capable of.

Part of me wanted to tell them we shouldn't be talking about this in the store, but a much larger part of me was delighted to have partners in crime aside from Rich. Not that he was a *bad* partner in crime; in fact, his past and current professions made him very useful at solving mysteries. However, those same professions tended to make him prone to lecturing me on personal safety and leaving things to the police.

Which, like... fair. But also boring.

Plus, Rich and I were a couple now, and for some reason that made me feel weird about using his professional skills to help me snoop around. Perhaps it should have made me feel more entitled to those skills, but instead it was kind of like mixing business and pleasure.

I hoped the feeling would pass. My first kiss with Rich had happened during a stakeout, so getting involved with crime was kind of part of our love story.

I made a mental note to leave that detail out if we ever got married and I needed to make a romantic speech.

But seeing Imogen and Norman so enthusiastic about

this crime—and helping Amy clear her name—had me more interested in hearing what they had to say.

Surely, three heads were better than one.

Also, seeing Norman this excited about *anything* was a thrill. He spent most of his days dozing in the chair while reading little bits of mystery novels. If anything, we were doing a community service by getting one of Raven Creek's elders involved in something so mentally stimulating.

I kept that excuse stored away for when I was inevitably lectured for getting too involved in the case.

The detectives should have known what would happen when they asked for my help.

I pulled up one of the squishy armchairs so I could keep an eye on the door but also participate in the conversation. Bob, delighted by the sudden appearance of my lap, took his cue and jumped onto me, curling into a little marmalade loaf before I even realized what was happening.

"Okay, tell me more," I said eagerly.

CHAPTER TWENTY

Norman Loughery cleared his throat as if he were about to deliver a Shakespearean soliloquy and began to tell me what he and Imogen had learned.

"There were six original members of the troupe, including Naomi. Two of them have left since then in addition to her: Eugene Larson and Reid O'Connell."

"They got writing jobs at *SNL*," Imogen explained. "I think one of them is now doing a recurring bit on Weekend Update."

"Oh, the guy who explains Gen Z speak to the hosts?" I asked. "He's hilarious." The gag worked especially well since the actor was in his late thirties pretending to be a college student. "I think we can probably rule them out as being involved. They're not here this week with the others, and I think they're successful enough on their own. I doubt they're too jealous about Naomi."

"You're probably right, though I don't think sharing a smelly 30 Rock writers' room for NBC pay is quite the same level of success as being an Oscar-nominated superstar. But their not being here removes means," Imogen pointed out.

"Oh, you're catching on quick," Norman said with delight. He looked over at me. "I was explaining to Imogen how we will narrow our suspect pool down by determining if they had the three most important things a killer needs: means, motive, and opportunity."

Mr. Loughery was just about ready to teach a grad school class on solving murder. I was starting to wonder if he really was just an avid reader, or if, perhaps in his younger days, he might have dabbled in a little amateur sleuthing of his own.

Actually, forget younger days, I was beginning to think Norman was a veritable Mr. Marple.

"Who does that leave us?" I asked.

"Three original members are still with the troupe today," Imogen continued. "Quinn Delancey. She had a few bit parts in some movies on Netflix, and according to her IMDb she starred in one Hallmark Christmas movie, but she hasn't done much since."

I resisted the urge to ask *which* Hallmark Christmas movie, knowing I'd likely seen it.

"Liam Mulvaney. He's been getting viral online attention lately for some crowd work he does during his stand-up. He's really cute—if you're into that too-perfect thing, yuck—so there are a lot of women in his audiences, and he definitely works the room. There are rumors online that he and Naomi were a thing. Like *recently*."

I leaned in. "Maybe *he's* the one who has a jealousy motive. If Naomi dumped him to get with Blaine, he might have retaliated."

"Possibly," Norman said. "But Imogen says that the DMZ has reported him dating a model much younger than Naomi in the past month."

I blinked at him, trying to process what the DMZ had to do with this.

"TMZ," Imogen corrected with a smirk. "They're an online gossip channel."

"Oh!" Mr. Loughery's cheeks reddened. "My goodness, that *does* make much more sense. I was wondering why the North Korean government would be keeping such close tabs on a relatively unknown comedian."

I resisted laughing as long as I could until my eyes were watering and my chest actually hurt, and then the laugh came out almost as an explosion. I clapped my hands over my mouth, but continued to snort, unable to stop myself, tears streaming down my face.

Apparently, I had really needed a good laugh after the stress of my morning and worrying about Amy.

I placed a hand on Norman's arm once I regained my composure. "I'm sorry, Norman. I wasn't laughing at you, just the delightful mix-up."

"Oh, don't worry about me, Phoebe. At my age, if I can't laugh at my own blunders, then what's the point of still being around?" He winked at me. "Now, Miss Imogen, why don't you tell us about the last original member?"

"Keidi, yes, that's Heidi but with a K, Crandle."

"Surely that's not her real name," I said, aghast.

Imogen smirked. "Thankfully no, she was born Heidi, but according to the lore of her tiny Wikipedia article, a casting agent once wrote her name down wrong and apparently she got the job because the director remembered her *weird name*, so she changed it professionally."

"That's awful." I wrinkled up my nose.

"It's certainly not something I would choose for myself," Imogen said. "But hey, if being memorable gets you gigs, I guess she thought it was worth it."

"What's Keidi's bone to pick with Naomi?" I asked.

"Well, apparently before Liam dated Naomi, he dated Keidi."

"Ohhh, a scandal. That's a lot of in-group dating. Never a good idea." I wondered if it was just a case of spending so much time with the other actors that they couldn't meet anyone outside the group.

"Right?" Imogen showed me a picture of the whole original group, all smiling from a small theatre stage. While I vaguely recognized some of the faces, it was hard to be sure if that was because of a role they'd played, or because I'd just seen them yesterday. Naomi's was the face that stood out the most, since she was so well known.

They all looked so happy it was almost euphoric, and considering a few of their brows were damp with sweat, they had likely just finished a particularly good performance.

"They look like they really like each other here," I said, looking at the photo on her phone.

"A lot can change when one person gets more famous than the rest," Norman noted. "Jealousy can be a bitter pill to swallow."

"I just wonder if it was enough to make one of them want to kill her," I wondered aloud.

My question was left hanging as the bell over the door chimed and I got up to help our newest customer. Except I stopped dead in my tracks when I realized it was Dierdre Miller.

Since Dierdre only showed up when she wanted something—and that something was almost never books or tea—I gave her a guarded smile.

"Good morning, Dierdre." I did not ask what brought her in.

I was hoping she wasn't planning to stay long.

"Oh, wonderful, just the people I was hoping to see." She looked at not just me, but also Imogen and Norman. The two of them exchanged a concerned glance. I was glad I wasn't the only one in town who didn't enjoy spending quality time with Dierdre.

"You wanted to see us... why?" I asked, trying to keep my tone pleasant, but I really just wanted to shoo her out the door.

She was a little *too* happy, and with Dierdre that tended to make me nervous.

"I've come with wonderful news," she declared, clapping her hands together. "Due to the auditions being cancelled following the... unfortunate incident that occurred, it was agreed upon by the theatre committee and the remaining members of Something Wicked have decided that a different approach was necessary to casting the fall play."

I had almost entirely forgotten about the play, which had been our reason for being at the community center in the first place. I couldn't believe the play was still going to be put on at this point. Certainly, Naomi's murder was reason enough to call it off.

Dierdre, seeming to read my mind, said, "The town council and the troupe decided it would be a good morale boost for the town to have something to participate in and look forward to. And it is such a long-standing tradition."

"Sure," I replied, still unclear what this had to do with any of us.

"I'm sure you're just dying to know why I've come, so I'll jump right to the point. Instead of basing things off auditions, which wouldn't be fair since the auditions weren't ever completed, the whole play has been cast via a lottery, using all the names of those who were planning to, or already had auditioned."

A sinking pit in my stomach told me where this was going only a moment before she made her big announcement.

"All three of you will be among our stars!"

CHAPTER TWENTY-ONE

Dierdre didn't wait around long enough to see if we might protest her declaration. She simply said she had a lot of other people to tell, and we should plan to be at the community center that evening by seven o'clock.

I couldn't even beg off for Imogen and me, claiming the store needed staffing. Dierdre knew all too well we closed at six. I wasn't clever enough to come up with another lie, either. I *had* been at the auditions. I had just assumed my complete lack of performing ability would be enough to dissuade them from selecting me.

This was one lottery I wished I hadn't won.

As soon as she was gone, it was evident my two Scooby Gang pals were not as bummed out about this turn of events as I was. Imogen and Norman shared a high five.

"Heck yeah!" Imogen declared with enthusiasm. "I've been wanting to get in on the annual play for *years*. They always cast the same ten people, I swear. This is our year, Norman."

"Yes, I am delighted. It has been quite some time since I last graced a stage, but I admit I am looking forward to it."

"You guys, this is the worst. Do you think I can give my role to someone who actually wants it?" I moaned, flopping back into my chair. Bob, who had been sent to the floor when Dierdre came in, eyed my position warily. He wanted to jump back into my lap, but didn't want to keep getting knocked out again whenever the door opened.

He opted instead to climb up behind me and settled on the fluffy cushion behind my head. His purring vibrated against my neck. Maybe I could train him to do the same thing at home to de-stress me after days like this one. It was doing a pretty good job.

"Oh, come on, Phoebe, it's going to be fun, and you'll be with friends. No one is expecting you to be Laurence Olivier. Everyone in town loves you, and they're going to cheer for you no matter what."

I took a moment to process this and realized that it might have been the single nicest thing Imogen had ever said to me. Or said *period*. How could I possibly back out now when I'd gotten a pep talk from the least peppy person I knew?

I chewed on my lower lip. "I suppose it couldn't hurt to see what role they've assigned me," I said. Perhaps I'd be lucky, and I'd have one line.

"Plus, look at the positive side of it," Norman said cheerfully. "There couldn't be a better way to get some one-on-one time with our entire list of suspects, now could there?"

At that, I brightened considerably.

When in doubt, I could always be cheered up by the opportunity to do a little snooping around.

I just hoped I was a better actor when it came to questioning people than I was when it came to reading lines.

· · ·

Mr. Loughery left around noon with a promise to meet us back at the shop so we could all walk together to the community center. Likewise, my shift ended before Imogen's, which thankfully gave me enough time to take Bob home between work and the first meeting about the play.

With Bob and Coco fed, they would be far less likely to murder me in my sleep for going out for the evening. I placated them with extra treats before heading back out and noticed with a smile that Rich had pre-set my coffee maker to brew a pot the next morning. I'd never been able to get it to work and had complained about it the other day.

It was not a surprise that he'd been listening, but it was still a treat.

After reminding my fur-children to behave, I headed back to the store. I was used to leaving the house while it was still dark outside to go to work, but for some reason it felt different to do it at night. I quickly scoured my porch to make sure no photographers were hiding in my bushes, then set off on foot to go back to the bookstore.

My bike or car would have been faster, but then I'd need to leave those at the store and return for them later. Plus, it was a nice evening, no rain, and cool enough to need a hat and mittens, but not in an unpleasant way.

Even though the shop was now closed, the light was still on inside, and as I went through the door I found Norman, Imogen, Daphne, and Honey all huddled together sharing steamy cups of tea.

"You two got wrangled into this as well?" I asked Daphne and Honey.

"Guess no one else agreed with Naomi's opinion on my audition," Honey said with just a hint of lingering bitterness in her tone. "I know it's a lottery; it just feels like the universe setting things right, that's all."

I hoped she just meant with the casting and not with Naomi ending up dead.

"Speak for yourself," I replied. "Because I'm not sure what I did to the universe to deserve this."

"Are you sure you're not destined for the stage?" Imogen asked. "Because you're being dramatic enough."

I snorted. "Okay, fair, fair. I promise to stop complaining and try to have a good time."

"That's the spirit," said Honey gamely. "Just remind yourself it's only community theatre."

"I'm not sure that helps now that I understand how invested everyone in town is in this whole thing, but as long as I'm playing, like, second lobster, I'll be okay."

"You'll be great no matter what," Norman piped in, his cheeks rosy with the excitement of what was to come. Seeing Norman after dark felt somewhat like seeing a teacher at the grocery store when you were in grade school. He was still him, but the circumstances felt all wrong.

"Did Frodo approve of you leaving for the evening?" I asked, referring to his beloved tuxedo cat. "Bob and Coco were *not* thrilled with me for abandoning them."

Norman chuckled. "He was sleeping on one of the heat vents when I left. I'm not even sure he noticed."

We gathered together, to-go cups of tea in hand, and headed out into the night, as I locked the shop up behind us. I smiled at the sign hanging over the doorway, reminding myself how lucky I was to be responsible for this wonderful place that my aunt had created.

I hoped she was proud of me, wherever she was.

Though she was likely considerably less proud of my puzzle-solving abilities.

Rich was just emerging from his apartment as our group headed out. "You guys look like you're planning on getting up to no good," he said, catching my eye amid the group.

"Oh, are you somehow the only person I know who *hasn't* been roped into being in the play?" I asked.

Rich took in the motley crew of us, a grin spreading over his handsome features. "I guess I'd better go get tickets for this thing, because there's no way I'm going to miss it now." He skirted around the others, wrapping an arm around my waist and planting a kiss on my temple. "I expect a full report tomorrow. I, unfortunately, will be trying to find out if someone has a cheating husband tonight." He tipped an imaginary cap to us, gave me one last squeeze and then headed off to his car.

I was sorry to see him go, but part of me was happy to be able to miss him. When I'd lived in Seattle, all my friends had been Blaine's friends. I never did anything social unless it was as part of being a couple. I had been in college the last time I'd had *real* friends of my own, the kind of people I could spend an evening with, just chatting, and enjoying that time.

Now, as I looked at the group moving down the sidewalk ahead of me, I realized that part of the reason Rich and I worked so well was that we both had our own lives separate from each other. It meant that whenever we were able to come together, we had so much to share. I *liked* that he wasn't my entire world.

We made our short walk to the community center, where about fifteen other people were gathered, most of whom I recognized to see, and a few I actually knew by name.

Charlie Bravebird, who ran the pet shop, was there, and to my genuine surprise, so was Detective Patsy Martin.

I left my group and hustled over to her, where she was hanging up her coat alongside several others. A brightly colored scarf was wrapped around her neck, and I realized this was probably the first time I'd ever seen her in anything other than one of the pantsuits she wore to work.

"Patsy!" I greeted. "I'm surprised to see you here. For some reason, I didn't take you for the theatrical sort."

"I will take that as a compliment, because I am decidedly *not* the theatrical sort." She inclined her head in the direction of a pretty woman in her forties with a dark bob haircut. "My wife Ruthie was selected by the lottery, and since I don't always get to participate in her hobbies, I thought I'd come and lend some moral support."

For some reason, getting this much personal information out of Patsy at one time stunned me into silence. Much like seeing Norman outside his usual armchair, learning that Patsy had a wife and a complete home life I didn't know about was equally surprising.

I kicked myself for not asking people more personal questions about their lives. Though, to be fair to myself, I usually only crossed paths with Patsy when murder was involved.

I stepped closer to her. "Be honest with me, you're here because you want to see if any of the acting troupe stick out as an obvious suspect."

Patsy raised an eyebrow at me and barely restrained a coy smile. "Why, Phoebe Winchester. Are you suggesting I'm a workaholic who can't put a case aside?"

"No, I'm saying if you're anything like me, you can't pass up an opportunity to keep an eye on things."

She smirked. "Speaking of which, I know we only spoke

about it recently, but have you had a chance to speak to Blaine yet?"

I made a face, which was apparently my involuntary response to hearing his name. It wasn't very mature, but at least it was genuine.

Patsy chuckled. "All right, I'll let you do that in your own time. But you have to let me do *my* job, okay? Just because you're helping out doesn't make you an honorary detective, which I think you might forget sometimes."

I gave her a look of mock horror. "Me? I am always a model citizen."

She rolled her eyes. "Sure, Phoebe. Come on, let me introduce you to Ruthie."

Ruthie Martin was shorter than both Patsy and me and looked like she exercised regularly. She was of East Indian descent, and her skin had a lovely coppery hue to it.

"Ruthie, this is Phoebe," Patsy said, and the other woman's eyes widened, which made me wonder precisely how much Ruthie knew about me.

"Phoebe, what a delight. I knew your aunt very well; she and I used to go for photography hikes together all the time. Patsy tells me your interests are a little more varied that Eudora's were." Her eyes twinkled.

"Ohhh, she's been telling you all about my worst habits. That's not fair," I said with a laugh. "I haven't been able to defend myself."

"She did tell me you have a marvelous cat."

"Bob. He's the best. You should come by and meet him. He's usually at the store with me most days. And if cats are your thing, we do adoptions."

Ruthie's eyes widened with evident delight, and Patsy paled. "Oh no, nope. She's not going in there; she'll leave with every cat you have *and* a stack of new books."

"And what's wrong with that?" Ruthie asked, putting her hands on her hips.

"Yeah, I think it's a great idea," I chimed in.

"I knew introducing you two would be a disaster." Patsy shook her head, but she was chuckling.

Dierdre appeared in the doorway that led from the community center lobby into the large auditorium where the auditions had been held, and where the play would be performed. "Good evening, everyone. We appreciate you being able to join us on such short notice. I'm thrilled you are all able to participate in our little play. Now if you'll follow me in, we'll make cast announcements, and let you know the rest of the rehearsal schedule. It will be quite tight with the show being only two weeks away, but I know we're going to make it our best one yet."

Two weeks didn't even seem like enough time for me to learn my lines on my own, but I wasn't about to voice this protest out loud. Evidently, the rest of the townsfolk were unsurprised by the schedule, so this must have been standard every year.

I still had a lot to learn about this town.

Everyone in the lobby filed into the auditorium and found seats close to the front. There was a long table set up on the stage with six chairs behind it, but no one was seated there yet. A stack of what I assumed to be the play's script were placed at one end of the table.

I sat between Norman and Honey, tapping my foot nervously. I knew we were doing an Agatha Christie play, but I'd never seen *And Then There Were None* performed. I was hoping it wouldn't be very complicated, given the short turnaround time to prepare.

A sound announced the opening of a door at the back of the stage, and soon Dierdre, an older man I recognized but didn't know, and the remaining members of Naomi's troupe all appeared. No one—perhaps excluding Dierdre—seemed all that excited to be there, but everyone pulled back their chairs with a clatter of shrieking metal legs and sat down.

I recognized several of the faces better after my morning chat with Imogen and Norman. Liam was sitting in the middle, next to the older man; Quinn was beside him, and Keidi towards the end. Only one of the newer members of the troupe was with them, and I felt bad for not knowing his name.

The only person who seemed happy to be at the table was Keidi, who was beaming at all of us like we were pageant judges. She waved to the assembled crowd, and one or two people waved back uncertainly. The rest of the troupe looked miserable, or in Liam's case entirely disinterested, his handsome face completely vacant of any real expression as he stared off into the middle distance.

Dierdre, on the other hand, looked like she was about to burst out of her own skin she was so excited. I wasn't sure I'd ever seen her this worked up about anything.

"Folks, folks!" She got up from the table and clapped her hands a few times, getting the attention of the already fairly quiet crowd. "Welcome, thank you so much for coming, I know you're all as excited as we are to get started, so without any further ado, I want to introduce our director, and he can tell you more about the play we'll be doing."

Dierdre waved her hands at the older man seated beside her, and he took this as his cue to stand.

"Hello everyone. My name is Pierce Townsend, and I am the regular season director at the theater in Barneswood. I'm excited to be dipping a toe outside my usual format with this year's play, and we'll be leaning into what Something Wicked is most famous for... Improv!" He paused for us to all respond, but the only response was a confused murmur buzzing through the crowd.

Meanwhile, I was frozen in horror.

If there was one thing I feared more than regular acting, it was improv.

CHAPTER TWENTY-TWO

When the crowd didn't respond the way Pierce had hoped, he cleared his throat and decided on a different approach.

"We'll be doing a stage version of Agatha Christie's *And Then There Were None,* which feels perfect for our spookier theme. As I'm sure most of you know, and I hope no one will shout about spoilers after almost ninety years in publication, the book revolves around a number of people on an island together who begin to die one by one. We decided this would make for a lot of fun with an added improv element. And we can see we do have more than ten people here, but we are planning to incorporate some flashback sequences as well as adding some elements of the supernatural."

Please let me play a ghost, please let me play a ghost, I chanted to myself. I could *definitely* manage jumping out and yelling *boo* at people. Hand me my Tony now.

"I'll be posting a cast list as soon as we're done here, but I'd like everyone to grab a copy of the script. Yes, there's a script even though we will be doing a fair bit of improv;

you'll see scene notes where we will break from the script to involve the audience. I think we'll have a lot of fun with this, and for the first few rehearsals we'll also have Something Wicked on hand to give us advice on how to make this the most impactful and fun experience."

I tried to lean into Pierce's enthusiasm, but this whole thing still sounded like it was going to be a complete nightmare. Pierce gestured towards Liam, who finally decided to stop disassociating long enough to remember he was in front of a crowd.

"Yeah, you guys, we're going to have an awesome time, and we'll run a little improv boot camp with you to make sure you're ready to *yes, and* your way to a standing ovation." He chuckled at his own joke, and Keidi smiled harder, so much so that I wondered if her cheeks were starting to hurt.

Quinn, who seemed to be especially annoyed or frustrated by the proceedings, simply grabbed the stack of scripts and shoved them down the table towards Pierce. Now that I was looking at her up close, I definitely remembered seeing her in a Hallmark movie, though I couldn't recall if it was the one where the woman saved the Easter candy company by championing giant chocolate bunnies, or the one where the woman headed to her hometown bacon festival. Whichever it had been, she had looked a lot happier in that role than she did currently.

I couldn't blame her. I was sure my face was pretty grim at the moment, too.

Not to mention, no matter what the tensions had been between Naomi and the rest of the group, at one point Quinn and Naomi had been friends. Losing a friend in such a shocking way, then being asked to go on with the show couldn't have been easy on any of them.

I was trying to see if any of the troupe members were looking extra cagey, but I had to remind myself they were all actors. Maybe not at Naomi's level of fame, but enough to book real gigs. They weren't going to make it completely obvious that they were hiding a deadly secret.

I almost felt like we should have been doing Edgar Allan Poe's *A Tell-Tale Heart* instead of a Christie. It would have been interesting to see how they reacted to a story about a guilty conscience.

Pierce gave Dierdre the scripts, and she handed them out, one making its way to all the cast members. There appeared to be about twenty of us in total. The script had eleven named characters, but then there were an additional nine roles that were just listed as *Sundry Cast*, who would evidently play multiple small roles throughout the play that didn't require a character name.

"The cast list is now posted in the lobby. We look forward to seeing everyone tomorrow night at seven o'clock to begin our first rehearsal and do a little improv boot camp."

Now that we'd been dismissed, we all filed out and into the lobby where anyone who had come as moral support hung back, while others crowded around a bulletin board where the cast list had been posted. Someone whooped with excitement, and a few others just mumbled their grudging acceptance. Sundry cast, I assumed. Meanwhile, that's what I had my fingers crossed for.

We approached the board once everyone had cleared out to check our assignments.

Norman was Judge Lawrence Wargrave, whom I recalled being one of the more important people in the book, and he seemed delighted by the casting, then a flicker of nerves caught up with him. "Oh dear, I do hope I'm able to remember all the lines." He started flicking through the script, scanning for his character's name.

I squeezed his shoulder. "You're going to do great."

Imogen had been cast as Emily Brent, who was meant to be an elderly woman, but also had a mean streak that I imagined Imogen would ham up wonderfully. Honey had the role of Ethel Rogers, and since they'd drawn more women's names than men in the lottery, it looked as if Daphne was going to be playing Tony Marston.

I scanned for my name at the bottom of the list with the other Sundry Cast, but it wasn't there. Perhaps I hadn't been added. I wouldn't tell anyone.

Then Honey said, "Oh Phoebs, I hope you're ready to dazzle us all."

My gaze drifted back to the top of the list where, just below Norman, I was entered alongside the name Vera Claythorne.

Somehow, I'd been cast in one of the leading roles.

I swallowed down a wave of nausea that threatened to knock me over, and reminded myself that everyone else was excited, and this was all just supposed to be fun. I certainly wouldn't ruin it for the others by complaining about getting a role that was *too prominent*. I did wonder, however, if trades were allowed.

"Oh, that will be... fun," I said, flashing a smile at the others, then looking through the script, seeing an unfortunate number of *VERA* among the blocks of text.

Maybe I'd be lucky and die early. I was going to have to re-read the book tonight to refresh myself on the complex plot.

I went to collect my jacket while the others chatted happily about their roles and started looking over their lines. Since it was going to be mixed with improv, I hoped flubbed lines would be looked at with forgiveness. I had a decent memory, but I wasn't going to be able to keep huge monologues fresh in my brain, especially not after working full time.

As I rifled through the coats trying to determine which of the many identical black peacoats belonged to me, I heard two voices that had an entirely different pitch than the rest of the crowd in the lobby. These voices were low, their tone clearly angry.

I darted a quick glance around the room to see if I could tell who was missing but couldn't. So, I took a few steps closer to the voices, which seemed to be coming from one of the corridors that led into the staff areas of the center.

I wasn't actually eavesdropping if I could hear everything from where I was standing, I rationalized. Pulling out my phone, I pretended to check my text messages while I waited, but noticed there was a new one waiting for me from an unknown number.

Phoebe, it's Blaine. I was hoping you might have a few minutes to talk later. I could really use a familiar face right now.

I groaned but then realized there couldn't be a more perfect opportunity to see what Blaine knew about Naomi's murder, and judge for myself whether I thought he was hiding something. And since Patsy and Kwan had asked me to use my relationship with Blaine to help them with their case, I had no reason to feel like I was overstepping.

I replied, *Let's meet for breakfast tomorrow at 10?*

Imogen would be at the shop to relieve me, and I wanted to meet Blaine in the light of day at a neutral location, rather than inviting him over to my home after dark.

Rich, I knew, was out on a stakeout, but I wanted to tell him. Rich wasn't a jealous person. He'd never shown a sliver of that kind of insecurity with me, but I also knew that hiding things from your partner was a surefire way to spoil a good thing in a hurry.

Meeting up with the dreaded ex tomorrow. I added the puking emoji in afterwards for good measure.

A few moments later, his reply came. Guessing the stakeout wasn't too exciting at the moment. *You want me to come along, pretend to be a tough guy?*

I chuckled to myself. *Nah, I can take him.*

Rich sent back the flexing bicep emoji. My heart swelled. I had worried that Rich and I switching from being *what if* friends to actually being a couple might change our dynamic and the friendship we had built since my arrival. But I was learning—and learning to accept—that it *was* possible to be best friends with the person you were regularly smooching.

It was such a relief to me that I could be falling in love with someone who I still really *liked*. I hadn't known until Rich that kind of dynamic could exist. When people around me would call their partners their best friends, I would inwardly roll my eyes, thinking they needed to get out more.

As it turned out, when you *liked* the person you were with, it made the relationship a heck of a lot easier.

Blaine messaged me back a moment later. *Sure. Meet you @ your Shop? 10?*

Sounds good, I replied, but judging by the twist of my face, I didn't mean it, and anyone looking at me would know that.

I shifted my focus, realizing that my stupid phone had managed to successfully distract me from my eavesdropping. Cursed devices. The people I'd heard were still in conversation, though, and they must have thought the lobby was too bustling for people to hear them, because they weren't doing much to lower their voices.

"Look, you can go if you want to, but I don't think we're getting paid for this if we split early," a female voice said, her tone clearly frustrated.

"I need the money as bad as you do, but I don't think it's smart for us to stay here. This place gives me the creeps."

I arched a brow, taking this insult against my small town very personally. There was *nothing* creepy about Raven Creek. How rude.

"You're being ridiculous; this town is so cute it feels like the set of a Hallmark movie."

The man made an audible sound of disgust. "You would know."

"Like I said, no one is stopping you from leaving, Liam, but if you don't want to look sus, then stop acting sus. Leaving town is only going to make them look at you more closely."

The Hallmark comment and her use of Liam's name helped me narrow down who the likely people having this discussion were. Liam was obviously Liam Mulvaney, and the woman he was speaking to must be Quinn. I hadn't realized the troupe was getting paid, but I suppose that had been naïve of me. Of course, they weren't dropping a week of their personal time to do this just because Naomi had thought the town was cute.

Though I'd spent the better part of an hour talking to Norman and Imogen about the various motives Naomi's fellow actors might have for killing her, that had felt like more of a game. Hearing the two of them talk about getting out of town and how to avoid suspicion was making the hairs on the back of my neck stand on end.

These people had been Naomi's friends; they'd known

her when she wasn't a household name. How could that relationship become so twisted that it might have been enough to motivate them to take her out permanently?

Obviously, it made the most sense that someone close to Naomi would be the one to kill her, and whoever had done it was close enough that they'd been able to poison her drink. Still, it was shocking to hear the way these two were talking. They didn't seem to care at all that Naomi was dead, just how they were being perceived and if they were getting paid.

Even if they *weren't* responsible for killing her, the conversation was cold enough to make my skin crawl.

Imogen waved to me from across the lobby, and I rejoined my friends, slipping my coat on. "You guys ready?" I asked. I wasn't sure if I should tell them what I'd overheard. I decided if the topic came up again tomorrow at the store, I'd share the vague comments with Norman and Imogen to see if they agreed things sounded a little suspect, or if I should just let it go.

I was also *very* curious to hear what Blaine had to say for himself, because he had been the last person to see Naomi alive. I might not *want* him to be the killer, but just statistically speaking, he was the most likely suspect.

Right now, I wasn't sure if I wanted to distract myself from this mystery by focusing on the play, or if focusing on the mystery would help distract me from the play.

Either way, the two were going hand in hand, and I had a feeling that as the next week of rehearsals unfolded, I'd discover a lot of things about these people that they would probably rather keep hidden.

The show must go on.

And so must the investigation.

CHAPTER TWENTY-THREE

When I'm nervous, I like to bake.

This wasn't always the case. Only a year ago, I was a lost cause in the kitchen, preferring to fall back on delivery meals after a long day of work rather than spending hours slaving away over a hot stove. Blaine had complained about this from time to time, insinuating that part of my wifely role should be to make sure we had dinner on the table.

I had politely reminded him that he was welcome to come home after his full-time job and cook for us if he'd like, but that I was tired after mine. That usually ended the argument, at least for a month or so.

But ever since moving to Raven Creek, I found that there was a Zen-like calm that could be found while kneading bread dough, and that there was a bizarre level of personal pride one could take in crafting a truly delicious scone. I wasn't a *baker*; that was Amy's area of expertise, and she could craft the most exceptional treats that looked as good as they tasted. But I could bake the heck out of a loaf of sourdough.

The morning of my meeting with Blaine, I was distracting myself by preparing my loaves for our lunch specials at the shop. The dough had risen overnight, and I was about to add my mix-ins, the thing that would make each loaf special.

We had a rotating variety of standards that our customers loved, but today I wanted to try something a little experimental. After having great success with our jalapeno-cheddar loaf, I thought I'd do a cheeky little spin on that. I chopped up some dill pickle spears into little cubes, and then chopped some fresh dill as well. Then, because cheese was always a good idea, I cubed up some aged white cheddar and mixed all the ingredients into my bowl. I'd seen variations of pickle loaves online where bakers had mixed pickle brine in at the first dough stage to make things extra-pickly, but I hadn't thought far enough ahead for that, so this would need to suffice.

I'd top the bread with a dill cream cheese and some smoked salmon.

For the sweeter option of the day, I *had* thought far enough ahead to mix several of my loaves with pumpkin puree. To that, I added some fresh chopped rosemary and chunks of white chocolate. The bread was inspired by Amy's cookies and would hopefully have a marvellously seasonal flavor. I'd top it with ricotta, dried apricot, honey, and a little bit of cinnamon.

With the loaves in the oven, I did a quick check of the front. The first hours of the day, I was by myself, but they were also the slowest. Bob had abandoned his usual chair by the fire and was sitting in the front window, a bit of the fake spiderweb brushing the top of his head.

Two women passing by paused and took a picture of him, giggling with delight as they walked away.

He slow blinked into the unseasonably sunny day, either oblivious to his fans or just soaking in their appreciation. As I approached the window, he looked up at me, his orange fur glowing in the sunlight, and I felt a pang of such love for this little animal that it actually made my heart hurt.

I owed a lot to the people I had met when I moved to Raven Creek, but it had been Bob who had been with me since the very moment I got out of my car. Bob, who had given me a reason to belong before I'd ever made a real human friend.

I picked him up, and he started to purr immediately, butting his big head into my chin and rubbing his face against mine. This was a cat's way of marking their favorite things. He was telling any other cats that might be in close proximity to my face that I belonged to him.

I pressed a thousand kisses onto his forehead, and then our mutual admiration party ended when the bell over the door jingled. I set him down, only because some customers might feel weird about being served tea by someone holding a cat, and turned to greet my new arrival.

"Good morning," I said brightly, then stopped in my tracks.

My new customer was Keidi, one of the troupe members who was at the play event last night. If she recognized me, it didn't show in her expression. She was smiling much the way she had yesterday, in a forced friendly way that made me wonder what the opposite of Resting B Face was, because I was currently looking at it.

"*Hiiiiii*," she said, her voice thick with vocal fry. "What a cute shop."

"Thank you. We have tea and some pastries on your right, and the bookshop is over here." I realized that was a pointless thing to say since shelves loaded with thousands of books were standing right beside me. "Were you looking for anything in particular?"

Keidi laughed. "As it turns out, there is a limit to how much one person can scroll TikTok, and I was getting sick of looking at my phone. I thought I'd take a walk around town since it was such a nice day, and then I saw your shop and thought maybe it would be good to get a book, so I don't actually rot my brain, you know?"

I smiled. "I am a big fan of using books to avoid brain rot."

Keidi seemed hesitant to start browsing, and I recognized the deer in the headlights look on her face. New readers, or readers just coming back to it after not picking up a book for fun in many years, could often go into a state of shock seeing the sheer number of options available. It could be hard to know what you liked, what was good, and what was a series, when you weren't deeply immersed in book conversations every single day.

Keidi appeared to be dazed by the shelves behind me, so I figured I'd give her somewhere more contained to start.

"You said you're a big TikTok user, right?" I asked. The video platform was one I didn't personally use, but Daphne was something of a pro at it, and our store evidently had a decent following on the platform thanks to her efforts. And people's obsession with Bob and the cats. Since adding the cat adoptions, our follower numbers had quadrupled.

Keidi nodded.

Daphne kept me up to date on what books were trending on the major social media platforms, and near the new releases wall, we had added a table specifically for books that had gained some online notoriety. The table was heaped with steamy hockey and mafia romances; popular fantasy novels; thrillers that people were obsessing over; and a metric ton of romantic fantasy books that seemed to all feature dragons on their covers in some capacity or another.

Seeing book covers she recognized, Keidi seemed to relax, and I left her to browse the table, promising to check in. It was taking what little self-control I had not to start grilling her about Naomi, but I didn't want to scare her away.

Still, after what I'd heard being said between Quinn and Liam yesterday, I was itching to see if Keidi had any insights about her fellow troupe members. I did have to remind myself, however, that Keidi was as much of a potential killer as anyone else. Just because she seemed nice, and she wanted to buy books didn't mean she was innocent.

Someone had killed Naomi, someone she knew, and that was a very short list in this town.

I wished the police could see that it *must* have been someone close to her and not Amy. Why on earth would Amy want to kill a movie star? Amy wouldn't hurt a fly. I felt almost personally offended that one of my closest friends had suspicion cast on them. And over what? A stupid cup.

I busied myself behind the counter of the tea shop so I could keep an eye on Keidi and a few other customers who had come in to browse, but it also helped take my mind off the whole Amy situation, because if I ruminated on it too long, I just started to get mad.

Amy had been back to work this morning like usual, but she wasn't herself. She still smiled, said good morning, had my order ready to go, but I knew something was off. She normally doodled little pictures or notes on my takeout boxes, and those doodles hadn't been present today. It was obvious to anyone who knew Amy well that her mind was on other things.

I wanted to help take that burden off her shoulders, but I couldn't do that unless I had someone else to point the police toward.

A few minutes before ten, Imogen came in. She was unexpectedly happy this morning, saying hello to the customers she passed, and greeting me as she headed to the office to deposit her jacket and bag. When she came back, she was holding her script for the play.

"You're really excited about this, aren't you?" I asked.

Imogen flushed, like I'd caught her doing something she shouldn't be. "I used to love being in plays in high school. I even briefly considered trying to do it professionally before my dad told me he wouldn't pay for school if I didn't get a useful degree."

"Ugh, I'm sorry. My parents were kind of the same way. They insisted that if we were going to go to school, it had to be for something marketable. My brother Sam became a lawyer, so at least they got one winner out of the deal."

Imogen quirked an eyebrow at me. "Phoebe. You're very literally a successful small business owner. Just because you're not a doctor doesn't mean you shouldn't be proud of yourself."

I blinked at her a few times, trying to chase away the sudden emotion her words made me feel. What kind of upside-down world was it this week that I was willingly having a meal with my ex, and Imogen Prater was giving me emotional pep talks?

Before I could reply to Imogen, the bell at the door tinkled, and in walked Blaine.

Blaine looked *terrible*. He had dark bags under his eyes; his clothing was so rumpled it looked as if he must have put on the first thing he'd found on the floor that morning. It didn't appear as if he had shaved in at least two days. He looked genuinely awful, and I wasn't just thinking that because I harbored resentment towards him.

"Yikes," Imogen said under her breath, confirming to me that Blaine did indeed look worse than usual.

"Hey Phoebe," he greeted, trying to smile but managing only a grimace. "You've got a nice place here."

"Thanks," I replied, not willing to move from behind the counter. I knew I should have been kinder, more compassionate, whatever the things a better person would be in the wake of his loss, but I found it very hard to conjure up any sympathy for him.

Maybe that made me a bitter ex-wife, but so be it.

"Phoebe," Imogen said, cutting me a quick, knowing glance. "Blaine looks like he could use some tea."

I stared at her stupidly for a moment, wondering why on earth I'd want to give my ex any of our lovely tea. Then Imogen nudged me hard in the ribs.

"The special tea we keep in the kitchen. For our best customers."

My eyebrows shot up. While Imogen was not *technically* on the list of people who knew about my witchy skills, she *had* worked with Eudora for many years. Eudora kept her more magical blends in the kitchen, and they were only sold by request. We actually went through a decent amount of all of them per month, because locals in Raven Creek had come to rely on Eudora whenever they needed a little boost in certain areas. Love, money, luck, sleep.

And truth.

Our Truth Be Told tea was not one of the more commonly sold blends, largely because most people didn't actually *want* to know the truth when they suspected something.

But in this case, I'd never wanted my ex to be more honest with me.

"Imogen, what a great idea."

Blaine had wandered around the store while Imogen and I talked, and seemed entirely oblivious to our conversation. Bob stopped at the door frame leading into the book shop half of the store and took one look at Blaine before hissing loudly, all his fur standing on end and his tail turning into an orange bottle brush. He glowered at Blaine before scampering back into the bookstore to observe from the safety of his usual chair.

Blaine blinked several times.

"Why do you have a rabid cat in here?"

I sighed. "He's not rabid; he just doesn't like you."

"He must be yours then," Blaine said, and almost sounded sad about it.

"He is."

"I never really took you for a cat person," he mused, still staring into the shop at Bob.

I crossed my arms over my chest. "That's probably because you never wanted any pets. So, I never had a chance to *know* if I was a cat person. It turns out I am."

Keidi, who had been browsing happily to this point and was hugging a brightly colored Emily Henry book to her chest, seemed to realize at that moment that Blaine had come in.

He likewise spotted her unexpectedly.

They both froze.

"What are *you* doing here?" Keidi snarled. Her voice was so filled with venom I got whiplash turning my head around to look at her. I thought I was the only one who hated Blaine that much.

"I could ask you the same question," he replied, though his voice was more level. "I didn't know you could read. Congratulations."

Keidi's mouth fell open, her cheeks turning red. Since she was the only actual potential paying customer of the two, I couldn't let this continue.

"*Hey*," I interrupted, coming out from behind the counter to stand in front of him. "Whatever beef you might have, I'm not letting you come into my store and insult my customers. So go wait for me outside. You're upsetting my cat, and you're being unbelievably rude, so go." I shooed him to the door. "I'll be out in a minute."

Once Blaine left, thankfully without a fight, I looked at Keidi. "I'm so sorry."

"You know him?" she asked.

"I was, unfortunately, married to him for several years."

Keidi gave me an assessing look. "Was he this much of a jerk back then?"

"In retrospect, yes, he has always been terrible."

"Then I'm sorry for you."

"Well, thankfully I'm not married to him anymore. But I take it you're not a fan?" This was curious to me because it seemed like Naomi had been head over heels. Had her friends seen something she hadn't?

"He's a real piece of work. I'm pretty sure he hit on every single woman Naomi knows whenever she wasn't paying attention. He tried to make a move on me once, and I told Naomi about it, but he lied and told her I'd been the one to come onto him. She was so blinded by love she believed him."

"I'm sorry. I wish I could tell you I was surprised, but that sounds like Blaine."

"I wouldn't be surprised if he's the one who killed her," Keidi said suddenly, then seemed to realize what she'd said and clapped one hand over her mouth. "Oh my gosh, please pretend I didn't just say that. He might be awful, but I shouldn't just go accusing people of such horrible things."

I couldn't pretend she hadn't said it, though. Was she alone in thinking Blaine was responsible, or did some of Naomi's other friends share the same sentiment?

This was hardly the place to ask, especially since Keidi was so obviously upset she'd even mentioned it. She hustled over to the cash desk with her book, and I headed into the little kitchen to make Blaine a cup of tea. The last time I'd tried to use the Truth Be Told tea on anyone, I had baked it into some scones, and the result had been a slightly too powerful effect that made Dierdre Miller uneasy about coming into my store even to this day.

I just brewed him a regular cup of tea in one of our to-go mugs, then added some steamed milk on top to make it a tea latte. Blaine was more of a coffee guy, but he was also too polite to reject something I put in his hands, so I knew he'd drink it.

Keidi was gone when I emerged, so if there had been any additional fireworks between her and Blaine, I had missed them. Blaine was lurking outside, looking at the last-chance book cart but not really paying attention to it. I grabbed my jacket because even though it was sunny; it was also October, and the weather had taken on a distinct chill.

I met Blaine out front and thrust the tea into his hands. He looked down at it as if I'd just passed him a living thing that he didn't know how to take care of. "What's this?" he asked.

"It's tea. Drink it. You look like lukewarm hell; that'll make you feel a bit better."

He grimaced. "Do I really look that bad?"

"Does your hotel room not have mirrors, or are you secretly a vampire who can't see his reflection? Yes, you look awful."

Blaine gave me a quick look that said I didn't need to be quite *that* honest, but I wasn't going to sugarcoat things just to be nice. Blaine hadn't done anything to earn my general kindness. A bigger person might have been able to look past the injuries in our history, but I was not a bigger person, and I wasn't trying to be.

The most obvious place in town to go for breakfast would have been the diner, Sweet Peach's, but that was my place with Rich. It was where we'd gone on our first date, even if neither of us had really known if it was a date at the time. We ate there frequently enough we no longer needed to look at menus to order, which was such a lovely feeling.

Being a *regular* somewhere was an experience I'd never had outside Raven Creek. I wasn't going to share that place with Blaine, no matter how good the pancakes were.

There was another place down Main that was popular with the tourist crowd because it leaned super hard into the small-town cute and cozy vibe, and they also made tasty food, which didn't hurt. Grandma's Griddle was close enough to walk to, so Blaine and I set out on foot. I probably could have made more of an effort to chat with him along the way, especially since the detectives were counting on me to find out what he knew, but I found that I was spending most of my energy tamping down the urge to push him into oncoming traffic.

I took steadying breaths since I knew this kind of low-boil anger wasn't good for me, but it was easier to avoid feeling it when he wasn't around. Having him walk beside me with his shoulders slumped forward and his free hand stuffed in his pocket like he was a miserable child being taken somewhere against his will wasn't doing anything to help my mood.

I knew amicable divorces existed and that plenty of people were on friendly terms with their exes, but despite how non-volatile our actual divorce proceedings had been, having him here now told me that I wasn't going to be one of those cool ex-wives who was super chill about all the betrayal that had led to our separation.

Forgive and forget was what people suggested, but it turned out I hadn't done either.

We made our way into Grandma's Griddle, and I was relieved to see that we'd arrived in the sweet spot in between breakfast and lunch rushes, and there were several open tables for us to choose from. The space was warm and inviting, and just being there took the edge off my anger.

The walls were done up with chintzy wallpaper; there were ruffly café curtains on all the windows, and the tables all had different thrifted tablecloths on them. There was a shelf all around the top of the walls that displayed a variety of tchotchkes, like teddy bears, teapots, old dolls, vintage goose-shaped cookie jars and more. It absolutely felt like walking into the dining room of a beloved grandparent.

We took a seat at one of the open tables near the door, and a plump, jolly-looking woman appeared practically out of thin air. Her round cheeks were flushed pink, and her smile was so infectious I found that the last of my anger towards Blaine had burned off.

"Morning, Phoebe," the woman said. It always

surprised me when people I didn't really know were aware of who I was. I rarely came here, but I knew the woman was the owner, Bessie Higgins. She was a periodic member of the knitting group who met at The Earl's Study every Friday, but she hadn't come in several months, making me wonder if there'd been a falling out, or if she was just too busy.

"Morning, Bessie," I replied, fixing a smile on my face.

Bessie looked expectantly at Blaine, waiting for an introduction, which he thankfully saved me from having to give. "I'm Blaine Winchester, nice to meet you."

"Oh," Bessie replied. The folks in town knew my last name was Winchester, but they also knew my family name was Black. Bessie had evidently done the mental math and realized Blaine wasn't my brother. "Well, yes. Hello. You kids want something to drink while you're perusing the menu?"

Blaine held up the tea I'd given him, and I was grateful Bessie didn't comment about the outside beverage.

"I'll take a praline latte, please," I said.

"Excellent choice, hon, I'll be right back with that."

She disappeared, and I watched, holding my breath, as he took his first sip from his cup. He made a slight face at first, then seemed to reconsider his initial reaction; he nodded in approval. "That's a really unusual blend," he announced finally. "What is it?"

"Oh, just something we have around the shop. I'm not sure I remember which one I picked."

He accepted this response and took another sip just as Bessie returned with my latte. The drink smelled of espresso and sweet praline syrup. I took a sip, and my brain lit up like the Fourth of July from the intensity of the sugar. It was wonderful, but I'd definitely be in a sugar coma later.

"Bessie, you snuck something else into this. What is it?" I asked, picking up a rich but subtle flavor under the sugar.

"I add a little bit of butter extract into the cup with the syrup," Bessie replied with a wink. "Really helps ground that sweetness, I think."

She was right, though I didn't think NASA could ground the sweetness. But it did help balance it with something richer, more creamy. I couldn't have this every day, but as a treat it was really lovely.

Bessie left us to look at the menus, and the vast array of home-cooked items available had my stomach rumbling in anticipation. I waited until we had ordered—corned beef hash for Blaine, waffles with banana and Nutella for me—and then I fixed Blaine with a stare, hoping the tea had had enough time to work its literal magic.

"Why did you want to talk to me today?" I asked, cutting right to the chase.

"Because I think the police think I did it, and you seem to have a good relationship with them." As soon as the words were out, his eyes widened, like he was shocked to have heard them coming out of his mouth. "That wasn't what I planned to say."

"Yeah, I'm sure it wasn't." I sipped my latte. I didn't want to go at him too aggressively with the questioning because he might figure out that he was saying things against his will and clam up completely. "Why don't you just talk to the police yourself?"

"I did, but I'm pretty sure they don't believe me, which is fair because I wasn't being entirely honest with them."

A look of pure horror settled onto his features, and I was sure the jig was up. These were things he'd never be saying on his own, and we both knew it. I figured I had about two minutes before he stopped talking altogether, shutting up from fear over what he might say.

"What weren't you being honest about?" I asked.

"That Naomi and I had a big fight right before she died, and she said she was thinking about calling off the engagement."

This time, both our eyes widened simultaneously. Well, that *was* a big thing to keep from the police. And it didn't do much to help take Blaine off the suspect list. If anything, it bumped him higher up. I'd come into this assuming he was probably a bad fiancé, but not a killer. Now I was wondering if he might be both.

"Blaine, did you kill Naomi?"

But my luck had run out. Blaine pushed back his chair and was out the door before I could even read the expression on his face.

He might not have answered, but his silence spoke volumes.

CHAPTER TWENTY-FOUR

I spent the rest of my workday in a daze. I was *dying* to talk to someone about what Blaine said—and hadn't said—but I also knew I had to be careful who I shared that with because it happened to involve the use of magical tea.

While rumors of my witchy abilities weren't *as* abundant as they had been for Aunt Eudora, I knew some people had their suspicions. And while I didn't think anyone would run me out of town with pitchforks and torches if they learned the truth, it *was* kind of a difficult thing to explain.

Oh yes, by the way, I have magical powers and can stop time periodically. Do you have any special skills?

Yeah, nope. That wasn't a conversation I felt like having *before* jumping into my conversation about whether or not my ex-husband might be a murderer in addition to being a scoundrel. That meant I needed to wait until Rich was awake so I could bounce things off him. As a PI, a former detective, someone who knew I was a witch, and also my current boyfriend, he seemed like the most ideal person on the planet to get into this with.

I texted him after my meet-up with Blaine and offered to bribe him with the uneaten corned beef hash I'd brought back with me. It took about an hour and a half for him to reply. When he was out late on stakeouts or doing work, he often slept well into the afternoon.

By about two o'clock, I got a text back. *I am sufficiently awake for whatever true crime theories you have managed to muster.*

Since Daphne had arrived, I didn't feel too bad for leaving the shop a little earlier than usual. I left Bob sitting in his usual chair, and I'd collect him before I headed home. Since Rich lived in the apartment over the store, going to see him was unbelievably easy. I stepped outside and went to the small doorway at the right side of the building, where a narrow staircase led upstairs. I knocked, and Rich must have been standing at the door waiting for me.

I held out the takeout container of hash as an offering.

"Grandma's Griddle?" he asked, perplexed.

"I wasn't going to take the dreaded ex to Peach's." I made a face.

"Fair enough, though I'm not sure if I should be offended that you're giving me his leftovers."

"I don't think they count as leftovers if he ran out the door before they arrived at the table. Think of them as a prize from the dine and dash fairy."

He took the box out of my hands and lifted the lid. "Well, I'm not one to look a gift hash in the mouth. This smells incredible. You know Bessie makes all her corned beef herself?"

Corned beef was one of those things that I understood got made *somehow* but vaguely assumed it happened only in factories. The idea it could be made in someone's kitchen was fascinating.

"I did *not* know that."

He stepped out of the way, and we moved towards his couch. Rich's apartment was not overly large, but it was very cozy and comfortable. He had really made it his own over the year and a bit he'd been living here. I wondered briefly if he wanted to stay here long term, or if he had started to wonder about all the space in my house and what he could do to fill it.

We weren't anywhere near having that conversation, but it didn't stop me from thinking about it constantly.

After Blaine and I had split, I hadn't been sure I'd ever want to share my space with someone again. But I was starting to soften to the idea.

Rich did have a much nicer TV than I did, after all.

He grabbed a fork and returned to the couch, offering me first bite, which I declined. "All right, tell me exactly what happened?"

"I gave him some of Eudora's truth tea, and oh man did he tell the truth."

Rich snickered. "I thought you'd learned your lesson about using that tea. I'm pretty sure Eudora stopped selling it to customers. Too potent."

"Boy, is it ever."

"Did he admit to killing Naomi?"

"Not exactly. He admitted he'd lied to the police about them having an argument, and that apparently Naomi was thinking about calling off their engagement."

Rich raised an eyebrow at me. "That's a pretty strong motive." He set the hash down on his coffee table and turned so he was facing me directly. "You asked him if he did it, I assume."

"I did, but by then he'd caught on to something being amiss. He was out the door before I even had the question entirely out of my mouth. I don't know if he ran because he didn't want to answer it, or if he was already running before he even heard it, but he's definitely got some kind of secret he wants to keep that way."

"I mean, everyone has secrets; I'm not sure that makes him a killer. You'd run out of there pretty quick too if you thought you might accidentally spill the beans about being a witch. We all have stuff we don't want to share. But I agree that sounds suspicious, and them having a fight right before she died doesn't look good for him at all."

"I don't know if I should tell Patsy and Kwan yet," I admitted.

"Why not?" There was no tone of judgment in the question, just curiosity.

"They're going to react like cops, even if they know there was a magical element to it. I'm having a hard time believing Blaine could have killed her, and I don't want to be the reason someone else gets arrested unfairly." I couldn't help but think of poor Amy.

But wouldn't telling the police what I'd learned help clear Amy's name?

Rock, meet hard place.

"I think that's fair, but we also need to make sure that if he *is* guilty, he's not going to suddenly skip town and vanish into the night."

I considered this. "I wonder if there's a spell I could use that would compel him to stay put. At least until we know what's going on."

Rich raised an eyebrow at me. "You don't think he had enough magic with that tea?"

"I don't even know if it's possible, but if it was, we'd at least know he wasn't going anywhere."

"Hmm." Rich contemplated this. I'm sure there were

some ethical considerations at play; it was sort of akin to magically handcuffing him here. "Well, if anyone would have a spell like that, it would be your aunt. Though hopefully it doesn't require him to drink anything, because I think you'd be hard pressed to get him to accept any beverages from you in the immediate future."

I snorted. "Just an idea. I mean the detectives *did* ask if I could help magically."

"I love how you interpret their requests in whatever way suits you best at the moment," he said with a laugh, but my cheeks still reddened. "Hey, I'm just teasing. I know you just want to do what's best to help solve the case."

"I want to figure out who did this. Not for Blaine's sake, but for Amy's. It was her cup that had the poison in it, and I think it's going to take a lot more than her friends vouching for her to convince the police that's just a coincidence."

"They have to do their jobs. I don't think they like it anymore than you or I do." He scooted closer and put his arm around me, pulling me to his side and pressing a kiss on the top of my head. He smelled *crazy* good, like bergamot shampoo and a really nice cologne.

Maybe *he* was putting me under a spell, because the smell of him and the warmth of having him close was making all my worries start to melt away. It wasn't fair, but I also wasn't mad about it.

"Hey, I have an idea," he said into my hair.

I looked up at him. "Oh?"

"Can you get off early tomorrow?"

"I have been told on numerous occasions I am the boss. So probably. Why?"

"Get Daphne to come in early. We're going to go on a scavenger hunt."

It took me a moment to understand what he was

saying, but once it clicked, my eyes widened and a thrill of excitement shot through me.

"Yeah?"

"Yeah. I'm dying to see what Eudora has planned for you."

CHAPTER TWENTY-FIVE

Before there could be a magical scavenger hunt, however, there was the first day of rehearsals. I had looked over my script several times since receiving it, even keeping it with me in the kitchen at the shop. As a result, it now had some sourdough splatters on certain pages.

It didn't seem to matter how much I looked at the words on the page; none of them stuck in my brain. Were cue cards an option? I was really hoping they might be willing to let me swap roles, but I figured I'd wait until I had a moment to speak to the director privately rather than making a big fuss about it. Surely one of the Sundry Chorus folks would be keen to take on a leading role.

Still, part of me felt almost obligated to carry on. My friends were *so* excited about the play, and I knew they'd be disappointed if I decided to swap roles. Yet another decision to weigh on me.

I'd stopped at home between my conversation with Rich and the rehearsal to drop off Bob, give Coco some love, and make myself a sandwich to take with me to the community center. It was a quick way to get rid of some deli turkey meat that would likely only be good a few more days, and some of the leftover pickle sourdough. I was surprised there was any of the sourdough left, considering it had been a massive hit.

I was happily munching on my sandwich when the rest of my friends arrived and settled in around me. Daphne was excitedly talking about what she was going to do with her extra hours at the shop tomorrow. I'd never known anyone as enthused about their job as Daphne was. And she had more than earned her full-time position.

In fact, thanks to her, we were doing so well with online sales I had almost depleted the huge stockpile of books I'd bought at an estate sale earlier in the year. I was going to have to start looking at notices again. That particular sale hadn't gone so well, ending with Bob finding a body, but hey, at least that happened *after* I'd won my auction.

I was glad Daphne wasn't annoyed by the extra time she'd be at work. It sounded like she was planning to make some new content related to our adoptable cats, and something to spotlight a few of our rarer first editions.

Soon, Pierce, the director, was on stage and clapping his hands for everyone's attention. "Hello, folks, glad to see we didn't scare any of you away with the scary I-word for *improv*. Today we won't be going over lines; instead, we'll be asking you all to come to the stage in groups of four, and we'll be having you do some improv dry runs with the experts."

With a flourish he held his hand out, and Keidi, Liam, and Quinn came out onto the stage. Everyone applauded, but it was a small crowd, so the sound of it wasn't big enough to fill the room. The troupe members hid their disappointment well, keeping superficial smiles plastered to their faces and waving at our motley little cast.

Before I knew it, I was up on stage with Norman, Honey, and Daphne, looking out over the theater. I think it helped my nerves somewhat to see that there were so few people there, and we weren't the first group, so I knew the other assembled members of our cast weren't going to laugh at us.

Still, my stomach was in knots, and I was sure I was sweating bullets.

Eudora had often told me that no one got very far in life without doing things that scared them, so for Eudora I took a deep breath and smiled, ready to tackle this crazy challenge the best I could. It's not like anyone else with me on stage was a trained improviser.

Well... except for the trained improvisers.

Liam came to stand at the end of our row. We'd already learned that the cardinal rule of improv was *yes, and*, which wasn't actually all that different from the first rule of covertly questioning murder suspects, which was to just go with whatever they were saying and let them paint themselves into a corner.

I nervously shuffled my feet and waited for the exercise to begin. All my friends were smiling, and the group before us seemed to have enjoyed themselves. If they could all have fun, so could I.

"All right, guys, you saw how this was done. It's easy. I'm going to set the scene with Quinn, and I just want you to join in when you feel comfortable. Okay, ready?"

We all nodded. Quinn came to stand beside Liam, and without a word spoken between them, Liam mimed holding a cup in one hand and swaying to unheard music. "Man, I can't believe it's actually been twenty years since we were in high school," he said, affecting a shouting tone to his voice like it might be hard to hear him over the music.

"I know," Quinn said, giggling like she might have had a bit too much to drink. "Mr. Murphy is still here. I think he tried to give me detention on the way to the bathroom."

A few titters from the small audience said that they were getting into it.

I felt an unexpected rush of enthusiasm and didn't dare let it go. I held my own imaginary cup and danced my way over to them. "Did you guys see Sammy Devlin? He's going around trying to convince everyone to run a naked mile on the track."

This sent up a howl through the viewers, and I felt a weird elation. People had laughed! At a joke I'd made!

Was this why people liked acting? I felt like there were fizzy bubbles in my head, and I could barely stay in character. I wanted to smile so badly.

"Seeing how Sammy looks now, I think a lot fewer people will take him up on it than they might have in high school," quipped Liam.

Daphne joined in a prissy cheerleader with a long-held crush on Liam—which might not have been acting considering how moony-eyed Daphne looked around him—and Honey played the part of Sammy the jock with rib-splitting perfection. When Norman came in as stodgy old Mr. Murphy throwing out detention slips to everyone, the small crowd was cracking up, and we got a big round of applause on taking our bows.

For the first time since Dierdre had mentioned the play, I wasn't dreading it. Yes, there was still a lot to learn, and I wasn't entirely confident I could memorize the whole script in two weeks. But if we were going to be allowed to wing it whenever we forgot something, then there was a chance... a small chance... I could actually make this work.

And I was surprised to find that I *wanted* to.

Rehearsal lasted almost two hours, and when we had gone through improv exercises in various groups and we all still liked each other, the mood seemed to be high all around.

Everyone filtered into the lobby, but I realized quickly that I'd left my bag behind and excused myself to retrieve it. The auditorium was already dark, someone having shut the lights off when they left, but I knew where we'd been sitting and there was a small light on the stage, so it wasn't pitch black.

I found my bag right where I'd left it under our seats and was about to leave when I saw someone move behind the curtains. At first, I thought I might have been imagining things. I also briefly wondered if it might be a ghost. No matter how many times Honey insisted on telling me that there was no such thing, I couldn't help but wonder.

I froze in place, daring not make a move. Then the curtain rustled again, and a moment later Keidi appeared. Gone was her permanent smile, her face now set in a focused stare, brows furrowed. When she peeked her head out from behind the curtain and scanned the auditorium, she must not have seen me because I was too close to the front. The stage was quite high, and I wouldn't have been visible from where she was because of how dark it was and the angle.

I watched with curiosity as she came out onto the stage, carrying something in her hand, and moved quietly towards something I couldn't see. She knelt down and, to my surprise, managed to lift one of the floorboards. Whatever she had been holding, she slipped inside, and then was gone in a flash, hurrying back behind the curtains and out of sight.

What on Earth?

I was itching to go up on stage to see what she had hidden, but Daphne peeked her head in the auditorium. "Hey Phoebs, you coming? We want to walk to Peach's and get some cocoa."

I took one longing look back to the stage but knew I wouldn't be able to explain myself if anyone from the crew saw me snooping around. With a sigh, I followed Daphne out, knowing that if I couldn't hunt for clues that hot cocoa was a good secondary option.

CHAPTER TWENTY-SIX

The next morning, after I went through my usual opening shift ritual and had been relieved at ten by the arrival of Daphne and Imogen, I stood shoulder-to-shoulder with Rich in my backyard. In one hand I held Eudora's second letter, and in the other the key.

The backyard of Lane End House was only a "yard" in as much as it was a green space behind my house. There was a small lawn, still green even in the dropping autumn temperatures, and the rear of the house also had a vegetable garden, a small tool shed, and affixed to the house was the new catio I'd recently had built for Bob and Coco so they could venture outside when the weather permitted.

Right now, it was chilly, but the sky was clear, so I'd opened the interior window that let them come outside. Bob, much more delicate in his sensibilities, hadn't come outside yet, but Coco was sitting on one of the shelves watching us with the intensity of a construction foreman.

"*Miaow*," she declared, her voice higher and more delicate than Bob's, almost like she had a different accent.

"Yeah, I'm not sure either, Coco," I called back.

"Do you always talk to them like you understand them?" Rich asked, raising a brow at me and glancing back over her shoulder to Coco.

"Sure. I get the gist of what they're trying to say. Plus, it would be rude to ignore them when they're talking to you, I think. Communication is a two-way street."

He stared at me, trying to decide whether or not I was making a joke. I wasn't, but I understood that not everyone was as co-dependent with their cats as I was. I wasn't ever going to have kids, so I'd kind of started treating Bob and Coco like they were my little fur children. If people thought it was weird, so be it. Rich, however, just seemed more curious than anything.

"That's actually very sweet," he said finally.

From behind us, Coco meowed her agreement.

The yard gave way to a wooded expanse. Only about a quarter acre of it actually belonged to me, but the woods just kept going for miles and miles out my back door.

It was not out of the question for me to see deer grazing in my yard, and other woodland creatures had been known to visit as well. I'd seen foxes, a few eagles, and more birds than I knew how to track.

Right now, there were no animals to be seen, just the looming woods. I was grateful it was such a nice day, because the old-growth forest could be dense and very dark. When I'd played there with Rich and Leo as a kid, it had felt like stumbling into a fairyland.

We had played there so much Eudora needed to leave markers showing us how to get back to the house in case we wandered too far afield. I wondered if any of the signs she'd made were still around.

"Do you think our fort is still there?" Rich mused, thinking along the same lines as me.

"I have no idea. I haven't been out here since I moved here."

"What?" He was incredulous. "All this prime hiking right out your back door and you don't use it?"

I shrugged. "I thought it might be nice to get some running trails going back when I first arrived, but I just never had the energy to put in the work. The growth it pretty dense, and there are lovely groomed trails all around town. But if you're volunteering to help make me a 5K track, then by all means." I smirked and took his hand, giving it a squeeze.

"Don't issue me challenges like that, Phoebe, I'm inclined to try."

"Rome wasn't built in a day. You can do it like Vin Diesel said in the cinematic masterpiece *The Fast and the Furious*... a quarter mile at a time."

Rich laughed, and the sound of it went right to my heart. "Did anyone ever tell you that you're a ridiculous human?"

"I feel like this town brings it out in me."

"Then I should write a thank-you letter to the town." He squeezed my hand back, then gave me a kiss that lingered just long enough for my toes to tingle.

"All right, stop distracting me," I teased when he pulled away. "We have to figure out where she's hidden the lock that this opens." I dangled the key in the air. "And you seem to think it's out *there*."

"You've tried every room in the house, right?"

"Anything even remotely lock-shaped, yes. No dice."

"Then, I think we need to remember where we went as

kids and try that. And I think the first step is to go looking for that old fort."

I wasn't optimistic about the fort's fate. We'd built it when we were eleven, and had hauled old wood scraps, palettes, and sheet metal out to make it. The Pacific Northwest weather and the passage of time in the woods must have obliterated it in the twenty-five years since we'd built it, but perhaps there might be some lingering traces.

Rich and I headed into the woods. He brought along a light backpack even though we weren't technically going for a hike. Still, he reminded me that we weren't as young as we used to be when we ran wild through the woods, and having a couple water bottles and some granola bars wouldn't be a bad idea in case we had to go further than we had originally planned.

I wasn't going to argue, especially since he was willing to carry them.

The first part of the old trail was easy, since it angled downhill, though after about a hundred feet that nice downhill angle got a lot steeper, and rocks were sliding under my hiking boots making me periodically stumble and grab Rich's arm for support. It was almost a shame we were already dating because this would have been the perfect opportunity for him to hold on to me just a little too long and make his first move.

Alas, we were well past the first move at this point, but he was still my knight in flannel armor as he caught me every time it seemed like I might twist an ankle and end our adventure early. The trail evened out some after we were hiking for about ten minutes.

I didn't remember it being quite so treacherous when we were younger, but the reality was that we'd been fearless and brimming with energy. We had likely flown down that hill at top speed, shrieking and giggling the whole way. Danger hadn't even been a concept for us at the time, though I know Rich had his own version of danger at home, which made the woods even more of an escape.

I was amazed how much the atmosphere changed in the trees. It was darker, but the sun being out created a dazzling stained-glass effect on the overhead leaves. The trees were all tall and huge around the trunk, and their bark was covered in thick moss. The forest floor was dense with ferns and other ancient-looking foliage.

While Raven Creek was by no means a noisy town, it was still evident that the world got so much quieter here. Birds were singing and flitting from branch to branch overhead, but otherwise it was just a mellow nothingness that I liked to imagine was the sound of trees breathing.

Rich moved with a purposeful sense of direction, but even he was going at a leisurely pace, looking around us, awed by the incredible power of nature. It was astonishing to me that this was all part of my backyard. Or backyard adjacent. Why *didn't* I come out here more?

Then I thought back to my half-falling descent and remembered it was because I'd probably end up with a broken ankle and then die alone in the woods when no one knew where to find me.

As we moved through the trees, I was surprised to find that some things were starting to look familiar. There was the rock shaped like a turtle, its shell covered in moss. The tree with a burl on its trunk that was so big we had called it the Pimple Tree because we were eleven and zits were the height of personal embarrassment. There was the little creek we had wanted to build a bridge for, but it was so shallow we just splashed through it.

Now, being a fully grown person, I could almost jump

across it, but there was a nostalgia in splashing into the smooth river rocks.

Before I knew it, we'd been in the forest for almost an hour, and Rich handed me a water bottle. I hadn't even realized how thirsty I was until I took a sip, and then I almost polished off the whole thing. As we paused to drink, Rich put a hand on my arm.

"Look." He pointed to something behind us.

As I turned, I immediately knew what he'd spotted. There was a little wooden plaque in the shape of an owl. The paint had almost entirely faded, but the ghost outline of an arrow was somehow still visible.

One of Eudora's trail markers pointing us home.

We were definitely going the right way. My memory hadn't been playing tricks on me. I just hadn't remembered how far out we had hauled all that stuff to make our little fortress. It must have taken us forever, but it didn't seem like it in my recollections.

Then I realized Eudora might have had a part to play in that.

If anything, I was surprised that thought hadn't occurred to me sooner. Of *course* nothing bad had ever happened to us. Of *course* we'd carried heavy wood and metal miles into the woods without any issue.

We had magic on our side.

Rich and I came around a bend and stopped dead in our tracks. If I'd been suspicious of magical involvement before, I was sure of it now. Because there was our childhood fort, and it was in the exact same condition it had been in the last time we'd ever left it.

Of course, we hadn't known that would be the last time, but children rarely know when they're about to reach the moment they outgrow something once beloved.

Seeing it, impossibly still in the same condition, my breath caught in my throat, and Rich and I shared a quick look. He seemed as surprised and dazed by it as I was.

"I was hoping some of it might still be here," he said. "But I never could have imagined this."

The fort wasn't much to look at, even with all four walls and the roof still intact. The frame was built from packing palettes and zip ties, with a few nails for good measure when we remembered to ask to borrow a hammer. The whole exterior was covered in corrugated sheet metal, which might explain *some* of its resilience, but certainly not all.

No, Eudora definitely had a hand in this.

The roof was covered in leaves and twigs, but the area around the little building was clear, the rocky border we'd built in a circle still visible. We had built a little fire ring as well, but we'd been told that we weren't allowed to start a real fire in it under any circumstances, so we just built a little tipi out of twigs and imagined a roaring fire while we ate raw marshmallows.

I could almost imagine the three of us passing the plastic bag and giggling like we'd gotten away with something. As if Leo's dad hadn't handed them to us.

As we approached the little shack, I pulled the key from my pocket, finding that it was unexpectedly cool to the touch. The fort had never had a lock—what were we protecting—but now that I was standing in front of it, I could see the unmistakable shape of a keyhole in the door.

Rich and I once again exchanged befuddled glances. I was glad he knew about Eudora and me being witches, because this was hard enough to explain on its own without having to get into the finer nuances of magic existing. Magic was the *only* way to explain this.

"That never had a lock before, right?" he asked, even though we both knew the answer.

"Never," I confirmed.

"Well then... what are you waiting for?" He nudged me with his shoulder, and the small gesture gave me the little flourish of courage I needed to stoop down and stick the key in the door. It fit perfectly, and when I turned it, there was a satisfying sound, like a very old lock being opened for the first time in decades.

I still didn't understand what the lock was doing there or how it was even latched, but I pulled open the door and looked inside the fort.

On the dirt floor of the fort were reminders of what it had once been: our safe haven. There were cans of pop that were so old the designs on the labels would now be considered retro. A few comic books were scattered around, their pages wrinkled from all the moisture in the air. A quilt and a few old throw pillows were piled up on the floor, and a little lantern sat on a wooden crate in one corner. We had taped some of our own drawings to the walls, depictions of this fort as a castle, and dragons hiding among the trees. Somehow, the tape was still holding even after all this time.

And there, in the center of the floor, was a wooden box.

CHAPTER TWENTY-SEVEN

Rich and I sat cross-legged and hunched inside the fort. It had been a fine size for three eleven-year-olds, but for two adults pushing forty, the space was a little tight. Still, it felt like the right place to open the box. I wasn't sure my curiosity would let me take it all the way back to the house before opening it.

Inside the fort, the sounds of nature were even more hushed, and if Rich hadn't been moving, I would have wondered if my time-stopping magic had been triggered somehow.

The box was made of a similar wood to the one back at the house, but this one had obvious hinges. I lifted the lid, and inside was another envelope of the same crisp paper as the others—no damage from moisture whatsoever—and underneath the envelope there was a small puzzle, the pieces disassembled and the final image unclear.

I looked up at Rich, perplexed, then opened the envelope as I handed him the box to look at. He picked up a few pieces, but it was clear he didn't know what to make of it either.

Inside the envelope was another short letter in Eudora's neat handwriting.

Darling Phoebe,

I hope you're not too annoyed with me for setting up this little hunt. I also hope you've learned the trick of finding each next piece of the puzzle. Sorry, I suppose that's a bit literal in this case.

You're close to the end now.

Love,

Eudora

I handed it to Rich to read over. "Huh, so I guess there's going to be a missing piece of the puzzle. But do you know what she means when she says *you've learned the trick*?"

I shook my head. "I have no idea; I feel like it was pure dumb luck that led me to the first clues. Or, more specifically, it was good ideas from other people. Bob was the one who took me to the horse. You're the one who took me out here."

Rich looked at me, grinning. "Maybe that's it."

"What?"

"Maybe the trick is that you need to find the right person—or cat—to help you. Maybe the whole point of this is that you're not supposed to do it on your own."

I thought about this, re-reading Eudora's letter, and realized it was actually genius if he was right. Eudora had no idea when I might stumble across the box, and what I might or might not know about myself when I did find it. I also might have uncovered it when I first moved—which would have happened if I hadn't put off cleaning the attic for a year—in which case, I wouldn't really know anyone in town.

Was this her way of helping me reconnect with my

past? To bond with Bob? To help me make Raven Creek my home?

I held her letter to my chest. "What a sneaky old witch," I said with nothing but love in my voice.

"She was one of the best," Rich said fondly. He looked around the little fort, his gaze filled with wonder. "I can't believe she managed to keep this old place standing all this time. It feels like we never left."

I felt a pang of remorse knowing that part of the reason we'd stopped coming was due to me. I had gotten older, started to think I was too cool to spend summers in Raven Creek with my aging aunt, and instead stuck around Chicago, going to suburban malls with my friends, or laying out on the beach. In retrospect, I was devastated to have missed so much time with Eudora. But the whims of teenage girls were terrible and mighty things.

"I have no idea how this place is even standing, but I wish she'd cast whatever spell this is on the front deck, because that would have saved me a lot of money." I smiled, knowing that Rich and Leo had done a lot of free labor to save my porch, but it still hadn't been cheap.

"I'm worried if we stay in here too long, this place might end up in the same condition. I'm almost afraid to sneeze."

I knew what he meant. Magic had kept this place in pristine condition, but Eudora wasn't around anymore to keep that spell going. One wrong move might undo all her work, and I didn't know how to fix it.

We crawled out, and I took the quilt with me when we left. The other things belonged here, though I would come back and tidy up the garbage at some point soon. At least it was contained for now. The quilt, though, I remember being a staple in Eudora's living room for years, and it was still in perfect condition. A quick wash and it would be as good as new.

It felt nice, to not only have the next part of my mystery secured, but to also bring home something that had been a part of Eudora's life. She hadn't made the quilt—her talents lay elsewhere—but it was a gorgeous jewel-toned piece with little triangles in a dozen different shades of merlot, purple, emerald green, sapphire blue, and more. I don't think it was meant to be anything, but it had always reminded me of the night sky.

I had actually wondered, in passing, what had become of it, and now I was pleased to know it could find a new home in my house, likely at the end of the bed where it would become a cat hair magnet.

When Rich and I got back to the house, the sky was already starting to get darker; the colors matching the tones of the quilt. The early arrival of night this time of year was always such a rude surprise, but even more so today because I hadn't realized we'd been gone that long.

We took the box inside the house where—thanks to a rowdy chorus of meowing—I fed the cats, and then called in an order for pizza delivery. Perhaps it was too much delivery for one week, but there were no other adults around to tell me not to, and I really loved pizza.

I would need to head to rehearsal early, in about an hour, and Rich had his usual evening work, but we still set out the puzzle pieces on my kitchen table. There were only about a hundred pieces, but without an image to guide us, it took a surprising amount of effort to get the little puzzle assembled.

When it was finally all together, Rich and I stood back in wonder.

It was an incredibly old picture of Lansing's Grocery.

Only the building looked nothing like the one that was currently sitting there. Still, the sign was unmistakable, and I knew which friend I needed to enlist for help next.

Looked like Leo Lansing was about to get roped into this little hunt.

CHAPTER TWENTY-EIGHT

Once again, my mission to unravel the rest of Aunt Eudora's clues had to be set aside due to other obligations. I had a *different* mystery to unravel at the community center, one that required I get there before the rest of my friends, lest they start asking me some pretty awkward questions.

When I got to the community center about an hour before rehearsals were slated to start, I was grateful to see that no one else was in the building. I had tried to find a sweet spot where I could explain why I was there early if I needed to—oops, forgot the time—but that it was likely no one else would have shown up yet.

The building was unlocked, because I'm pretty sure the community center never locked its doors, so I was able to sneak in unnoticed. A few lights had been left on by the daytime staff, but for the most part the building was dark.

I moved quietly through the lobby and into the auditorium. I knew there must be other ways to access the stage, but this was the only one I was aware of. The room was so silent I was grateful for the carpeting down the aisle towards the stage, because otherwise I was sure each click of my boots would sound deafening.

I took one of the side stairs up to the stage and quickly looked around. Up here, I was standing right under one light, and if anyone came in or looked onto the stage from behind the curtains then I'd be spotted immediately. I had to hurry if I was going to see what Keidi had buried under the floorboards yesterday.

Maybe I was overthinking it, and it was something totally innocent, just a weird little ritual she did before shows. Before I told the police what I'd seen, I wanted to make sure it was even worth mentioning.

As predicted, my footfalls sounded especially noisy as I crossed the stage and tried to figure out which of the boards she had lifted. I knew the rough location, but it wasn't an exact science when all the boards looked almost exactly the same.

I touched my toe to a few of them until one gave a little under my weight, and I stooped down to lift the corner. Inside it was dark, but there was a small space between the stage and whatever was stored below it. I couldn't actually see what was hidden within because the stage light was almost right behind me, and it was casting a terrible shadow.

I took out my phone and engaged the flash, then snapped a few photos of the inside of the hiding place. Before I had a chance to look at the quality of the images, though, I heard voices distantly in the building.

Letting the floorboard drop back into place, I tapped it firmly with my toe and then hustled off the stage and back out into the lobby, which was still empty, but a few more lights had been turned on. Since it was still much too early for rehearsal to start and I didn't want to bump into any of the improv crew, I snuck quietly out the front door, and headed in the direction of The Earl's Study, so I could walk back again with the rest of my friends.

I waited until I was a block away from the community center before looking at the photos on my phone, and when I did, I stopped dead in my tracks.

There, on a bottle with all sorts of warning labels and demands for safety, was a label that clearly read *Arsenic*.

What was Keidi doing with a bottle of arsenic, and why was she hiding it under the stage at the community center? I had a pretty good idea of the answer to both those questions, and it made my blood run cold and a sweat break out over my forehead.

Behind me, the sound of approaching footsteps caught my attention, and I didn't dare look back to see who they belonged to. It might be an innocent coincidence, but I wasn't going to risk it. I picked up my pace and practically jogged the last few blocks to my store, grateful that I was a regular runner, so it wasn't difficult to outpace someone behind me unless they actually decided to start chasing me.

The footsteps did seem like they were speeding up initially, but once I reached the front door of The Earl's Study, knowing witnesses were right behind the glass, I paused to look back.

No one was there.

Either my imagination was working overtime, or the person following me had given up once they realized they wouldn't be able to get to me before I got to safety.

My heart was pounding as I stepped into the shop, and I was glad to find Imogen and Norman were sitting together near the fireplace. Norman spotted me and gave a warm smile.

"Phoebe, I was disappointed not to see you and Bob

when I came in this morning. I hope everything is okay. Imogen claimed you took the bulk of the day off, but I declared it simply impossible."

Imogen rolled her eyes. "I think he was worried I might be a method actor, and I'd bumped you off to get into the spirit of things for the play."

"No, just took some time off to spend with Rich, got some stuff done over at the house. I promise Imogen didn't kill me." I forced a smile at them, but my hands were shaking so badly I had to shove them into my pockets. We had been discussing the case right here only a few days ago, and I felt certain I could tell them what I'd found. But was I putting them at risk by sharing those details? If someone really *had* followed me from the community center, then who knew what other desperate lengths they might go to?

I had come in hoping to share my news with someone, but now, looking at their expectant faces I wasn't sure I wanted to turn it from a little logic game into something real.

I *did* know I'd have to tell Patsy and Kwan, though. This wasn't something I could write off as mere coincidence. I knew Naomi had died by poisoning, and there it was, poison right under the floorboards.

Once again, I mused that Poe's *Tell-Tale Heart* would have made a much more suitable play for us to perform this year. I wished I was in the headspace to make a joke about it out loud.

Instead, I decided not to wait to send the photo off to the police. I texted it to Patsy with a brief explanation of seeing Keidi hide something the previous day and this being what I'd discovered.

Did you touch it? was the response I got back.

It was almost enough to make me roll my eyes. Not a

thank you for uncovering important evidence, not a *great job*, just *did you screw up my crime scene*.

What was I, an amateur?

I chose not to answer that question to myself and assured Patsy I had only touched the floorboard and nothing in the hidey hole. She didn't write back, so I pocketed my phone and went to check on the adoptable cats.

There were only three cats in the four condos, and it made me smile more happily. I knew a family had come in earlier that week and had absolutely loved a cat named Milkweed, who was an adorable fluffy gray lovebug. Now Milkweed's condo was empty, and either Imogen or Daphne had added a new Polaroid to our successful adoptions board.

I was sorry I wasn't here to see him go home, but thrilled that I'd get to send word to Barneswood Animal Shelter that we would need a new tenant. They'd already know about the adoption since the requests all had to be cleared through them.

"Milkweed got adopted," I said out loud.

"He did," Daphne said enthusiastically. "They picked him up this afternoon. He was purring so loudly in his carrier you could hear it through the whole store." She came over and showed me a video she'd captured on her phone to post online, and sure enough the rumbles of his happy purrs were audible even with her volume reduced.

Honey tapped her watch. "Hey guys, not to break up the feline adoption lovefest, but we should get going if we don't want to be late."

We were barely at the end of the block when I spotted a squad car go by with its lights on. A moment later, an unmarked police car with a magnetic light stuck to its roof went zipping past us down Main. I was pretty sure I saw Patsy behind the wheel.

"What do you suppose all that's about?" Norman asked, his arm looped through Imogen's as she followed along at his slower pace.

"No idea," I said, though I was positive I had a *very* good idea. There wasn't enough crime in Raven Creek for anything else to warrant two police cars at the same time. Sure enough, when we got to the street leading to the community center, the lights were flashing out front of it, and a tiny crowd of onlookers—mostly our fellow cast members—were huddling together gawking.

The temperature had dropped considerably now that the sun was down, and I could see my breath coming out in puffs as we got closer. The few people who were gathered together to watch were shuffling from foot to foot to stay warm. No one had dressed to spend a long time outside.

"Did something happen?" Honey asked Ruthie as we approached.

Ruthie shrugged. "I'm not sure, but that's Patsy's car, so maybe it has something to do with Naomi Novak's murder?"

"You don't think one of the troupe members did it, do you?" Daphne asked, and I could tell she was hoping that Liam specifically wasn't involved. Her little crush was not very subtle.

I shared a knowing glance with Norman and Imogen. I might not have told them about the poison, but they'd been right there with me putting together our list of suspects. There was no shortage of jealousy and bitterness working behind the scenes with Something Wicked.

We joined the cluster of our castmates waiting to see what would happen next. We didn't have to wait long, as the community center's front doors opened and out came Patsy, along with a uniformed officer, who had Keidi handcuffed and was nudging her towards the waiting squad car.

"No, you've got this all wrong," Keidi protested. "I had nothing to do with Naomi's murder. Please believe me." When she saw us all watching, she turned on her megawatt smile, even though her mascara was streaked, and it was obvious she had been crying. "This isn't what it looks like folks, don't worry. I'll get this all sorted out in no time."

The uniformed officer held the top of Keidi's head as he ducked her into the back of the cruiser. In the doorway, Pierce, Liam, and Quinn were grouped together, though it was hard to tell what they were thinking from their stony expressions. Dierdre Miller, on the other hand, was standing a few feet in front of them, dancing from foot to foot like the ground was hot underneath her. "There must be some mistake," she kept saying.

As I glanced at the rest of the troupe, I found that while Pierce and Liam were both looking at Keidi in the car, Quinn was looking right at me.

A shiver went down my spine.

The expression on her face wasn't a friendly one.

I suddenly had a good idea of who had been following me earlier.

CHAPTER TWENTY-NINE

Rehearsals were, for obvious reasons, cancelled that night.

We ended up back at Peach's as we had the previous night, huddled together in a big booth, plates of onion rings and fries between us, as I learned the hard way that jalapeno poppers and hot cocoa were not a flavor combination made in heaven.

Everyone was quiet for the first little bit, then suddenly Honey said, "I'm not going to lie, I thought Phoebe's ex did it."

"Same," came a mumbled chorus from the others at the table, and then they all gave me an apologetic look.

"Oh, don't worry about me, guys. Up until tonight, I was pretty sure it was him, too."

Norman munched thoughtfully on a French fry, dipping his in a little saucer of ranch dressing he had requested. I wasn't going to throw stones at his dip choices, since I liked to dip my fries in barbecue sauce.

"I don't know if Keidi makes sense." He was looking up at the ceiling, like he needed to stare somewhere else to put all his thoughts in order. "I know she and Naomi both dated Liam, but is jealousy over old lovers really such a fresh wound that she would lash out now?"

"They dated?" Daphne said, astonished. She looked a little disappointed.

"Pretty common in acting groups like that for people to end up dating each other, I imagine," Norman said.

"Where did you hear that?" Honey asked, obviously interested in the gossip.

"TMZ," Imogen answered, saving Norman from making a mistake about the name again. "It was over a year ago that Liam and Naomi split, and apparently he was with Keidi right before he got together with Naomi."

"And Blaine must have been Naomi's rebound from Liam," I commented. "She really traded down."

"No kidding," Daphne said.

We continued to share all the deep-fried goodies, and it felt nice to talk about this with the others, though I still didn't feel comfortable explaining that I'd been the one who got Keidi arrested.

"Maybe Blaine framed her," Imogen said.

I bit my tongue.

"Or maybe they were in on it together," Norman said. "Perhaps they were lovers."

"If her reaction to him in the shop the other day is any indication, I doubt it," I said. "She seemed to detest him. Said he was always flirting with Naomi's friends and once tried to make a pass at her."

"That would be something someone might say if their illicit relationship didn't work out. A good way to cover a broken heart is to act like you hate someone." Honey said. She then saw my expression and laughed. "I'm not accusing you of covering *your* broken heart. I believe your dislike is very, very real."

"Good."

Everyone continued to bandy about ideas about why Keidi had been arrested, but each time something new got mentioned, my guilt ticked up a notch. I could never be an actual criminal. I would snap under interrogation in a heartbeat.

"Keidi hid a bottle of arsenic under the stage floorboards yesterday," I blurted out, then slapped my hand over my mouth, stunned at my own lack of resolve. So much for keeping it a secret.

My friends didn't even skip a beat or demand to know why I was only just telling them now. "You saw her?" Imogen asked.

"Yes, when I went to get my bag yesterday."

"How do you know it was arsenic?" Daphne asked.

"I went back today before I met you guys." I showed them the picture on my phone, and a collection of gasps went around the table like a wave.

"That certainly does look bad for the young lady," Norman said solemnly. "It's a sad thing, what jealousy can bring out in people." He gave his head a shake. Norman had been married to his wife since they'd graduated from high school. I felt like jealousy hadn't likely been much of an issue in their relationship, but being with the same person for sixty years was likely a bumpy road at times no matter how true that love was.

I wasn't sure if I'd ever been *jealous* of Blaine. What I'd felt had been much more akin to betrayal.

There was much discussion about Keidi and the hidden poison, which devolved into a discussion of how one would even go about *buying* arsenic, which turned out to be a much more complicated mystery than that of who had killed Naomi. As it turned out, buying incredibly potent poisons wasn't as easy as just finding a seller online. There were a lot of hoops to go through.

I suppose finding out how she had acquired the poison would be a job for the police, because uncovering details like that was a bit beyond the scope of my investigative skills. It was scary to think she had managed to get her hands on a poison like that. Arsenic felt like such an old-fashioned way to kill someone. I imagined it was a bit easier to get some in Agatha Christie's era.

After about an hour at Peach's, we paid our bill and headed back out into the evening. Honey lived just a few doors down, and Daphne was on the same block, so they went off together. Imogen lived in the opposite direction and bid us good night with a smile.

Norman lived quite close to me, so I offered him an arm and we set off in that direction. The night air had gotten very cold, the way it did when the threat of snow was on the breeze. Our temperatures were still warm enough during the day to fend off the white stuff for a bit longer, but that didn't mean it couldn't fall at all. Just that it wouldn't stick around.

"Have you lived here your whole life?" I asked.

Norman nodded. He moved slowly, but it was nice to just take a meditative stroll. Sometimes people go so quickly they don't really stop to enjoy the world around them. I was often guilty of just that. Going at Norman's pace gave me a chance to really soak in the Raven Creek autumn.

The leaves had all started to change a few weeks ago, and now there were brilliant glowing patches of orange and yellow hanging over the streetlights. The temperature made me long for soup and sweaters, and I had started to wear my coziest socks. The ladies of the Knit and Sip crew had given me several pairs the previous Christmas, and they were all wonderful.

I loved the way autumn felt, especially here. While it was often rainy, which added to the overall chill, it was also so beautiful it was sometimes hard to take it all in at once. The way morning fog would cling to the pines, like someone had taken a thick blanket and pulled it over the whole town. Or how the birds would suddenly look all different, as migrating species began to move south from their breeding territory in Canada to return south for the winter.

I was also enamored with the way society had demanded that we shift flavors for the season. The arrival of pumpkin spice and praline. How sage and rosemary started to sneak into dishes. Candles were all named for fallen leaves and mulling spices.

Fall was wonderful.

Norman and I pointed out various yard decorations to each other as we passed. There was no shortage of them, considering how obsessed this town was with the holidays. Since it was one of our biggest claims to fame, I wasn't surprised to see that cars were passing slowly down the street to take in the sights, and at least one group had stopped to pose in front of a particularly elaborate graveyard set up.

I was surprised by how active the street was until I realized it wasn't even eight thirty yet, so of course people would still be out and about. The dwindling sun was a problem. I'd started to adjust to seeing the sun less since I'd moved here, thanks to how gray and rainy it was throughout the year. But losing light earlier and earlier as we hurtled towards the winter solstice was tough.

I'd bought myself a sunrise lamp to make it easier to get up in the dark each morning. The cats thought it was magic, considering it woke me with birdsong instead of a beeping alarm. They would spend several minutes each morning looking for the birds before giving up and going back to sleep.

Norman's house was a sweet little mid-century bungalow. While his yard décor wasn't as over-the-top as that of some of his neighbors, he had still made the Raven Creek effort. There were several ghosts hanging from the overhead branches of the trees that lined his walkway. In the low light and the breeze, they looked almost real with their fluttering sheet bodies and haunted faces. Pumpkins were neatly lined up on each of the steps, but rather than being carved they had glow in the dark plastic pieces added for faces, like a Mr. Potato Head.

Norman saw me looking and smiled. "My grandkids got me those last year. It's a bit hard on the old hands to do all that carving anymore, but this way they can help me decorate. No knives or pumpkin guts needed."

I had yet to carve my own pumpkins, not wanting them to rot before the big day—or get nibbled to bits by squirrels —but I knew it was going to take me at least a full night of effort to get them all done. I was impressed with Norman's workaround.

"That's a fun idea. They look great."

They looked a little like Picassos with noses for mouths and teeth in their foreheads, but hey, at Halloween things could be as messy as need be. Next to Norman's front door was a sign that said *Welcome Boys and Ghouls* which made me chuckle.

"Thank you for walking me home, Phoebe. You're very good to me, you know. Your aunt always spoke so highly of you, but I wanted to tell you how much I appreciate you letting an old man like me take up space at your shop day after day."

My heartstrings tugged. "Norman, we love having you there. The place doesn't feel the same on the days you don't come. And you know Bob loves having a reading buddy."

Norman smiled, the deep wrinkles around his eyes creasing. "He's one of the best parts of my day. You know, my wife and I used to joke that when we retired, we would finally get to catch up on all the reading we weren't able to do while we raised our kids. And when we did retire, we had so much to do still that we barely managed to read anything then, either. It wasn't until Grace died that I finally realized it was time to slow down and really enjoy each day like it might be my last. I know I'm not getting any younger, but I am glad I'm finally doing what she and I said we should do all those years ago."

"I'm sorry I never met her."

"You two would have gotten along swimmingly. She was a big fan of trying to unravel little local mysteries, too." His eyes twinkled merrily, and he nudged me with his shoulder. "She spent a lot of time with your aunt."

"Oh, I can imagine they probably got themselves into a lot of trouble," I laughed.

"You have no idea. But your aunt, she was a special lady. Gifted." He looked at me meaningfully, and I wondered just how much he knew. "I think there's a lot of her in you." He held my gaze for a long time, and deep down I understood what he was trying to tell me, even though neither of us were saying it out loud.

I smiled. "I'm not quite at Eudora's level yet. But I'm trying."

Norman put a hand on my shoulder and gave me a very grandfatherly look. "You're going to accomplish great things, Phoebe Winchester. But please be careful. When people bury their secrets, they tend to get pretty defensive about keeping them that way. The more secrets you uncover, the riskier it can be. Just be smart."

I'd heard a lot of warnings about the dangers of my predilection for poking around into mysteries in this town, but for some reason Norman's struck a real chord.

Had I really helped find Naomi's killer, or had I just managed to draw attention away from the real murderer?

And if so, how far would they go to stop me from meddling any further?

CHAPTER THIRTY

The next morning, I got to Amy's as early as possible, wanting to share the news of Keidi's arrest with her before the town gossip mill managed to bring it her way.

When I got to the Sugarplum Fairy, it was still dark outside, and the dark was likely to drag on all day because it was pouring rain. I had parked behind our stores and started a fire for Bob—and for the comfort of the shop—before heading next door.

Amy was already hard at work, the bakery smelling of yeast, sugar, cinnamon and all those wonderful things. She was humming a tune to herself as I came in, and when she looked up her smile was bright enough to chase back all the clouds.

"Good morning," I said. "Man, you look super happy. What's the deal?"

"Me?" she cooed. "I don't know what you could possibly mean." She finished filling up the display cabinet in front of her with incredible-looking pumpkin tarts, cranberry scones, and pumpkin cookie sandwiches, then came to meet me at the front counter.

"Okay, you're practically glowing. I came here to tell you something I thought might cheer you up, but if you get any cheerier, you might explode. Spill the beans, sister."

Amy leaned over the counter, her cheeks flushed. "Leo is moving in."

My mouth dropped open in surprise, then I let out a little squeal of delight, grabbing her hands and shaking them. "Amy, that's *amazing*; congrats."

Leo and Amy had started seeing each other over the summer, but it had been obvious right away this was no short-term fling. They were both getting older, both had been single a long, long time before becoming a couple, and with this news, I wouldn't be surprised if there were wedding bells in the future before they even hit their first anniversary.

But I was getting ahead of myself.

"What happened?"

She busied herself making a latte for me, like she needed to do something with her body, or she'd just start skipping around the shop like a lunatic. Which she deserved after the week she'd had.

"I made him dinner last night, and he told me that when he found out I'd been taken in, he knew that he never wanted to let me out of his sight again, that he would never let anything bad happen to me. Oh, Phoebe. I know the police were just doing their jobs, but it might just be that being taken for questioning was the best thing to ever happen to me. He said it made him realize that time was precious and we're not getting any younger, and that he knows in his heart that being with me is what he wants."

She set the latte down in front of me and then raised her hands to her heart. "I *never* thought I'd hear something that romantic in my life. I've always been..." Her voice drifted as her hands went to her ample hips. "Well, I've never been anyone's first choice before. But Leo makes me feel like I'm the *only* choice he's ever wanted, and it makes a lot of lonely years feel very worth the wait."

"Amy, I'm so happy for you two." I'd need to tell Leo separately that he was a smart man to snag this wonderful lady. "I assume he's going to move into your place." My tone was teasing. Leo lived in a little apartment at the back of the grocery store.

Amy made a little face at me, as if trying to imagine moving all her things in there and using a postage stamp-sized kitchen for the rest of her days. "Yes, he's going to start bringing stuff over this weekend. No sense in putting it off."

"If you guys need any help, let me know. Though I can't imagine he has all that much stuff to bring."

Amy laughed. "I'm pretty sure he's only going to need about six inches of closet space. The man only owns about five shirts that aren't Lansing's Grocery uniforms."

At the mention of Lansing's Grocery, I was reminded of the puzzle from Eudora and knew I'd need to speak to Leo sooner rather than later. I would head over to the store after Imogen got to work and congratulate him while also gathering some more information.

If Rich was right about his theory, it would make sense that I'd need to talk to Leo in order to find the next answer. Every step of the way, Eudora was connecting me to parts of the town, helping me deepen my roots.

I quickly caught Amy up on the drama of the previous night, and it was clear she was relieved that the police's attention would now be focused somewhere else. Today was really turning out to be a good one for her.

I collected my pastries and my drink and told her we

needed to make a plan for a double date so Rich and I could properly help her and Leo celebrate this big life milestone.

Back at The Earl's Study I felt lighter than I had in days. Amy was happy; Naomi's killer might have been found, and everything was going to be back to normal in time for Halloween.

I did wonder if Keidi's arrest would interfere with the play going forward, but since we hadn't gotten any notifications that tonight's rehearsal was cancelled, I figured this crowd really stuck with a *the show must go on* mentality. If Naomi's murder hadn't stopped the play, then Keidi's arrest likely wouldn't either.

The morning dragged by slowly, the pouring rain keeping most would-be customers at bay. I spent most of my time sorting through our loose-leaf tea, making a list of what needed to be restocked, and also what blends I would bring back for Christmas, which would be our next major flavor season after Halloween.

Was I getting ahead of myself with visions of candy canes and sugar plums? Absolutely. But the retail gods demanded Christmas as soon as the calendar page turned to November. It wasn't like I could make a Thanksgiving tea. Rosemary, sage, and thyme were all wonderful flavors, but not necessarily ones I wanted to drink.

Besides, my one true flavor love was candy cane. The world might be mad for all things pumpkin spice—and I loved it in moderation—but candy cane just made me so insanely happy. I wasn't sure why.

I pushed the notions of peppermint and chocolate to the back of my mind to think of later and finally gave up on trying to do work. The shop was clean, the bread loaves were baked and cooling. I took an Earl Grey Shortbread cookie out of the display cabinet, made myself a cup of

Pumpkin Earl Grey to go with it, and sat on the stool behind the cash desk. I'd be able to see anyone who came in, but I didn't think anyone would be coming anytime soon.

Rain fell in sheets outside, and the rare pedestrians I saw were huddled under umbrellas and moving as fast as their feet could carry them. I hadn't even bothered to put our skeleton outside today. It was much too wet for him to be selling off our bargain books.

I picked up an old whodunit off the clearance cart, the author's name unfamiliar and the cover sporting a seventies design with garish colors and images of a pearl necklace, a pile of desserts, and a bottle marked *poison*.

Taking the book back to my place behind the desk. Soon I was absorbed in the story, one that felt oddly familiar. The book was about a famous actress inviting several of her friends to her lavish country home. There she planned to stage a play that she hinted would reveal some uncomfortable truths about everyone present.

The night before the play, the actress was found dead, having eaten a poisoned pastry.

What followed was a classic whodunit formula in which a roguish detective arrived on site and started to talk to each of the suspects in turn. But all of them had good reason for wanting the actress to keep their secrets hidden. Torrid affairs, thievery, a stolen manuscript, even another murder were all skeletons in their closets.

By the time Imogen arrived, I was halfway through the book, and though the writing wasn't great—it *was* steeped in marvelous 1920s slang—the story itself was what had me engrossed.

"I don't think I've ever seen you read at work," Imogen said, astonished. She lifted up the cover of the book I was reading and made a little face. "We have thousands of books in here you could have chosen from, and you went with something off the bargain cart? Phoebe..."

"Hey, I'm not saying it's good. But also, I'm not saying it's bad. It's giving me Ngaio Marsh if Ngaio Marsh was a mediocre white man."

Imogen nodded knowingly. "I'm just glad you finally learned that sometimes it's okay to do nothing. I'd be surprised if we end up with a single customer today." She peered into the bookstore. "I see even Mr. Loughery decided to stay home."

"I can't say I blame him; today is the kind of day for curling up in bed, or next to the fireplace, and just listening to the rain. It's definitely *not* a day for going outside. I might tell Daphne just to stay home, and we can close early if it stays like this."

Imogen shrugged. "I'm here now, so might as well stay open. Makes no difference to me if I read here or at home." She winked.

Rather than join me in reading, however, she set about re-organizing one of the tables in the foyer. It had been set up with some popular kid and teen books, and that had done well for us around back to school, but Imogen had an uncanny ability to know what table displays would do well at any given moment.

In the wake of Naomi's death, I half-expected her to set it up with books about Hollywood scandals, or maybe some books that Naomi had starred in the film version of, but she went a totally different avenue. Soon the table was covered in cookbooks, and there were a few knick-knacks she had added as well, including some tea towels, and recipe cards.

Once she finished, she stood back and gave the table a nod of approval.

"For Thanksgiving," she explained. "Never too soon for people to feel inspired to eat."

I grinned. "Hey, you think you can fend off the crowds by yourself for a bit? I need to run down to Lansing's."

"I don't know how I'll mange," she replied in her most blasé tone.

"You're the best, thank you."

"I know. But I'm glad you've realized it too." She winked as I headed to the back for my jacket, and then I made the short dash out the back door to my car. The rain was so powerful I could barely see the road in front of me as I navigated down the block to the grocery store.

No wonder no one was coming into the shop today; it was miserable out.

The grocery store was almost as empty as my shop, with one bored cashier flipping through a gossip magazine at the front counter, and a stock boy elegantly stacking oranges in the most perfect pyramid I'd ever seen.

I knew Leo would be around, so I slowly passed by each aisle until I spotted him in the milk section, checking dates on all the gallons.

Leo was a big man. His presence filled a room just by being in it, but despite his height and large build, he was the quietest man I'd ever met. I wondered sometimes if he was just so large that he'd tried to make other parts of him smaller in order to make those around him feel more at ease.

"Hey, Leo," I greeted warmly.

"Mornin' Phoebe. You came out in this weather? Brave."

"I actually wanted to ask you about something. Do you have a minute?"

Leo glanced around the empty aisles. The soft tones of instrumental music overhead were the only noise in the entire store. "Yeah, I think I can spare a second." He smirked and closed the cooler door. "What's up?"

"First, Amy told me the good news. I'm so happy for you two." I didn't give him a chance to duck away before wrapping my arms around him in a big hug. There had been a point, right after I moved, where I thought Leo might harbor some long-standing childhood crush towards me. And before Rich and I had finally figured things out, I'd debated whether Leo might be a better match for me, but I was so glad things had turned out this way. Leo and Amy made a perfect couple, and I was happy that things with Rich and me were progressing nicely.

I wasn't even miffed that Leo and Amy were moving in together before Rich and I had even talked about it. Their pace didn't need to be our pace. And neither of them had ever been married and had that fail. Rich and I had to unpack a little individual baggage before he could move his into my house.

Leo's cheeks were flushed, and he rubbed his hand on the back of his neck. I swear he was about two seconds away from saying, *aw, shucks*. Instead, I saved him the embarrassment by continuing.

"Also, I've made Amy promise that we're going to have a double date soon. No excuses."

"That would be nice. I'm glad you and Rich finally stopped pretending like you weren't crazy for each other. You two have been in love since we were ten."

It was my turn for my cheeks to color. There was probably an element of truth to his hyperbole. Rich—Ricky as he'd been then—was definitely my first crush, the first time I'd worried about how a boy might perceive me.

"Speaking of Rich, he and I found something strange, and I'm hoping you might have some ideas about it."

"Oh?"

As quickly as possible, I tried to explain Eudora's scavenger hunt, and our discovery of the untouched fort in the woods. Then I showed him a picture of the completed puzzle, with one missing piece.

He scratched his beard thoughtfully, holding my phone and looking at the image like he was trying to solve a riddle. "You know, I'm pretty sure I've seen this picture before."

He handed back my phone and jerked his head sideways to indicate I should follow him, and he led me through some swinging double-doors marked "Employees Only." Down a hallway lit with flickering fluorescent lights, we found our way into a small office.

The space was petite but clean, with a computer on the desk and a neat pile of papers sorted into a tray on one corner. On one of the walls was a whiteboard with the monthly staff schedule written out, the printing so tidy I found myself wondering if it was Leo's or if he had someone on the staff, do it to be legible. For some reason, Leo didn't strike me as a legible-handwriting kind of guy.

Maybe I just couldn't picture him holding a whiteboard marker and writing out the whole thing. He was just so big the marker might look silly in his hand.

Leo went over to a small bookshelf in one corner of the room, then pulled out a leather-bound album and set it on his desk. As he flipped through it, the effect was like a slideshow of the history of both the grocery store and the town. There were photos of Lansing's through the ages, back to when Leo's grandfather had run it. It was wild to see all the old signage, different brands, and even the clothing and hairstyles of the customers and employees who were in the pictures.

Finally, Leo landed on a page, and there was the exact

photo that Eudora had used for the puzzle. This one was a little more yellowed, but the image definitely showed the same storefront, with the old Lansing's logo. A little note under the picture in Leo's book said *Customer Appreciation —June 1956.*

"Wow."

"That was only about a year after the place opened," Leo said.

I looked down at the image and focused on the missing square, trying to figure out what Eudora had intentionally left out. It looked to be a square right over the front doors.

When I looked closer at the picture, I was perplexed.

"Leo, that number isn't the same as it is now." I tapped the address.

"Oh yeah, no. This isn't the original Lansing's." He said this like I should just know it, but I was stunned.

"What do you mean?"

"The original building was pretty small. Grandpa moved over to this location about ten years after the first one opened. This store opened in 1965."

"So where is the original Lansing's?" The number on the front of the image wouldn't tell me what street it was on, and the Lansing's branding made it hard to recognize what the building might look like now without it.

"Town bought it. It's the library now."

I almost laughed.

Of course, Eudora would send me to somewhere packed with books.

CHAPTER THIRTY-ONE

As much as I wanted to head right to the library and look for my next clue, I returned to the shop instead. It was almost as dead as before, except for one exception.

Blaine was sitting in one of the armchairs by the fire.

"How long has he been here?" I asked Imogen.

"Showed up about five minutes after you left. I told him he could come back later, but he said he was just going to wait for you." She gave me an apologetic look.

I was honestly stunned that Blaine would have wanted to see me again after what had happened with the Truth Be Told tea, but perhaps he didn't realize it was the tea that had put him in a confessional mood.

Most people would believe just about anything before they believed in magic.

"Blaine?" I left Imogen at the counter and stood in the doorway of the bookshop, feeling like that was close enough.

Blaine was staring absently at the cat condos, where my three feline adoption prospects were all wisely ignoring him.

"Hey. Oh. Hey, hi." He got to his feet in a hurry and made like he was going to come towards me, but I took a step back, making him pause. I wasn't sure if he had planned to hug me, or if he even knew, but I was good at my minimum safe distance.

"Sorry," he said, though he didn't really seem to know what he was apologizing for.

"What are you doing here?" I asked.

"I heard about Keidi getting arrested."

"And?" That wasn't really a solid explanation for him being in my shop.

"I just... Phoebe, do you think we could just have a conversation? Like people who used to care about each other?"

I narrowed my eyes at him and felt renewed anger bubbling under the surface. How dare he act like I was being unreasonable, like I didn't have every right to still be mad at him?

"Did you care about me when you..." I took a deep breath, closed my eyes, and counted to ten. "You know what? I'm not going down this road again with you. If you want to talk, you can say whatever you have to say with Imogen here. I'd tell her all the details anyway, so you might as well save me some breath."

Blaine looked nervously past me to Imogen, and though I couldn't see what she was doing with her face, Blaine blanched. He seemed to be seriously considering just leaving without saying anything, but then reconsidered.

"Keidi didn't do it," he said finally.

"There's a fair bit of evidence to suggest she did," I replied, but my curiosity was too piqued to be ignored. "How do you know she didn't do it?"

I thought back to his words at Grandma's Griddle the

other day, and how close it had seemed to him confessing something. Was he about to do that now?

"I just... Look, I know Keidi, and I know what her relationship was like with Naomi. They were like sisters. They could get under each other's skin, but Keidi would never do anything to hurt Naomi."

"Even though Naomi called her a liar when Keidi ratted you out for hitting on her?"

Blaine's face paled. Guess he hadn't expected me to know about that.

"That's not what you think," he said.

Funny thing was, this wasn't the first time he'd said those words to me. I didn't believe him then, and I didn't believe him now. "Sure. Whatever. But if you have something tangible to prove Keidi didn't do it, you should take that information to the police."

I watched him, trying to gauge his response to this, and just like I predicted, he looked horrified by the thought. Blaine had one of the worst poker faces I'd ever seen. You'd think for a guy who lied as much as he did, he would get better at it over time, but apparently not.

"Could you talk to them? You are friendly with them." His expression was so nakedly hopeful it was hard to look at him.

I didn't see any traces left of the man I'd once loved. But maybe that had less to do with him and more to do with me. I was a very different person now than I had been when we were married, something I was grateful for every single day. The old me might have considered helping him.

"Blaine, I don't know Keidi. I'm not going to go to the police and tell them she's innocent."

"Especially not after you called them to put her in jail,"

Imogen said under her breath. I was close enough to hear her, but Blaine wasn't.

I looked back over my shoulder, but she just smiled at me innocently. That was the last time I was telling anyone about things I'd uncovered while investigating.

"You think she did it," Blaine said flatly.

"I don't know *who* did it, but I want to give the police a fair chance to figure that out. Someone needs to be held responsible for what happened to Naomi. You were going to marry her; don't you want to know what really happened?"

He blanched, and for a moment he looked so pale and nauseous I worried he was either going to pass out or throw up in the middle of my bookstore. I didn't want to deal with either of those situations, so I hefted a long sigh.

"I'll talk to the detectives. I'm not going to vouch for her, but I'll tell them what you told me. For whatever that's worth."

His expression lightened immediately, and he crossed the room, grabbing my hands and squeezing them. I jerked back, especially when it looked like he might try to hug me.

"Thank you, Phoebe."

I wasn't sure he should be thanking me, but at least he was leaving, so I'd done *something* right. As Blaine headed back out into the rain, I turned to Imogen and rolled my eyes.

"What was *that* all about?" I asked, throwing my hands in the air.

"Oh, it's not obvious?"

"What?"

"That Blaine and Keidi were hooking up."

CHAPTER THIRTY-TWO

I spent all afternoon thinking about Imogen's assessment of the Blaine and Keidi situation, and I had to admit, the longer I considered it, the more I realized she was probably right. Even though Keidi had enthusiastically denied any involvement with Blaine when she'd been in my shop, in retrospect it might have been a case of the lady protesting too much.

But if Keidi and Blaine *had* been involved, then that didn't do much to help prove her innocence. If anything, I felt like it was just more likely she *had* killed Naomi to get her love rival out of the way.

And thinking back on Blaine's words at our breakfast, he'd admitted that Naomi was thinking of calling off the engagement. If she'd discovered that Keidi and Blaine were carrying on behind her back, that would certainly be a valid reason to put an end to their marriage plans.

After lunch, I left Daphne and Imogen at the shop together and decided to make good on my promise to Blaine and talk to the police. I still wasn't sure how much I was going to tell them about my chat with my ex while he was under the influence of magical tea, but I'd probably need to share *some* of it. Blaine *had* asked me himself to go talk to them, so in a way, he was giving me permission.

At least that's what I told myself.

The rain was at least serving one helpful purpose: the paparazzi were all steering clear of the police station today. This let me park right by the door and hustle inside with my coat held over my head. Inside the station felt darker than usual thanks to the heavy gloom of the afternoon storm.

The station had decided to do its own part to decorate for Halloween, which was a change since the last time I'd been in. There were cobwebs strung up in the corners of the lobby, and a pumpkin garland stretched across the back wall behind the reception desk. On the desk's counter were three plastic jack-o'-lanterns and one big glass pumpkin bowl filled with candy.

While one seat at the receptionist desk held a human woman, the chair beside her was occupied by a plastic skeleton positioned to look like it was working on a computer. I chuckled.

"Morning, Phoebe," said the receptionist. "You here to see Patsy? Detective Kim is in Barneswood today."

I wasn't sure if I was relieved not to have to explain why I was here, or to worry that everyone at the police station knew me by name.

"Here to see Patsy," I confirmed.

"You can head right on in." She barely glanced up from her computer.

I made my way to the police work floor. There were two uniformed officers there working at their own desks, but neither one seemed distracted by my presence as I headed toward the back of the room and found Patsy sitting at her desk working away at her computer.

She glanced up as if expecting someone else, then did a double take to see me instead. "Phoebe, nice to see you. I wasn't expecting you today."

I dropped into the chair beside her desk and hoped I wasn't dripping anymore. "You have time for a quick chat?"

"I do, actually."

"Have you talked to Keidi?" I assumed they must have since she'd been in custody almost twenty-four hours, but there was also the possibility she had lawyered up and wasn't saying anything, which would have definitely slowed the investigation down.

Patsy gave a thin smile then sighed. She shook her head slightly, but I felt like it was more of a gesture to herself rather than a *no* to me. "What a mess, Phoebe."

"Uh-oh, I don't love the sound of that."

"We thought we'd cracked the case wide open. But now we're back to square one again. We had to let Keidi go this morning."

"*Why*? What about the poison?"

"That's just it. The bottle isn't poison."

I blinked at her, utterly confused. "What do you mean?"

"Turns out the only thing in that bottle is off-brand headache medication crushed up. And when we looked up the manufacturer on the label... they're a stage prop company. It's not *real*; it's something meant to be used in a play."

I was horrified. Embarrassed. She must have seen the look on my face because she shook her head again. "We thought it was real, too. It looked very convincing. And it was convincing to Keidi, too. She admitted that she hid it to protect someone, but when we asked her who, she clammed up, wouldn't say anything else. When we found out it wasn't real poison, we had to let her go. You can't hold someone for hiding Tylenol." She shrugged. "So, she's protecting someone, but we don't know who. And the craziest part of it all was, we finally got the toxicology report back on Naomi's coffee. No poison."

"Wait... what?" Now I was extra confused. "But she died by poisoning, didn't she?"

Patsy shook her head. "Apparently not. But the tox screen did find that there was something unusual in the drink. Peanut butter powder."

I thought back to my brief interaction with Naomi as she sniffed teas at my shop. *There's no nuts in this, is there? I'm allergic.*

I'm allergic.

"Naomi was allergic to nuts," I said.

Patsy nodded.

So, Naomi hadn't been poisoned, but the presence of peanut butter powder suggested she hadn't just accidentally had a nut latte. Someone must have added it intentionally. "She was still killed, though. And by someone who knew about her allergy."

"Most likely. But unfortunately, that doesn't help us narrow things down very much. Anyone who was close to Naomi would have known about her allergy. I think she's even mentioned it in interviews. Certainly, anyone who ever worked on a set with her would be aware of it. Everyone we already considered a suspect is still a suspect."

"Except Keidi," I said.

"You think so?" She was being patient, almost like she was testing me.

"Well, if she had been the one to put the peanut butter powder in Naomi's drink, why go to all the trouble of hiding the fake arsenic—that she thought was the real murder weapon—to protect someone else? Seems like a lot of effort to cover her own tracks, since she couldn't have known I saw her hiding it."

Patsy sat back in her chair. "Yes, that was the conclusion Kwan and I came to as well. However, she's not out of the doghouse just yet. She's covering for someone, which means there's someone she believes capable of committing the crime and she doesn't want them to get in trouble. She was willing to be held here overnight to avoid talking about them. To me, that says she either knows who killed Naomi, or she knows something she doesn't want us to find out."

This seemed like as good a time as any to dish on what I'd learned. I wasn't sure it was going to point them to the right mystery person, but I knew given Blaine's sketchy behavior they probably needed another chat with him.

I explained to Patsy what Blaine had said that morning at the shop, and then some of what he'd said under the influence of my tea—specifically about Naomi considering ending the engagement—and what Keidi had said to me about Blaine the day before.

"That's an awful lot of he-said-she-said," Patsy said with a sigh. "But it certainly merits some additional investigation. Thank you, Phoebe. I might need to commission some of that tea of yours for the department." She laughed to indicate she was joking, which was a relief because that tea was probably too potent for its own good.

"That tea is too dangerous for me to let out of my sight, quite frankly."

"A little truth goes a long way," she said. "I think too much of a good thing can be dangerous; you're right."

"So, what next?" I asked.

"You're in the play, so you'll be around all these people for the next couple of days. Keep an eye on Keidi and the others, see who she's spending a lot of time with, see what's going on with their dynamics. You don't need to talk to anyone, just give me an idea of anything that looks a little suspicious."

We both knew I was going to talk to people, but it was sweet of her to pretend that I might just observe and report.

"Hey, Amy is off the hook now, right? With everything else that we've learned."

Patsy lifted a familiar pink cup and jostled it. "I never really thought Amy was our killer. But this work requires us to follow every lead. No, I don't think Amy is responsible for Naomi's death. Even if it was her drink that delivered the fatal blow. Someone else did this."

I almost mentioned that it was Amy's *cup* that delivered the drink, but not the drink itself, since Amy didn't make cider, but it seemed like a moot point now that Amy was off the hook.

A feeling of pressure lifted off my shoulders. I'd gotten invested in this case to clear Amy's name. I was glad that Patsy wasn't holding any of Amy's past actions against her. There was a huge difference between trying to spook a jerky boyfriend who had hurt her sister and maliciously poisoning an A-list actress.

If anyone could see the difference, I knew it would be Patsy.

"That ex-husband of yours, on the other hand..." Patsy said. "I gotta say, things aren't looking so great for him."

My mouth formed a thin line as I considered this, and I had to ask myself a serious question.

Was I willing to keep digging into this to find the killer, even if that killer turned out to be someone I once loved?

And I found that I was.

I really, really was.

"So, what next?" I asked.

"You're in the play, so you'll be around all these people for the next couple of days. Keep an eye on Keidi and the others, see who she's spending a lot of time with, see what's going on with their dynamics. You don't need to talk to anyone, just give me an idea of anything that looks a little suspicious."

We both knew I was going to talk to people, but it was sweet of her to pretend that I might just observe and report.

"Hey, Amy is off the hook now, right? With everything else that we've learned."

Patsy lifted a familiar pink cup and jostled it. "I never really thought Amy was our killer. But this work requires us to follow every lead. No, I don't think Amy is responsible for Naomi's death. Even if it was her drink that delivered the fatal blow. Someone else did this."

I almost mentioned that it was Amy's *cup* that delivered the drink, but not the drink itself, since Amy didn't make cider, but it seemed like a moot point now that Amy was off the hook.

A feeling of pressure lifted off my shoulders. I'd gotten invested in this case to clear Amy's name. I was glad that Patsy wasn't holding any of Amy's past actions against her. There was a huge difference between trying to spook a jerky boyfriend who had hurt her sister and maliciously poisoning an A-list actress.

If anyone could see the difference, I knew it would be Patsy.

"That ex-husband of yours, on the other hand…" Patsy said. "I gotta say, things aren't looking so great for him."

My mouth formed a thin line as I considered this, and I had to ask myself a serious question.

Was I willing to keep digging into this to find the killer, even if that killer turned out to be someone I once loved?

And I found that I was.

I really, really was.

CHAPTER THIRTY-THREE

Since I was already out, I decided I might as well make my way to the library. I considered calling Rich to join me, but knew he was likely still asleep, so I figured I'd tackle this one on my own.

Even though the point of the activities seemed to be to connect me with important people in town, I'd already checked that box for this task with my visit to Leo. I had no doubt that the next clue would point me to someone else, though I was out of ideas for who else might be on Eudora's list.

It really could be anyone. Just because I already had connections forged with the first three helpers—one of whom was my cat—didn't mean there weren't new people to find, people she meant for me to know that I didn't yet.

I found parking close to the front of the library—a building I hadn't yet been to in Raven Creek—and made a dash for the door. Because it was still pouring, I didn't have a chance to really look at the outside of the building for long, but it was evident even from my short run up the path that it was the same one from the picture. There were no lingering relics of the building's past, though I did notice a little bronze plaque, but with the weather being what it was, I wasn't going to stop to read it.

Inside the library, the air was musty, but in the lovely way that any place filled with old books managed to be. I'd heard once that the smell bibliophiles love in old books was actually the scent of decay, but since everything around us was slowly decaying, that didn't take away from my enjoyment at all.

I took a deep breath, enjoying the warmth and dryness of the place, and noticed there were a dozen or so hooks just inside the door for patrons to leave coats and umbrellas to avoid bringing the Pacific Northwest damp inside with them.

I obligingly hung up my coat and fixed my ponytail before leaving the entry and heading into the library itself.

The building was a small single-story, but they had managed to cram in an incredible number of books into the relatively diminutive space. I could see how converting a grocery store into a library made sense. The main room would have already been completely open and set up for rows of shelving. Though the shelving was now lovely old wooden shelves instead of the standard metal grocery store fare. The floor had likely been tile once upon a time—easier to clean up spills—but was now covered in weathered gray carpeting, and where the produce section had likely once been there was a nice sitting area with worn-in armchairs and a selection of new magazines displayed against the wall. On the opposite side of the circulation desk—where I imagined the bakery had once been—was the children's section, with an area dedicated to kids' seating and a few toys, plus lower shelving that would allow little ones to access books in their own.

It had been a long time since I'd been in a library, but my love for this kind of environment came rushing back to me. This was a gathering place, somewhere people could come to learn, to immerse themselves in fictional places, to take a break from the outside world.

Libraries truly were a wonder.

Despite the fact I owned a bookstore, I made a resolution to come to the library more often. Very few places on earth felt like home the way a library could. I found myself smiling without even realizing it.

"Hello," a small voice broke through my reverie and called my attention back to the circulation desk.

Behind the counter was a little woman, whose age was so uncertain she could have been fifty or she could have been ninety. Her dark hair was streaked with silver and pulled into a bun on the top of her head, and she couldn't have been more than five feet tall. She also looked as if someone had imagined the perfect librarian and then she'd been brought to life. She wore reading glasses on a chain around her neck and had a cardigan buttoned over her plaid dress. The way she was smiling at me made me think of beloved schoolteachers from my past.

"Hi there." I kept my voice low, not sure if whispering was still expected in libraries or not.

"No need to whisper, love," she replied, a bit of a British accent coloring her words. "No one but us in here at the moment."

"I have a bit of a strange request," I said, approaching the desk.

"I'm sure I've heard them all. But let's have it. What are you looking for? Something out of print, esoteric, perhaps wondering what banned books we have available?" Her eyes were lilac-colored and positively sparkling with mirth.

"Actually, I'm not even sure if I'm looking for a book at all."

"Magazine? DVD? We have a small selection of video games." She clasped her hands together in front of her, and nothing seemed rushed about her tone or her stance, like she could have waited all day for me to tell her what I needed.

"I actually think there might be something here for me?" I asked, feeling more foolish by the moment.

"Oh, a hold. Sure thing, love." She lifted her glasses to her eyes and turned to the computer sitting next to her, a surprisingly new model given how old everything else in the library appeared to be. "What's your name?"

"Phoebe Winchester. But I don't have an account."

Still, she was either ignoring me or hadn't heard me say it, because she was busy typing away into the computer.

"My *goodness*, Ms. Winchester." She lowered her glasses to the tip of her nose and stared at me over the top of them. "Twenty-four years is quite a *long* time to have a book overdue. We quite wrote this off. But there is an outstanding balance of fourteen dollars and twelve cents that we have to clear up before I can release your hold to you."

I stared at her.

She stared back.

"I'm sorry; there has to be some confusion. I don't have a library card here."

"Sure you do. It looks like it was initially a subsidiary card for Eudora Black." When she met my eyes this time, there was no denying that her expression was hinting at something. She met my gaze steadily, practically imploring me to just go with this.

Like she knew something.

"Okay." I raised one quizzical brow at her, but she just

smiled back, pleased with the decision I'd made and offering me absolutely no more hints to go on.

I pulled out my wallet and handed over fifteen dollars cash, waving away her offer to give me change.

"Back in a jiff," she said, before disappearing down an aisle behind the desk. When she returned, there was a slim book in her hand, which she scanned and slipped a pickup reminder tag into.

The book wasn't one I'd ever come across in my exploration of the bookshop, nor anything I'd seen in recent book catalogues.

It was a small, colorful guidebook called *How to Get the Most out of Your Garden*. I flipped through the pages, but there was no envelope inside. Confused, I thanked the librarian and put the book in my bag.

I was all the way back to my car when I realized I had never asked what book it was I'd forgotten to return.

CHAPTER THIRTY-FOUR

The saying in theatre was that *the show must go on,* and as cliched as that might be for a small-town performance of *And Then There Were None*, it seemed as if Pierce Townsend and the members of Something Wicked took it very seriously.

I was impressed to see all the local actors had returned as well, given how inviting it would have been to skip rehearsal and stay home tonight. My only relief was knowing that if the book I'd collected *was* my next clue, it wasn't as if I could go digging in the garden in all this rain, anyway.

My search would have to continue when the weather got a little nicer.

Eudora couldn't have just put everything around the house like a normal person?

Well, no, of course not. Because my aunt had never really *been* a normal person.

And now I was sitting on the floor of the auditorium stage in a circle with the other cast and members of the troupe, and we were doing a ridiculous trust exercise that felt pointless given how close our performance loomed, but it was apparently meant to tell us enough about our co-stars that we felt like we could rely on them.

"Two truths and a lie is a very simple game. You will share three facts about yourselves. Two will be true, one will be a lie, just like the name implies. Then the rest of the members of the circle must try to guess which fact is a lie." Pierce beamed, clearly thrilled with himself, as if he had invented the game.

I tried to keep my pep up, but I'd played variations of this game in different office settings, in my college dorm, and at summer camp in my teens. The only thing I ever learned is that people loved to pick truths that made them sound more interesting and a lie that was typically harmless.

You didn't actually learn to trust anyone, because what inevitably happened was that most people sold the lie too well. So rather than trusting, all you learned was that the people around you were excellent liars.

Since I'd played the game before, I quickly thought of my own answers, which was good because I ended up being chosen to start.

"Hi everyone. My name is Phoebe Winchester. Today I had to pay a library fine for a book I took out when I was twelve. I have two cats named Bob and Coco." I looked over to the troupe members, including Keidi, who were all sitting beside each other. "And I'm allergic to peanuts."

Keidi was so busy looking at her own shoes I wasn't even sure she'd heard me. Liam's face remained completely passive. But Quinn once again had her gaze fixed right on me. While it was hard to read her expression—it wasn't guilt or worry—it wasn't anything *friendly*.

Since Bob and Coco were probably better known around town than I was, the rest of the group was split guessing between my library fines and my allergy.

The game carried on like that, but I found that every time I looked back over at Quinn, she was staring back at me. I could feel the weight of her gaze even when I looked elsewhere.

Patsy might have told me just to watch the others, but I had a feeling Quinn had something to say, and I wasn't going to miss the opportunity. When the game was finished, we broke off into pairs to work on-line readings, and I made a beeline across the stage, coming to stand in front of her.

"I could use a scene partner," I said, waving my script.

For a moment I thought she might beg off and find someone else, but when she looked around, it was evident that everyone else was already paired up. I smiled innocently.

"Fine."

We moved to the lobby, since every group was fighting to find some privacy and avoid the din of too many people talking. Quinn didn't seem like she was in much of a hurry to initiate conversation. Part of me just wanted to get right to the point and ask what her deal was, but I knew that wasn't going to get us very far.

"I know this might sound silly," I said. "But I really liked your Hallmark movie."

This at least was entirely true. I'd checked her IMDb page, and her movie was one about a princess falling in love with a ski instructor. It had been very cute. I was also hoping I might get a little warmth from her if I opened with a compliment. For a moment, the daggers she'd been shooting me for no apparent reason vanished and her face brightened.

"You saw that? Wow. Not many people watch the non-Christmas ones. It was my first big job, and I was *so* nervous about it. Thank you." There was the faintest hint of a Southern drawl as she spoke, something that hadn't been there previously when I'd heard her speak. I wondered if it was her real voice or just an accent she put on sometimes to seem more approachable.

I wasn't entirely sure why she'd been acting so cold to me before, but with one compliment, Quinn seemed like an entirely different person. I was mystified, but hopefully it meant she might open up to me more.

"It's got to be hard, getting roles like that."

"Any roles, really," she admitted. "I mean, even stuff like this is usually very competitive. There were so many people lined up the day we came for auditions. I'm actually kind of sad they decided to do a lottery draw because we saw a couple of really great auditions that morning and those people ended up not getting picked." She paused for a long moment, then as an afterthought said, "Not that I'm sure y'all won't be great."

It didn't escape my notice that she said *y'all* as in the whole cast, and not just me specifically.

Maybe that was why she'd been acting so coldly towards me. Perhaps she knew I didn't take this seriously—or at least as seriously as some of the others—and it made her angry that a bigger part had gone to someone who didn't even want to be in the play. Honestly, if that was the reason, I almost respected it.

While my opinion of the play had changed some since my first day of rehearsals, it was true that I'd been brought into this against my will, and I'd rather be almost anywhere else rather than running lines with a D-list actress. But I was here, and I was going to give it my all.

I tried to emphasize this in my next comment. "I've been so nervous," I admitted. "I'm not great at any of this, but I just want to do a good job, and I don't want to make anyone else around me look bad."

Quinn seemed to soften even more, further confirming my suspicions that her dislike wasn't rooted in some weird vendetta, but that she just didn't like people taking acting gigs who didn't really care about acting.

"Oh, I can help you with some of that. I used to get *so* nervous before all my performances, but Naomi taught me some techniques that really helped me. I still use them even now."

"You and Naomi must have been really good friends," I said, since she had given me the opening. "I'm sorry for your loss."

"Thank you." She looked down, inspecting her chipped nail polish. "We used to be close. Things changed a lot when she got super famous. I mean, I guess that's kind of how it always goes. But she didn't have as much time for us because she had all these new friends in Hollywood and her new boyfriend." She rolled her eyes, which immediately made me like her more.

"You're not a fan of Blaine?"

"He's your ex, isn't he?"

I guess I could expect that to have stayed secret for long. If the press knew, I suppose it must have hit the local gossip circuit as well.

"He is. And don't be gentle on my part, I'm not his biggest fan either."

This made her smile, and her shoulders relaxed a little.

"I guess I just didn't see how he fit into her life. He's not... I mean he's not very interesting."

I laughed out loud before I could stop myself. Maybe it wasn't very nice of me, but I couldn't help it. "No, he's really not, is he? You spent time with him?"

"Not much; we only really met him when this event got planned. They've been together for a while, I guess. She couldn't shut up about how great he was in the group chats. It was very Scheana talking about Rob hanging that TV in under seven minutes, y'know? Like, we get it already; you think he's great."

I had no clue whatsoever what she was talking about or who Scheana and Rob were, but I just nodded because she seemed to think this was a universal cultural reference.

"Like she kept talking about how much we were going to adore him. Blaine's so smart, Blaine's so funny, Blaine this, Blaine that. It was so *boring*. And then we met him and, like, no offense to you, but he's just like... a guy."

I probably couldn't have imagined a better way to describe him if I tried. I also noted that her Southern accent had vanished, making me wonder if I'd even heard it in the first place.

"He is indeed just a guy," I agreed. For some reason, this was what stuck with me of all the things Quinn had said. Blaine *was* just a guy, and not a very remarkable one at that.

He'd done me the biggest favor of my life when he'd cheated on me and shown me his true colors. If I'd still been married to him when Eudora died, there was no way I'd be living this life now. I'd have sold Eudora's house to Dierdre, like she had wanted when I'd first come to town. I never would have found the hidden deeds in Eudora's bookcase that made me the inheritor of half of Main Street and its various rent-payments. I never would have met Rich again and fallen in love.

I wouldn't have Bob.

There were so many gifts I'd received because I'd been open to them. Because there was room in my life to start over.

In a way, I owed Blaine a thank you, because without his selfish actions, I would still be stuck in a life I didn't feel anything for, going through the motions of what seemed right.

Instead, I was happy to get up every day. My life was filled with friends who were *mine* and not just people I knew through him. I was in such a better place now than I'd been when I rolled into Raven Creek on a nearly empty gas tank one year ago.

I realized I'd been harboring a lot of pent-up anger towards my ex, when what I really should have felt was gratitude.

Quinn might not have realized the impact her simple insult had, but I felt like a full year of weight had been lifted from my shoulders. I'd been so *mad* at him, and for what?

I was a better person now.

So, I could be a bigger person.

I could also figure out who had killed his new fiancée so he could have that peace of mind knowing there was at least some justice in the world.

Unless of course *he* had killed her, in which case my uncovering the truth would be a pretty big bummer for him.

CHAPTER THIRTY-FIVE

I spent the next fifteen minutes with Quinn, and while we were meant to be running lines, I found that once the floodgates were open with her, all she wanted to do was talk. I wondered if she was missing a female connection with Naomi gone and had just been waiting for a friendly ear in order to release her innermost thoughts.

Her innermost thoughts, as it turned out, were about as deep as a kiddie pool, but I wasn't about to dismiss her now that I'd gotten her going.

After she mentioned Naomi a few more times, I found myself asking, "Who do you think could have done it to her?"

Quinn paused, like the question had short-circuited her brain. I almost felt bad for asking until she took a deep breath, like she was preparing a soliloquy.

"Well, to be totally honest—again, no offense—I thought it was Blaine. Like, just between us, I think things were getting kind of rocky between him and Naomi, and maybe he was so desperate to keep her from leaving him that he just, like, snapped or whatever? But if he *did* kill her, then he's a better actor than any of us, because he is like... in *bad* shape since it happened. Have you seen him lately?"

"I have." I recalled how hollowed out he looked, his waxy skin, his unshaven face. But was that grief or was it guilt? The two could look an awful lot alike sometimes.

"Like, not even the best method actors could pull that off. I think he's really crushed that she's dead." She paused then, her face suddenly struck by a terrible thought. "I mean, not to say *I'm* not also crushed that she's dead. We were friends, but I guess I just know that Naomi wouldn't want us ruining perfectly good Botox with tears that can't bring her back, anyway."

I wasn't a doctor, but I was pretty sure Botox didn't work that way. I let Quinn go on thinking whatever she wanted to, though.

"So, if you don't think it's Blaine, then who else?" I was hoping she might point the finger at Liam, someone else it would be easy to pull aside for a chat.

"Well, I briefly thought it might be you, if I'm being honest. You were the one to find her, and she's with your ex. But I've seen the way you act whenever anyone talks about him, and now that I've talked to you, I'm pretty sure you're innocent."

Ah, perhaps that explained her intense glares and the reason she had been so still around me. I thought she might leave it there, but instead, she leaned in closer. "Have you seen that creepy guy that used to follow her around like a pathetic little puppy dog? Her stalker?"

The word *stalker* certainly carried with it some scary connotations. "You mean Howie? Yeah, unfortunately we've met." I could still picture his round face staring through my living room window. Shudder.

"Is that his name? Naomi always called him the Mole Man."

That nickname was unfortunately very fitting for Howie, who appeared as if exposure to regular sunlight wasn't a big part of his standard routine. Or leaving whatever underground layer he usually inhabited. I didn't like to stereotype people, but Howie did radiate *Mom's Basement* energy.

"She wasn't very fond of him, then?" I guessed.

"I don't know if she was actually scared of him, but she definitely hated it when he showed up to her events. It started off innocently enough. You know how fans will wait for autographs at movie premieres or the back door of plays? That's how she first met Howie. He showed up at a premiere or two, and she didn't think much of it. Just another fan, right? Well, I guess what happened is that one day she recognized him and said something totally innocent, like, *nice to see you again*."

Quinn didn't need to elaborate; I already knew what must have happened after that. She went on anyway.

"I guess that was all it took for him to decide that Naomi was secretly in love with him, and it just spiralled from there. Now he knows wherever she's going to be and shows up there."

"How long has this been going on?" I asked, and suddenly I couldn't help but remember the sound of footsteps trailing behind me when I'd left the theatre the other night. The unmistakable sound of someone following me. I'd thought it might be Quinn, but now I wasn't so sure.

My spine tingled.

"Almost two years. I think she tried to get a restraining order against him at some point, but because he was just showing up to public spaces, there wasn't much anyone could do to help her. So, she just had to get used to the creepy Mole Man showing up everywhere she went. He would show up in different cities if he knew she was on location. He sent her flowers on her birthday. He was just always around. I saw him here on our first day in town. I don't even know how he figures out where she's going to be before the paps even do; it's crazy. He's crazy."

"Did he ever try to hurt her before?" Not that his behavior wasn't threatening enough. I couldn't imagine having someone constantly in my shadow, everywhere I went. Unless I counted Bob. I'd never be able to let my guard down. I wondered what it must have been like for Naomi, who also had to keep up her movie star persona and couldn't lose it on him in the streets for fear of how it might look in the media.

Howie had probably known that, too.

Did he carry that camera around with him everywhere just to document whatever Naomi was doing? How many photos had he taken in two years? The thought of it was enough to make my skin crawl. Poor Naomi.

It was also an angle I hadn't thought of before.

I'd assumed Howie was just a nuisance rather than any kind of real threat. He hadn't really crossed my mind as a suspect, because I'd thought Naomi's killer had to be someone who knew her well.

But who would know her better than a stalker?

Who would read and watch every interview to feel like he was connected to her?

Maybe it was time to take another look at the man who had been out in my bushes.

Before I could ask Quinn more about Howie and his behavior in the past, Pierce's voice came booming out from the auditorium. "All right, my little thespians, let's get together and do a little scene run-through and then you can go home for the night."

Quinn and I returned to the theater, and my head was buzzing with new ideas. The biggest hiccup in Howie being the potential killer was kind of a major one: there was no way Naomi would take a drink from him. She wouldn't let him get close enough to her to even offer it.

Even with motive and being in the same town, would it have actually been possible for Howie to have enough access to Naomi to kill her? That was certainly a big hurdle to overcome, and one I wasn't sure Howie was smart enough for, even if he was motivated.

As we took to the stage and worked through one of our scenes, I was surprised to find that my lines were tumbling out without any issues. I even threw in an improvised line about carrying my own luggage that had our improv experts and my fellow actors laughing. This did result in a stern lecture from Pierce about not forgetting to keep our composure on stage, but he was smiling as he lectured us, so it was clear he was also enjoying himself.

Apparently, the key for me to remember all my lines was to be thinking about murder instead of acting.

Who said multitasking didn't work?

CHAPTER THIRTY-SIX

I was on cloud nine leaving our rehearsal. I'd been so worried about being a total failure at this, but apparently the key was just to get out of my own head. The whole crew were ready to get home and dry since it was still pouring, so I offered Mr. Loughery a ride while the others split up to their own cars to get where they were headed.

"How did you get to rehearsal today?" I asked. He was a big walker, but given the present state of the weather, I would have been shocked—and a little dismayed—if I learned that he'd come all the way by foot. Since he'd avoided the store during the day, I assumed he knew better, but he also hadn't asked any of us for a lift.

Come to think of it, I wasn't even sure Norman had my phone number to ask. It had never been necessary before.

"Oh, my neighbor Emma-Jean was doing her weekly grocery run. I just caught a ride with her. Can't say I'd have come if she hadn't been going out."

I gently slapped his arm with the back of my hand. "Norman. All of us were going to be headed there anyway, and picking you up is no more than a five-minute drive for any of us in town. Next time you don't want to walk—*anytime*—I want you to call me, okay?" I reached into my glove box and pulled out a notepad and paper I kept there, then jotted down my phone number and handed it to him.

"And not just for rides, either. I know you started out as a regular, but we're friends now. And friends are there for each other no matter what. If you need to go get groceries or go to Barneswood. Heck, I'd take you to Snohomish if you need to go. Though I'm not sure why anyone would need to go all the way to Snohomish, but you get what I mean."

Mr. Loughery was looking at me, taking in my speech, and I could see the faint sheen of tears in his eyes. He took my hand after accepting the note with my number and gave me a squeeze. "Phoebe, when your aunt died, I worried that this town had lost one of its truly great people. But what a gift she gave us in you." He pressed the back of my hand to his lips and gave it a peck. "I'm glad to know you."

That was almost enough to set *me* crying, and I could barely look at him without losing it. "I'm happy to do it. And I'm glad you came into my bookstore."

He opened the door and his umbrella in a well-practiced two-step gesture and then waved me off before running—a more semi-speedy amble—up to his door.

Once I knew he was safe inside, I drove the short distance home, surprised and pleased to see Rich's car parked out front and the living room and kitchen lights on. I did notice that the living room curtains were drawn. I smiled at the small protective gesture, since I usually left the curtains open when I left the house so Bob and Coco could watch Bird TV while I was gone.

I made a run for the front door, but still managed to be soaked by the time I got under the protective cover of the porch. Now that the sun was down, the rain had a definite chill to it. I squinted out into the downpour just to make sure none of the raindrops were sneakily snowflakes in disguise.

No, definitely all rain.

I got inside, and the smell of stew immediately enveloped me. My stomach grumbled loudly, now reminded it had been quite some time since I'd last eaten. I also noticed that while Bob came out to greet me, he wasn't wailing at the top of his little cat lungs about being starved.

I peeked my head into the kitchen where Rich was wearing one of Eudora's old aprons and shaking some garlic powder into the pot on the stove.

"Did you feed the cats?" I asked.

"I did. Bob wasn't going to let me have a moment of peace until he had his dinner, so I obliged. Hope that's okay."

"That's amazing, thank you. Did Coco actually show up?"

Rich grinned from ear to ear. "She *did*. Not for long, just enough time to scarf down a few bites before vanishing again, but she existed in my presence for at least five minutes."

"Dang. I'm impressed."

"So was I."

I left him to his stew preparations and headed upstairs for a quick shower just to warm up from the cold layer of rain that coated my body, and to pull on some comfy sweatpants and a sweatshirt. I wanted to be the kind of girl who looked cute and put-together around her boyfriend, but I also wanted to be comfortable, and tonight, comfortable was going to win out.

Back downstairs, Rich had set up dinner at the small

kitchen table. The house had a formal dining room, but it was much *too* formal for two people, and it was also a long-term storage space for items of Eudora's I still hadn't finished sorting through.

A year into the process, I could *almost* see the table again, and I was about ready to bring someone in to help me sell off some of the items that I didn't want to keep or give away.

It was hard to part with anything, knowing it had once been important to Eudora, but she had acquired a lot of stuff in her life, and I doubted she would be mad if I helped some of it find a new home.

But because of the disaster that still existed in the dining room, plus it just being too fancy for everyday meals, it had become my habit to eat in the kitchen. That was when I wasn't eating on the couch in front of the TV.

Rich's stew smelled insanely good. The official foods of fall, in my opinion, should be soup and stew in my opinion. Hearty, warm, delicious. Anything that made it feel like you were eating a hug. Rich had surprised me with his cooking skills the first time he'd made me dinner, and I was more than happy to let him continue working away in my kitchen as long as he wanted. The man could *cook*.

With wine poured and our dinner served, I told Rich all about rehearsal—he seemed genuinely happy for me about my lines—and he told me as much as he could about his current case. He never gave me his client's names or any kind of details that might tell me who they were. While his client base lived in several towns all within about ninety minutes of Raven Creek, there was always a chance I might know someone he was working with personally, and he obviously couldn't share their sordid life events with me.

But he did like to tell me about anything funny that

happened to him during his stakeouts. The previous night had evidently been difficult because a dog who lived next door to the person he was trying to follow kept noticing Rich in his car and going into bouts of loud barking throughout the evening. Ultimately, the dog had chilled out, but it had made for a challenging night.

"Next time I'm bringing steak along with me. I'll bribe the stupid thing."

"Maybe he's not stupid at all and that was his master plan."

"Touché."

Once we finished dinner and cleaned up the table, we took two frozen ice cream cones into the living room and turned on our cheerleader drama. I draped my feet in Rich's lap, and he squeezed my toes until I was warm.

"Do you think Howie could be the killer?" I asked.

He checked his watch, smiling to himself. "Two hours. I'm proud of you, Phoebe."

"Two hours?"

"It took you two whole hours to mention Naomi's murder. That might be a record."

My cheeks flushed, but he squeezed my toes playfully. "Don't get like that," he said. "I'm just teasing. You know I love your little Miss Marple brain. Now remind me who Howie is."

"Howie's the guy who was spying on us through the front window." I pointed to the window, which I realized as I did it wasn't necessary. Rich knew what windows were.

Rich immediately bristled at the mention of our little spy. I guess he hadn't been paying attention when we learned his name. He'd been too busy staring daggers into the guy. "Does Patsy think he's involved?" he asked.

"I don't know; I haven't talked to her about it."

"Then what made you think of it? He hasn't been back here, has he?" I felt him tense like he was going to get up and check, but I made my legs as heavy as possible, keeping him pinned in place.

"Woah there, stand down, buddy. No, he hasn't been back. I got to talking to one of the other actresses in Naomi's troupe, and the guy wasn't just a super fan; he was a stalker."

"Huh, can't say I'm surprised given how he behaved here the other night. But an actual stalker? Those are quite rare."

I recounted everything Quinn had told me, and by the time I was done, Rich looked horrified. I didn't mention anything about being followed the other night, because I didn't think it would help anything. If it happened again, I'd bring it up, but there was always a chance I'd misread the situation, and it had just been a random pedestrian. I was trying not to worry about it myself, so there was no need to notch Rich's anxiety up any higher.

"Definitely sounds like legit stalker behavior. That must have been incredibly scary for her. Especially seeing him show up here, when it's such a small town. Did Blaine mention anything about him when you talked?"

Come to think of it, he hadn't. "No, and maybe that's a bit weird, too, isn't it? You'd think considering how amped up he was to prove that Keidi was innocent, and how weird he's being in general that he'd love to point the finger of blame on someone else who is even more obvious of a suspect than he is."

"Hmm. I think you need to mention all this to Patsy and Kwan. If this guy did kill Naomi and he's been paying attention to you, then he might have noticed your little habit of asking a lot of questions about major crimes. I don't want him to think you're a liability. You know what happens to killers when they start to feel threatened."

I shivered a little, because I did know. All too well.

"Oh!" I jumped up off the couch and ran back into the foyer. Coco, who had been sneakily watching us from the stairwell, went scrambling up the steps when she saw me coming, the *tick-tick-tick* of her claws following her up as she vanished from sight.

I brought my bag back into the living room where Rich was leaned forward, trying to figure out why I'd suddenly vanished.

"Speaking of investigations, I found the next clue. Kind of."

"For the murder?"

Oh, right. Not everyone could follow my internal train of thought when it careened wildly from one topic to another only moderately related one.

"No, from Eudora."

He gave me a funny look, since I *had* just gone from him warning me to take my personal safety seriously to talking about a magical scavenger hunt, but I was really going to need him to keep up.

I pulled out the book I'd collected at the library. "Apparently this was on hold for me. And I had an overdue book from over twenty years ago I had to pay off."

"What book?" he asked, looking at the slim gardening manual with puzzlement.

"I have no idea; I forgot to ask her before I left."

"Was there a letter?" He opened the book, but the only thing that fell out was my pickup receipt.

"No, no letter. So, I think one of the books here must be the clue to point me to the next step."

"How did you even end up at the library? I thought the next stop was the grocery store."

"It was. Leo had the picture that matched the one from the puzzle. Apparently, the original Lansing's location was where the current library is."

I picked up the little receipt that had fallen out of the book and made a small noise of delight. The slip wasn't just for the return date on my gardening book. It also listed the book I had apparently taken out when I was still a child. I held it up for Rich to see, and he let out a little laugh.

"How do you suppose she managed that?"

The book I'd paid for was one called *Honey Do: A Kids' Guide to Beekeeping*. It was a book I could safely guarantee I'd never once taken out as a child. But the name was a dead giveaway to my next location.

Though I was mystified how my aunt had managed to point me in the direction of Honey when Honey hadn't even lived in Raven Creek when the book had been checked out.

Maybe one day I'd figure it out.

Or perhaps I'd learn to accept that there were some mysteries I would never solve.

CHAPTER THIRTY-SEVEN

In the morning, I left Rich fast asleep in my bed as I donned my running gear and prepared for a dark loop around town. It wasn't raining at the moment, which I wanted to take advantage of. Since it rained so much here, I knew the smart thing to do would be to buy a treadmill so I could run no matter the weather, but for me running wasn't so much about the exercise as it was the experience.

I loved to be outside. I loved to breathe the fresh air and feel it sting my cheeks when it was getting colder outside, like it was now. None of that would be available to me indoors, so I just got in my outdoor runs whenever the weather was nice enough to let me.

The idea of going now while it was still dark wouldn't normally bother me, but after Rich's words of warning last night, I was feeling a little uneasy as I tied up my running shoes. I wasn't used to feeling an inkling of fear associated with my run, and just feeling it now made me irrationally annoyed.

I lived in one of the safest towns in the country. A lot of people didn't even lock their doors in Raven Creek. I barely remembered to lock my car, but I did still lock my house door. That was a habit that wasn't likely to fade from my city-girl brain any time soon.

Especially not after some of my previous experiences.

But I *loved* my morning run. It was my time alone with my thoughts, just me and the running trails around town, the sidewalk and the dirt under my feet, the sound of my running playlist in my ears. I didn't have a lot of stress in my life these days, thankfully, but running did help keep my mental state in check.

I didn't want to give up that peace just because there was someone in town who had done a terrible thing.

With my lightweight puffer coat and good leggings on, I was protected from the early morning chill. Part of the reason I felt so safe at this time of day was because I was probably one of the only people in Raven Creek who was awake. Me, and Amy, and that was likely the sum total.

I loved being up when everyone else was dozing. It hadn't always been that way. I used to relish sleeping in whenever my schedule allowed it, and never would have used the phrase *morning person* to refer to myself. But that had all changed when I'd taken over the shop. Necessity required me to be there by six whenever I was opening—which was all week—and as a result I had somehow become what I once dreaded: an early bird.

But there was a freakish kind of satisfaction to accomplishing so much of your to-do list while most people were still off in dreamland.

I gave Bob a quick pat before leaving and then headed out on my usual route. The air felt damp, lingering traces of all that rain making my skin feel slightly tacky as soon as I was a block into my run. The temperature was borderline cold, making me glad I had dressed appropriately. I'd warm up quickly as I went, but in those first minutes as my body adjusted, I felt the late-fall chill turning my nose and cheeks rosy red.

The weather made me irrationally excited for Christmas, which I knew it was much too soon to think about, but with plans in place for my family to come visit me for the season, I was putting the horse before the cart in terms of my holiday enthusiasm. Or perhaps I was putting the sleigh before the jack-o'-lantern.

My morning run usually lasted about forty minutes, and I was halfway through it when a strange sensation came over me. I muted my playlist and took out one of my earbuds, wondering if I was just feeling paranoid because of Rich's warnings, but I couldn't shake the unmistakable feeling that I was being watched.

I slowed to a stop, removing the other earbud and turning in a full circle, trying to determine if there was anyone out and about. Sometimes I might see someone on the residential streets letting their dog outside. And periodically my run time aligned with that of the town paperboy, Malcolm. But no Malcolm, no dogs.

My breath was visible in the air as I tried to slow my pulse, but between the run and the adrenaline of my freshly stoked nerves, I was wired.

Then, suddenly, came the sound of feet on pavement.

I wheeled around to the direction they were coming from but only had enough time to see a dark figure, then a bright flash of light. Dazed by the light, I was momentarily blinded, and felt the heavy weight of a body collide with me, knocking me to the ground.

The wind whooshed out of my lungs, making it hard to breathe, and I covered my head and face with my arms, expecting another blow to land. Instead, the footfalls moved in the opposite direction, growing quieter until they were gone altogether.

It took me a minute to get my wits back about me. I just lay on the ground looking up at the still-dark sky and the plumes of my rapid breathing.

What had just happened?

I clambered to my feet, my butt damp from the rain left on the path and my palms gritty with wet dirt. I did a mental check, and the best I could tell I wasn't seriously hurt, just surprised and probably a little bruised. I wasn't going to hang around to see if the person who attacked me would come back for round two. Instead, I ran home as fast as I could and didn't stop until I was through the door.

To my surprise, Rich was awake and came out of the kitchen when I stomped back inside and locked the door behind me, my breath short and frantic.

"Woah, are you okay?" He set the coffee mug he was holding on the stair railing post and came over to me, holding my shoulders while his gaze took me in top to bottom, trying to see what had me so spooked.

I explained through short wheezes what had happened, and the expression on Rich's face changed from one of concern to one of anger. His hands dropped from my arms, and he grabbed his jacket from the hook by the door.

"What are you doing?" I asked as he slipped it on over his T-shirt. He was still wearing his pajamas, which I don't think he realized or cared about.

"I'm going to go find whoever did this to you," he said matter-of-factly.

It was enough to make me laugh. The fear had pushed me right up to the edge of my limits, and now all I could do was laugh at the absurdity of my boyfriend tramping outside in his plaid pajama bottoms to give some unknown stranger a piece of his mind.

Rich was shaken from his angry stupor by my laughter. He looked down and realized what he looked like in that moment.

"I appreciate the gesture, I really do, but they're long gone by now. And besides, I'm pretty sure I know who it was."

"Oh?"

The glare of the flashbulb was still making me see stars when I blinked.

"I think it's time to visit our resident celebrity stalker and see what he wants."

CHAPTER THIRTY-EIGHT

There were plenty of lovely bed and breakfasts in Raven Creek, places where even celebrities like Naomi Novak would feel comfortable. But there was only one motel, and it was on the outskirts of town. Depending on the day, it could give cute retro vibes, or if it was gloomy and grey like today, it could skew a little Bates Motel.

The Welcome Inn was run by a family who had lived in Raven Creek for at least three generations, and the motel had been there all that time, offering weary travellers inexpensive accommodations at a cheap price. The neon sign over the parking lot was from the fifties and had been up so long that the design had circled right back from out of date to cool again.

It advertised air conditioning but not Wi-Fi. There was evidently also a pool on site, but I assumed it wasn't open for the season.

It was also the most likely place for a guy like Howie to be staying.

I'd had to take care of the shop before we were able to go confront my likely attacker.

Knowing Imogen was *not* an early bird, I'd texted Daphne to see if she could come in and cover my morning shift. While I waited for her reply, I had Rich take me to the store—with the added bonus that he could go upstairs and change—and I got the order from Amy's and started basic morning prep. Daphne replied to my message with a series of thumbs up emojis and a big grinning smiley face, and said she'd be in by eight. That gave me exactly enough time to get the shop ready to open and the sourdough baking before Rich and I made our way to the motel.

Daphne showed up just before eight looking impossibly perky for the hour and giving me a quick hug before I left, telling me how excited she was to have the morning shift. If I'd known she was such a fan, I might have to start considering letting her come in for six instead of me.

But then I wouldn't know what to do with my time.

Rich parked in front of the old motel, and I eyed it carefully. There were four cars parked in front of the motel rooms, and an old Ford truck parked beside the office. One of the cars by the rooms was a little red Honda with a bumper sticker that said, "Naomi Novak for President."

"He's definitely not subtle, I'll give him that." I pointed to the sticker. "At least we know he's here."

"At least we know his *car* is here. He might be running around on foot assaulting people." He glared at the car like he might be able to channel his feelings towards Howie through it. I don't think the Honda was impressed.

"Come on, tough guy. Let's go see if he's in. And maybe turn the machismo down a couple of notches. You're at a Marlon Brando in *Streetcar* and I need you at a Guy Pearce in *L.A. Confidential*."

"Would you settle for Steve McQueen in *Bullitt*?"

"As long as you mean the stoic and restrained part and not the car chase part."

"I love that car chase," Rich said as he got out of the car.

I followed behind him, and we bypassed the main office to go right to room four, where the Honda was parked. The curtains were drawn. I guess Howie didn't want anyone impeding his privacy, which was funny, all things considered.

Big evergreens hung low over the roof of the motel, their branches heavy with water from all the recent rain, and their marvelous smell permeating the air. The Welcome Inn had put a carved pumpkin in front of each room, which was a super cute touch that I might have appreciated more if we weren't here to confront someone for attacking me.

I knocked on Howie's door, figuring it would be best for me to take the lead.

"Bruce Willis in *Die Hard*," Rich whispered.

"If you keep bartering, I'm going to say *Paul Blart Mall Cop*."

"Ouch."

The door opened a crack, the chain in place, and Howie's pale face peered out at us through the small opening.

"What do you want?" he asked.

I bit my tongue and squeezed Rich's arm to keep him from saying anything that might cause us to get a slammed door to the face rather than answers. Once I regained my own calm, I said, "I could ask you the same thing, Howie. Why did you knock me over this morning?"

I didn't think it was possible for him to get any paler, but he somehow managed it, looking completely ashen. "I don't know what you're talking about," he blurted, the completely lost any potential plausible deniability when he added, "You can't prove anything."

The desire to facepalm in front of this man was incredible. A criminal mastermind he was not. So, was it really possible he might have been the one to kill Naomi when he couldn't even stop from confessing to a minor assault? We weren't even cops.

"Howie, we just want to talk to you. I think there was a reason you did what you did, and I'm not sure if it's for attention, or because you're trying to send me a message, but either way, I can give you the opportunity for both now that I'm here."

For a long moment he just stared at me, then at Rich, his eyes narrowing into slits. Then he closed the door in our faces, and I was sure that was it for us until I heard the distinctive sound of a lock chain being removed and the door opened wide enough for us to pass through.

"Leave it open," he instructed, then pointed towards the two chairs at a table near the door. He sat on one of the two double beds in the room, the one farthest from us.

Next to the door was a pair of running shoes, their treads caked with dirt.

I stared at them pointedly, then back at Howie before I sat down in the chair closest to the door. Rich stayed standing, leaning against the frame of the open door, so if Howie had hoped that might be an easy route of escape, he was now sorely mistaken.

Howie's camera was sitting on the table, and I picked it up.

"Hey, you can't—"

I gave him a look that silenced him mid-sentence and turned the camera on, reviewing his most recent photos. I turned the view screen around to face him so he could see the picture of me in the dark, my expression more surprised than scared as the flash blinded me right before he knocked me down.

He hung his head.

I started to flip through photos for the past few days, finding several more of me taken from a distance. At the store, going home, at the library.

"This is so creepy, Howie. Is this what you did to Naomi?"

His cheeks flushed red, and he didn't answer.

"Why are you following me?"

"Because you were the last person to see her. Because you were both in love with the same person. You're the closest thing to her still alive."

I stared at him, then looked back down at the camera, where the photos were now all of Naomi. Naomi walking Main Street, Naomi at the private airport, Naomi in Los Angeles, grocery shopping, at a farmer's market, out on her bike. Everywhere Naomi went, there was Howie.

I was about to ask him another question when Rich's phone pinged. He didn't step outside to check it—he normally would—but when he did, his expression changed completely.

He darted a quick glance in my direction.

"What is it?" I asked.

"Blaine just turned himself into the police. He's confessing to Naomi's murder."

CHAPTER THIRTY-NINE

We weren't so lucky to avoid the paparazzi this time when we arrived at the police station. Thankfully, Rich was plenty familiar with the lay of the land, and as soon as we saw the swarm of cameramen and reporters outside the front door, he took us around back.

In the back of the car, Howie was sulking, hunched over and sitting low in his seat. Rich had refused to leave him unattended after what he'd done, and so it was decided he would come with us. He didn't seem thrilled about it, especially since I'd held onto his camera to show Patsy and Kwan his little photo series of me.

Even if he wasn't responsible for Naomi's murder, he wasn't going to walk away without some repercussions for his actions. Naomi couldn't defend herself from him anymore, but I could do that much for her.

I was feeling surprisingly sick to my stomach at the idea that Blaine had confessed. No wonder he'd been so quick to leave our breakfast, and so adamant that Keidi was innocent. It had been him all along.

But *why*? Imogen, Norman and I had gone through a

whole list of *why* for the various people in Naomi's life, but I found it almost impossible to believe that a man I'd once been married to could be capable of murder.

There were a lot of things I'd misjudged about Blaine, but this one seemed beyond all imagining.

Blaine Winchester, a killer?

I couldn't make my brain process it, but if Patsy's text to Rich was right, then he was here admitting to it himself.

While a few of the nosier reporters had circled around the back to shout questions at us, the number was much smaller than the group lurking around outside, likely hoping to score a picture of Blaine.

We got inside without too much difficulty and headed for Patsy and Kwan's desks. I pointed Howie to a seat at an empty desk in the middle of the room, where he dutifully sat and stared at his hands.

"He confessed?" I asked Patsy as I approached, putting Howie's camera down on her desk. She looked at the device with some confusion, then back up to me.

"He did. Don't suppose that tea of yours lasts for several days, does it? Then I might need to consider him under the influence of..." She peered around us to where Howie was sitting and reconsidered her words. "Outside influence."

"No, the tea wears off after a couple of super awkward hours. This is all him."

"Well, I texted Rich because he said he's willing to tell us everything that happened, but he'll only do it if you're here."

I looked from Patsy to Rich. "Why didn't you text me, then?"

"I tried, but you didn't answer." I checked my pockets and realized that I must have left my phone back at the shop with Daphne. I hoped things weren't falling apart at

The Earl's Study, because I'd have no way to know. Though I hadn't missed my phone up until that point, I suddenly felt a bolt of anxiety for its absence.

Funny how attached we can get to such a silly thing.

"I just assumed Rich was either with you or would be over the store if he wasn't, so there was a good chance he'd get to you sooner than I could."

"I hate that I'm so predictable."

Patsy laughed. "You are *anything* but predictable, Phoebe. But I can't force you to talk to him. I know you're not a big fan of his, and it might be hard to hear what he has to say, but we could really use the assist on this one."

I nodded. After my discussion with Quinn, I'd already started to feel differently about Blaine than I had even a few days earlier. That didn't mean it wouldn't be tough to hear him admit to murder, but Naomi deserved answers, even if they were painful for me to hear.

Patsy took me to the back of the building, where I knew the lone interrogation room was placed. I was pretty sure it was just a converted closet, because this wasn't the kind of town where an interrogation room was regularly required. There was only one holding cell.

I'd never actually been inside the interrogation room, but once I was, I was further convinced it was just a closet. For one thing, it didn't have one of those windows with the two-way mirrors. Or one-way mirrors? I wasn't actually sure which one it was, but this room didn't have one. Since my exposure to interrogation rooms was entirely limited to what I'd seen on TV, I assumed all of them had a mirror in them, but maybe I was just being scammed by Hollywood.

This room just had one small wooden table in the center and two chairs. There was a camera in one corner of the ceiling, its red light glowing, so I assumed that would be how they would capture any incriminating statements Blaine made.

Blaine was sitting on the opposite side of the table from the door, staring down at the wood surface like it might be able to tell him all the secrets of the universe. Instead, it just shared that Swedish people can make great cheap furniture.

I took the other chair and sat down. My stomach was flip-flopping like crazy, and seeing him there, looking so broken and defeated, I found that I didn't have the faintest sliver of hatred left for him. For the first time in a very long time, the only thing I felt was sad.

"Blaine," I said, trying to snap him out of whatever state he was in.

After a long moment, he finally looked up. There were massive dark circles under his eyes that were so bad I initially wondered if someone had punched him, but it was just the hollowed-out appearance of a man who probably hadn't slept all week. His stubble was quickly approaching a beard, and his eyes were red-rimmed and glassy from crying.

He didn't look like a killer.

He looked like a shell.

"Hey," he croaked. "I'm glad you came."

"Can you tell me what happened? The detectives said you confessed."

A tear rolled down his cheek, and it was a gut punch to see. Whatever had happened, the guilt of it was clearly crushing him. Still, if he had killed her, then he needed to face the consequences for that, even if I did feel empathy for his obvious pain.

"I didn't mean, too, Phoebe. I promise you. It wasn't my plan. But I killed her, I know I did."

"Okay. Can you just walk me through it?"

"When Naomi was going through the auditions, she asked me to go get her another drink. She liked the one that she got at that little bakery and wanted me to go get another one while she was working. When I got there, I saw that there was a hazelnut chocolate latte on the menu that looked really good, and I ordered it for myself. Phoebe, I don't know what happened. I was so careful because I know Naomi is allergic to nuts. Normally I won't even eat them around her, but I thought I'd be able to have my latte while she was working and then get rid of it and everything would be fine."

He dropped his face into his hands, and his shoulders started to shake as he cried.

I was perplexed, but I was also starting to put the pieces together, and as I did, my brows started to rise. I reached across the table and touched his hand, getting his attention back on me.

"Blaine, you think you killed Naomi by accidentally giving her the wrong drink?"

He looked up, nodding, and wiped his tears away with fisted hands like a toddler might.

I shook my head. "No. They tested her drink. What killed her was peanut butter powder that someone added intentionally. Amy doesn't use peanut butter powder in her drinks."

Blaine stared at me, and his expression was so unchanged for the longest time I wasn't sure he had understood me.

"Blaine, you didn't kill her," I explained.

"B-but, I gave her the drink. The drink that killed her."

"Then someone else must have added something to it

before it got to her. I swear to you, it was peanut butter powder that killed her. Did you get drinks for anyone else?"

He nodded. "For Liam and Keidi. They got the same thing as Naomi did. Phoebe, you're sure I didn't kill her?"

I smiled and patted him on the shoulder. "Yeah. I'm sure."

He started to cry again, but this time it was different. This time it seemed to be from relief.

If Blaine's drink hadn't accidentally killed her, though, then it was one of the others. And if Blaine had left them out at the audition, then someone might have had an opportunity to access them.

Liam and Keidi were certainly both worth a second conversation with.

But I was thinking of someone else.

Someone who had followed Naomi everywhere she went since she'd arrived in town.

I burst out of the interrogation room and looked out at the desks across the police work floor.

All of them empty.

Howie was gone.

CHAPTER FORTY

There was considerable hullabaloo over the missing stalker, especially after I showed Patsy the pictures on his camera and explained what had happened to me that morning during my run.

How had Howie managed to escape from the middle of a police station? He was so quiet and unassuming he must have just blended right into the background long enough for people to stop noticing him, then he just slipped out.

He hadn't been under arrest, after all. It was possible he had just gotten up and walked away.

I was sure the focus on Blaine and his confession—now retracted—had caused more than enough distraction for the other man to leave. Howie was the kind of person that people just didn't pay attention to. It was probably one of those things that helped him become such an efficient stalker.

"He's on foot," I reminded them. "I doubt he's going to walk all the way back to the motel. He's probably gone to lie low somewhere."

Patsy and Kwan were headed out to their car, while

several available uniformed officers made their way to cruisers. The police force in Raven Creek wasn't very big, and I suspected the people now looking for Howie represented all of it.

I figured that's why no one said anything when Rich and I joined in, getting into Rich's car and pulling out of the lot.

The amassed gathering of media out front shouted things to the police, but just as Rich and I were about to drive by, I touched his arm. "Hold on." Once the car was stopped, I rolled down the window and waved to Winnie York, who came over quickly.

"You got a scoop for me, Phoebe?" she asked eagerly.

"I might, Winnie; it depends. Did you see a plain-looking bald guy come by? Happen to notice where he went?"

"Yeah, sure. I know who you're talking about. Thinks he's a journo just because he's got a camera and an insider."

I stared at her. "An insider?"

"Sure. He was bragging to us the other day about how he's got an in with one of Naomi's camp, and that's how he always knows where she's going to be. Says he could scoop any of us all day long because he's always a step ahead."

Rich and I exchanged glances. There were only three people who could be Howie's insider, and only two of them had coffees Blaine had picked up. So, either Keidi or Liam were involved in this more than they had let on.

"Which way was he headed?" I asked Winnie.

She pointed down the block towards the community center. "Seemed to be in an awfully big hurry. Does he actually know something we don't?" She looked in the direction he'd gone.

"Not in the way I think you're thinking. But Winnie, if

things shake out the way I think they might, I promise to have the detectives give you an exclusive, okay?"

She huffed a little chuckle. "I don't think you can promise that. Can you at least tell me why your ex is in there?"

I paused, not wanting to throw Blaine to the wolves when it turned out he wasn't really responsible for his fiancée's murder. "He had some important information that helped the case."

"You sure he hasn't been arrested and you're just covering for him?" Winnie raised a challenging eyebrow at me.

"I can say with absolute certainty that Blaine Winchester didn't kill Naomi Novak."

"Now that's news that's fit to print. Thanks Phoebe."

Rich didn't wait for instruction, having made the same assumptions I did. I'd barely spoken to Liam through this whole thing, since all signs had seemed to point in other directions. Now I was wondering if that had been intentional.

Or had Keidi managed to fool everyone into thinking she was innocent, in what might be the performance of the year?

Either way, there was something rotten in Naomi's friend group, and the best-case scenario was that one of her supposed friends had been giving her location to a stalker.

The worst-case scenario was that one of them was complicit in her murder.

As we pulled up in front of the community center, I was surprised to see a new banner in place advertising the play. It hung proudly over the entrance, which was now decorated in its Halloween finery with potted mums, decorative gourds, and a skeleton wearing a Shakespearean ruff.

The moment we were out of the car, I could hear shouting coming through the community center's open door.

"You *idiot*," bellowed a male voice, which I quickly assumed belonged to Liam. "How could you be so sloppy? Why would you start harassing that stupid shop owner?"

Okay, rude.

Rich and I paused inside the doors as our eyes adjusted to the much dimmer light inside. There was no sign of anyone in the lobby, but the voices were coming from somewhere close. I pointed towards the doorway to the staff area, the place I'd previously heard Quinn and Liam talking.

Now it made a lot more sense why Liam would want to split town right after Naomi died.

"I told you to get it done and *leave*. If you'd just hit the road like you were supposed to, no one would have ever known what happened," Liam snarled.

"I'm sorry," came Howie's meek voice. "But you didn't tell me what was going to happen. You said she was only going to get sick, that she'd be in the hospital for a few days, and I could get some pictures. She wasn't supposed to *die*."

Liam made a snorting sound, and I exchanged a quick look with Rich, wondering if we should go in now or wait until Patsy and the others had caught up to us. Surely, they couldn't be that far behind.

"Well, I'm sorry you thought that, but what happened, happened. And now I'm sorry again, because if they're onto you, I can't just let you tell them what happened."

Then another voice interrupted this, and I was genuinely surprised. Keidi said, "What are you going to do? You can't kill him, Liam?"

"Shut *up*," Liam growled. "I can't deal with your incessant whining anymore. And that stunt you pulled with the arsenic bottle? What were you even thinking?"

"I *thought* I was protecting you."

"You thought I was stupid enough to leave the murder weapon just hanging around with my things? That was for the *play*. I didn't think this Podunk town would have any halfway decent props." His tone was aggravated, and it was clear he was running thin on patience.

There was a pause, then Keidi let out a squeal of alarm. I knew whatever was about to happen, we couldn't just wait for the police to show up. If we did, Howie might end up dead.

As much as the guy sucked, that didn't mean I was just going to stand around and let him die.

Rich moved before I could, running for the door and shoving it inward. The swinging door hit someone hard, and a loud *oof* sound followed after the heavy thud. I went after him, and when we came through the opening, Howie was on the floor and Liam was pointing a gun in the general direction of... oh, of us.

"You're going to want to put that gun down, Liam," Rich cautioned.

"I can shoot you just as easily as I was going to shoot him," Liam countered, pointing the gun at Rich. My pulse hammered, and I darted a frenzied gaze between the two of them. Could I jump at Liam and knock the gun from his hand, or should I push Rich sideways out of the path of the bullet? Both options would make it vastly more likely for me to get shot than Rich, but the last time someone had tried to shoot me my fickle time-stopping abilities had kicked in to save me.

I had to hope they would work again if push came to shove.

Before I could try, I caught Rich give me a quick look and shake his head.

I froze.

"Liam, you don't want to do that," Rich said, his voice completely calm, absolutely no tension in his body. "Because then you have three more bodies instead of one. And you might have gotten away with it when it was just Naomi being poisoned, but three gunshot victims are going to be a lot harder for you to get away from."

Liam didn't look like he was hearing any of this. His once-handsome face was twisted into a mask of pure rage, and he started moving the gun between Rich, me, and Howie on the floor. At the moment, he didn't seem to care how many bodies he piled up.

His finger was hovering uncomfortably close to the trigger of the gun, and I could hear my own pulse throb in my ears, slowing... slowing...

But time didn't stop.

My palm was itching to lift and see if I could do to Liam what I'd done to the last person who had threatened someone I cared about, but I held off. Rich had shaken his head. He wanted an opportunity to do this himself, the way he'd once been trained to.

"Hey," Rich said, his soothing voice bringing Liam's attention back his way. "Right now, you haven't killed anyone, have you?"

Liam stared at him, suddenly processing the words, actually *hearing* Rich for the first time since we'd arrived.

"No..." Liam said cautiously.

"Then why make this worse for yourself? Get a good lawyer, someone who knows how to spin. Howie has a history with Naomi; she's spoken to the police about him in the past. A good lawyer, some reasonable doubt... You can still walk away from this, kid."

Liam's jaw ticked. Howie sucked in a breath like he might be about to protest, but I kicked him in the leg so all he said was, "Ow!"

I noticed Keidi standing beside Liam, and she was trembling, but I could also see that her attention was on the gun instead of him. I wasn't sure if she was just afraid of it, or if she was making the same mental calculations I had been. Since she wasn't looking at me, I had no way to get her attention to give her the same silent message Rich had given me.

I fixated on her, begging her with my mind, *don't move, don't move, don't move*.

She didn't.

Her trembling stopped.

Her whole body had gone rigid, like she was suddenly a statue.

No one else in the room seemed to notice the change, but my heartbeat quickened. If she actually *was* frozen, that was an entirely new facet to my strange special ability.

I really wished I didn't need to be in mortal danger to unlock new magical skills.

I noticed that a door at the end of the corridor had opened, and Patsy was leading a small group of officers with her. She held a finger to her lips when she saw me spot her.

"Can I ask you one thing, Liam?" I said, and immediately regretted it as the gun pivoted to me. I swallowed hard but forced myself to keep going. Liam hadn't yet heard the police approach, and if I was talking, that was one more thing he was listening to instead of their footsteps. "Why did you do it? I know you didn't kill her... not with your own hands. But *why*? That's what's bothered me this whole time."

Liam scoffed. "I'm not sure I can expect *you* to understand." His lip curled into a sneer. "You were married to the same loser she was going to walk down the aisle with. Can you imagine going from *me* to that guy? And I'm sorry if that sounds conceited, but what could a guy like that possibly offer her?"

I didn't have an answer for that.

"I think she was planning to call off the engagement," I said. Having heard this from multiple people, including Blaine, I was starting to piece it together. She might not have believed Keidi's story originally, but it had probably started Naomi thinking, made her start paying more attention to Blaine's behavior, and made her realize for herself what kind of a man he was.

Maybe she had just figured out it was smarter to cut and run before the big day.

It was pretty clear from Keidi's pleading and her attempts to hide Liam's fake poison that she was still devoted to—and probably in love with—her ex-boyfriend. You had to be crazy about someone to go to those lengths. So, the idea that Keidi and Blaine had been involved was obviously not true. Though I completely believed that he had tried to hit on her.

Blaine wasn't going to come out of this looking great, but at least he wasn't going to go to jail for murder.

"You got Howie to make her a special drink, didn't you? A little mixture of cider and peanut butter powder. That wouldn't have tasted very good. Was that the plan all along, that she would only try a little bit? Did you want her to die, or were you just planning to incapacitate her? Play the hero? And it just didn't go the way you thought it would."

I understood now that it didn't matter which drink Blaine had purchased for Naomi, because Liam had another plan in place with Howie the whole time. I was willing to bet Howie had brought along the cider and powder on his own, and just swapped the generic brown cups out before Naomi got her order.

Liam sniffed. "I tried to give her an epi-pen, but it was too late. So, I just left her there." He shook his head. "I had no idea it would happen that fast. She only had a sip."

"You know that saying, don't you, Liam?" Patsy asked as she nudged her weapon into his back. "Play stupid games, win stupid prizes? Well, Naomi paid for your stupid game with her life."

Liam didn't seem to notice or care that the police had the drop on him. He spun the weapon towards Howie, and screamed, "This is all his fault. You have no idea what you're doing. Tell them the truth, Mole Man." Spit was flying from his mouth, and with the weapon shaking in his hands he wasn't making a compelling argument for his own innocence.

On the floor, Howie mewled and covered his head with his arms.

"I wanted to save her!" Liam bellowed, and spun around, the gun fanning across the officers behind him.

Keidi still hadn't moved an inch.

Patsy moved fast, swiping her own hands down, still holding her weapon, and the added weight of the gun in her hands knocked the weapon out of his. It clattered onto the floor, and one of the uniformed officers hustled over to grab it.

Liam looked frantic, his eyes on the door behind them

like he thought he might be able to bolt, but Patsy shook her head.

"You can go easy, or you can go hard, but either way we're taking you out of here, you understand?"

I wondered, briefly, if Liam might choose to go the hard way, but after a moment of watching him vibrate with rage, the tension seemed to leave him all at once and he just sagged forward, before putting his hands on top of his head to await the handcuffs.

Beside me, Rich let out a long exhale and shook his limbs as if they had stiffened up on him while he'd been speaking.

"You're a nutcase," I said. "You should have let me try to zap him." This latter part I said low enough that only he and I could hear him.

"No offense to your zapping skills, babe, but they are... untested. And I think I did a pretty good job talking him down without magic."

I took his hand. "You did, but don't you ever scare me like that again."

Rich smiled at me, pulling me into his side and squeezing me close. "Likewise." Over my head, he seemed to catch sight of Keidi, and he stiffened, then pushed me back gently, turning me in her direction. "Is she okay?" He waved a hand in Keidi's direction, but she didn't so much as flinch.

"Oh, um..." I shrugged helplessly. "Like you said. Untested."

"You did that?"

"I think so. She looked like she might make a move for the gun, and I panicked." I wasn't sure if I knew how to undo it. My time-freeze magic just wore off on its own after a very short period, less than a minute or two. I'd never frozen just one person while everything else stayed in motion, so this was new territory for me. I walked up to Keidi and placed a hand on her shoulder. The moment I touched her, whatever spell I'd put on her lifted and she let out a shaky sigh. I thought at first she might freak out. I wasn't sure if she'd been able to see what was happening while she'd been frozen.

But no freakout came.

She saw Liam being led away by the police, while other uniformed officers handcuffed Howie. "Wh-what happened?" she stammered.

"I think you were in a little bit of shock from seeing the gun," I suggested. "That's super normal. The police stopped him before anyone got hurt."

Since everything around her pointed to this being the truth, she nodded mutely.

"I am going to need you to come with us, Miss Crandle," Patsy said, stepping in and taking over the conversation. "You might not have killed your friend, but we're going to have to talk to you about attempting to cover up Mr. Mulvaney's crimes."

There was something kind of poignant about Keidi going to such efforts to cover up Liam's crimes by hiding the fake bottle of arsenic, when he actually *had* been involved in poisoning Naomi. He must have given Howie access to the back areas during auditions and while Naomi was on stage; he had dosed her new drink with the peanut butter powder. Blaine—thinking he'd been the last person to touch the drinks—assumed he was responsible for the murder. Meanwhile, Liam had been in the dressing room to dose Naomi with an EpiPen. He must have ducked out right before Blaine and I arrived when he'd realized the pen hadn't worked.

Norman and Imogen had been right when they'd broken down all the reasons why someone would want to kill Naomi.

In the end, it had all been over simple, miserable jealousy.

And it had been pointless, too, since Naomi was planning to end things with Blaine anyway.

Liam could have just waited another week or two, and he might have been able to win her back.

Instead, Naomi was dead. Liam, Howie, and potentially Keidi would all be doing jail time, and Blaine had lost his fiancée.

Talk about a grim third-act turn.

Agatha Christie herself would have approved of such a twisted finale.

CHAPTER FORTY-ONE

It only took about two days for things in Raven Creek to return to status quo following the arrests. With Liam and Howie shipped off to the larger police station in Barneswood, and Keidi and Quinn allowed to return home with the promise that they might be required to return to Washington to help the investigation at any time, the town was once again quiet and drama-free.

Pierce had even accepted that he'd be on his own to teach us improv for the final week before the play, and we had adapted surprisingly well to taking lessons from only one person instead of four. In fact, the cast was turning into a well-oiled machine as we approached the big performance day.

People in Raven Creek loved gossip, but with it being so close to Halloween, they were far more invested in making sure the town looked as festive and spooky as possible. The uptick in tourist traffic and some unexpectedly lovely weather was keeping everyone too busy to think about Naomi's murder. Someone had left a memorial for her outside the community center, and it was overflowing with flowers, candles, cards, and teddy bears, but it seemed to be the only lingering part of the story that was left.

I, on the other hand, still had a mystery I needed to solve.

Honey looked up when I came through the door. She'd been hunched over-the-counter reading from a large book when I entered, and her face brightened when she saw me.

"Hey, hey co-star, how you doin'?" Her energy was always so wonderfully infectious I felt my shoulders relax and I smiled back.

"I think you might be a better actress than I originally thought," I said, my voice teasing.

"Oh?" She raised a brow, but there was a faint hint of s smirk on her lips, so I suspected she knew exactly what I was talking about. "What could you possibly mean by that?"

"You had me completely convinced that you had no idea what was happening when I started this little scavenger hunt."

Honey smiled. "In fairness, I didn't actually know what any of the other clues were. And I don't know what comes next. I just knew I had to wait until you showed up looking for the clue from *me*. Did you find the book?"

I pulled out the little volume on gardening, and Honey took one look at it and laughed. "Well, that makes a little more sense now, I suppose."

She reached under the counter and pulled out a wooden box of her own, though this one was intricately carved and made of some kind of wood I wasn't familiar with. She opened the top, and there was a lump of material inside, which she withdrew and placed in front of me on the counter.

"I would have told you sooner, but she made me swear

not to say anything until you figured it out yourself. And you can't just break promises to Eudora Black."

I nodded solemnly. "Tell me about it."

I unwrapped the little bundle on the counter, and inside there was a gold hand trowel and another letter.

Dear Phoebe,

Congratulations, my love, you've made it! The last clue.

This time around, you have everything you need. Just get some advice on growing the best tomatoes, and you'll find everything you've been looking for. And hopefully, along the way, you've found some people who are going to help make the next steps a little easier.

I can leave you lots of gifts, Phoebe, but never forget that friendship is the greatest gift of all. I hope the helpers you've met will become a little Raven Creek family for you, as you were for me.

Now onward to the last stop.

Much love,

Eudora

I handed Honey the note for her to read as I flipped through the little gardening book I'd picked up from the library. *Get some advice on growing the best tomatoes.* I knew the book couldn't have been a red herring; it had to have meant something.

Inside there was a chapter on vegetables. The book indicated that the best place to grow tomatoes was a sunny part of the garden where they could really soak in the light.

I also happened to know that there were several labelled garden stakes still in my garden from Eudora's last planting.

Snapping the book shut, I looked at Honey.

"You want to go solve a mystery?"

"Do you even need to ask?" She grabbed her coat from behind the desk and came around to my side to follow me.

Outside it was a glorious fall day. The sun was shining, the leaves were in their autumnal finery, and littered the ground like confetti, crunching under our feet as we walked.

It wasn't a hardship, enjoying the unseasonably warm weather and taking in the over-the-top decorations that filled almost every yard. There were full graveyards, one had ghoulish figures lined up like robed ghosts all looking out towards the street, another had opted for a massive inflatable pumpkin, and one at the end of the block had purchased not one but two of the twelve-foot skeletons and they appeared to be peering in through upstairs windows.

As cool as that looked, I couldn't have handled it myself. I still got freaked out by the Halloween wreath on my door, thinking it was someone creeping outside. The skeletons would have given me a heart attack.

My own yard was finally up to snuff thanks to some help from Rich. Carved pumpkins adorned the front steps, and ghosts peeked out from behind the pillars on the porch. In the yard itself, I had added several animatronic witches who cackled and mocked anyone who walked up the pathway. One even took off her own head while chuckling. They were my nod to the witchy history of the house.

Who said I didn't have a sense of humor?

The coven was set chattering by Honey and me walking by them, and she gave them all a little side-eye as we passed but didn't make any questions about my decorating choices.

In the backyard, the garden was dormant under a pile of leaves and grass cuttings, waiting to be revived in the new year, but that didn't stop us from heading for the back corner, where a little stake marked *Beefsteak* was poking out of the ground.

I used the gold trowel Honey had given me to start digging a hole. The soil was damp and cold under my knees even through the fabric of my jeans, and soon I had to dig my lightweight gloves out of my pocket. It was nice out, but it was also still October.

The cold weather had turned the ground hard, and it was a lot of effort to dig down. I knew whatever I was looking for had to be deeper in than a foot, otherwise I would have stumbled across it by accident while planting that summer. Even now as I built up a pile of cold, damp earth beside me, I wondered if I had misunderstood Eudora's clue, and I was just wasting my time digging in the completely wrong place.

Then, my trowel struck something solid.

I looked up at Honey, who must have heard the sound of it because she huddled closer, trying to peer into the hole without blocking my light.

I continued to dig, now clearing an area around the object, which appeared to be made of wood and was quite a bit larger than anything Eudora had left me up until this point. My heart was racing because I knew this wasn't just another clue; this was what she had been leading me to. Right in my backyard the whole time.

When I finally had the rectangular box dug loose, I handed the trowel to Honey, and with some unladylike huffing and puffing I managed to pry the box out of the dirt and set it on the ground beside me.

It was about eight inches thick, and at least two feet long and a foot and a half wide. It also weighed a good thirty pounds, though I wasn't sure how much of that was the box and how much was whatever was inside.

The box itself was in perfect condition, showing no signs of wear or decay from its time in the ground. Who knew how long ago it had been buried. The clues varied wildly in their age, from a book that Eudora must have taken out during one of my last summer visits, to items that were likely left behind only when she knew she was dying. This little hunt of hers had been a long time in the making, and I was dying to see what was inside the box.

The only problem was I didn't see a way to open it.

"*Aaargh*," I groaned, collapsing backwards onto my butt in the soil. "Another box with no keyhole? No nothing?" I lifted the box up slightly to look under it, then leaned over to look back in the hole, but there was no additional letter from Eudora. No more clues to help me solve this last puzzle.

"Did you ever open that first box you found?" Honey asked.

I shook my head. "No."

She raised an eyebrow at me, and I immediately understood what she was getting at. She helped me get to my feet, and I carried the heavy box back into the house, setting it on the kitchen table. Then I went to the living room, where the box I'd gotten at the start of this hunt was sitting on the coffee table, the key to Rich and my secret hideaway on top of it. I set the key aside and took only the box into the kitchen with me.

I placed the smaller box on top of the larger one, and there was immediately a change in pressure in the kitchen. The hairs on my arms stood on end, and Bob scurried out of the room, then stopped to watch us from the hallway, his eyes round and dark and his ears perked at attention.

I moved closer to Honey, and we watched as both of the items on the table started to glow a vibrant purple color, the light shimmering like it was filled with glitter, the way snow sometimes did under the right light.

Then, the glow faded, and the items were both just wooden boxes again. Except something had changed.

Now, there was a very clear lid on the smaller box.

I approached the table cautiously, and the air around it smelled distinctly of Eudora's old favorite perfume, a blend of cedar, sandalwood, and amber. I paused, just breathing it in for a moment, feeling like she had just been in the room.

When I lifted the lid from the box, there was another key nestled inside on velvet. This one had a gold hue to it and was surprisingly warm when I picked it up. It was also much smaller than the one that had taken Rich and me into the woods.

The moment the key was in my hand, a small lock appeared on the top of the larger wooden box. I heard Honey's sharp inhale behind me. I was glad she was here, because otherwise I might have convinced myself I was imagining all of this.

With my hand trembling ever so slightly, but still comforted by the scent of Eudora's perfume, I unlocked the larger box knowing whatever came next, it would be okay.

Once the lid was off the big box, I could see what it was Eudora had been leading me to all this time.

Of course, it was a book.

Only it was unlike any other book I'd ever seen. The cover was made of a dark, supple leather, and there was a braided gold cord wrapped around the thick volume. The cover had no title on it, but there were beautiful gold symbols etched into the leather, showing the moon in its various stages, and other lovely details.

"Phoebe, do you know what that is?" Honey asked, the pure delight evident in her tone.

"A book?"

She came to stand beside me and looked down at it reverently. For a moment, it looked like she wanted to touch it, but then she pulled her hand back. "That's Eudora's grimoire. Her Book of Shadows."

I gave her a funny look, not totally understanding her meaning.

"Phoebe, Eudora left you her spell book."

My eyes widened, and I gently pulled the book out of the box. The leather was soft under my fingertips, and as I untied the gold cord, I was able to open the book and see inside. There were pressed herbs and flowers tucked between the creamy pages, and everywhere I looked was Eudora's distinctive handwriting.

Underneath where the book had been was a note on the same paper as the rest. This one wasn't in an envelope.

It read.

Phoebe,

May it serve you well. My only regret was not teaching you myself.

This is the next best thing.

Much love,

Eudora

A tear slid down my cheek, and I brushed my fingers over the words on the note.

How many times had I wished she could have been here to help me? How often had I thought this whole process of becoming a witch would be easier if Eudora could only guide me through it?

It turned out she'd been trying the whole time.

I just had to know where to look.

CHAPTER FORTY-TWO

I was never going to be a natural actor.

I lacked the confidence and bravado a real actor needed to get on stage every night or go in front of a camera and pretend to be someone else.

But, as I stepped over Honey's "body" on the stage and said, "What a way to go," the audience laughed along with me. I might not be an actor, but I understood what drove them to it. The absolute thrill of the attention when it was all going in your favor. The way delivering the right line at the right time could turn your entire day into something magical.

And I was starting to know a little more about what *that* felt like too, now that I had Eudora's spell book.

I'd learned a few interesting things about it.

Like, for one, I was the only person who could see the writing inside. I'd shown it to both Honey and Rich, and to them it just looked like a blank book with some pressed flowers inside. They weren't able to see the precise spells, the words Eudora had used and had passed along to me.

It was just mine.

I had also started to make things happen intentionally, and not just because I had stumbled onto the right intention or the right wording. With Eudora's help, I had cast a comfort spell over Coco that had somehow convinced her I wasn't a demon coming to take her away.

She now spent most of her days sitting in the living room window, and when company came over, she knew she was safe in the house. She wasn't going to run up to greet anyone, but she no longer went into hiding for hours on end simply because someone came through the front door.

I'd cast a repair spell on the front porch and had spent an hour afterwards jumping up and down on the old boards like a kid splashing in puddles because they suddenly felt brand new under my feet.

And I'd been a little self-serving when I cast a memorization spell on myself so that I'd have the guts to take the stage for our presentation of *And Then There Were None* the night before Halloween.

That one had worked a little too well because I'd ended up memorizing the entire script and not just my own lines. But better to be *too* prepared rather than under-prepared.

As the moment drew near for me to take my curtain call and die, Pierce—who had taken the part of the narrator for the play—sent his demands into the audience.

"What's a cause of death?" he asked.

"Choking!" someone in the audience gleefully shouted.

"All right, choking!" Pierce announced. "And what's an object someone can choke on?"

"A marble!" came a small voice, clearly from a child.

"All righty. Our poor Vera's time is drawing to a close. She may soon be meeting her maker." The spotlight dimmed on Pierce, and the stage lights went up, showing me as I casually stepped over all the other members of the cast who had died over the course of the play. *And Then There Were None* was a rather death-heavy book as the name implied, but these deaths were incredibly varied. Norman had died by a paper cut from a flower catalog. Imogen met her maker when she tripped over a taxidermied giraffe leg. Honey had fallen off a cliff and was devoured by hungry sea lions.

Our night had been a live-action round of Mad Libs, and we were having the time of our lives. I stepped around Norman's body, and he gave me a little wink from the ground while he suppressed a chuckle.

There was a small table at center stage, and I made my way over to it, pretending to examine the surface. "I'm certain I can take a break from looking into this mystery to try one of these marvelous-looking candies," I announced to the audience. "I do wonder how they make them so perfectly round."

The child who had suggested marbles was clearly delighted because there was a loud giggle in the audience and their little voice stage-whispered to someone, "Those aren't candies!"

I resisted the urge to smile. On the floor, Honey's shoulders shook slightly from the effort to repress a laugh.

I popped the imaginary marble into my mouth, then after a moment, began to mimic choking, my hands going to my throat as I made grunting noises. I turned to the audience and pointed to my back, then mimed getting the Heimlich. They all laughed. I dropped to the floor in an empty space between Imogen and Norman and then passed away.

As deaths went, it was pretty grand.

. . .

When we had all taken our final bow to a standing ovation from our friends and fellow townspeople, we removed all our thick stage makeup and changed back into our street clothes, which felt like a sigh of relief but also a bit of a sad goodbye.

I hadn't wanted to be in the play at all to begin with, but it turned out that participating had been the highlight of my Halloween. The murder of Naomi Novak had been an unexpected and melancholy turn of events, but knowing her killers were behind bars had given us all the sense of closure we needed.

The show must go on, after all.

And I think she might have been proud of us for what we'd achieved.

Out in the lobby, there were plenty of people still milling around, making friendly conversation or waiting for a chance to get their coats. Standing right outside the staff doors, a tall, handsome man was leaning up against the wall, holding a bouquet of gorgeous pink roses.

When Rich spotted me, his face lit up, and he closed the short distance between us, wrapping his arms around me and planting a lingering kiss on my lips. My toes tingled much the same way they did whenever I knew a spell was working. Not because I'd cast a spell on Rich, but because this thing growing between us was its own kind of magic.

"You were amazing," he declared proudly, kissing my cheek. "Sensational." He kissed the tip of my nose.

"Compliments *and* kisses? A girl could get used to this." I beamed up at him.

"Gross," Imogen said as she passed by.

"Immie, don't be mean," Daphne scolded in her wake.

"They're cute."

Imogen looked back at me grinning. "Sure, but they make us single people feel bad." I knew she was just teasing. No one loved being single the way Imogen loved being single.

I smiled at Rich and gave him one last kiss before I disentangled myself from him, and took the bouquet he'd brought, smelling the sweet roses and marvelling again at how lucky I was that the way everything had changed only a year ago had brought so much joy into my life.

This was what Eudora had wanted for me when she hid those clues.

To find a home.

To find peace.

To find love.

And as my friends and I left the community center laughing and recalling the highlights from the play, heading towards Peach's for celebratory burgers, I knew I'd found everything she'd hoped for and more.

ACKNOWLEDGMENTS

I'm so happy to have you all back in Raven Creek for another adventure. This book was never a sure thing (as it goes in the publishing industry), but I feel like I could never stop writing about Phoebe and Bob, even with no publisher. I'm grateful to everyone who has decided to follow along on the ride.

You may have noticed there are no recipes in this book, and I'm sorry. I know quite a few people enjoy those additions to the text, but I just didn't have the time to put them together for this edition. I hope to bring them back in next year's Christmas entry, however, so fingers crossed that works out.

A huge thank you to my dear friend Rachel Terleski for being the first eyes on this book and helping me tweak it before it was fit for print.

For my incredible new cover artist Adrian DKC, WOW am I ever so glad fate brought you to me. I was terrified I wouldn't be able to get the same vibes for my cover as the work done by the wonderful Mary Ann Lasher on the first three covers (as she has retired!), but Adrian took my design requests and made something that really captures the heart and soul of these books. I'm eternally grateful.

As always, to my mother, for being a ceaseless champion for me and my writing. To my soul cat, Nutmeg, my very own Bob, and to my chubby calico Margot, on whom Coco is based.

And last, but never least, to the readers who keep all of this going. I could never have enough thank yous in the world to really show my appreciation. But here's a start: THANK YOU.

ABOUT THE AUTHOR

Gretchen Rue lives in the Canadian prairies, which affords her ample time to read during six months of winter. She plays cat mom to seven mostly indifferent fur children. When she isn't sipping tea and working on her next novel (as both Kate Wiley and Sierra Dean as well), she enjoys painting, hiking, and watching baseball.

- facebook.com/SierraDeanAuthor
- instagram.com/sierradeanauthor
- patreon.com/sierragretchenkate
- youtube.com/thecountryauthor

ALSO BY GRETCHEN RUE

THE LUCKY PIE MYSTERIES

A Pie to Die For

Live and Galette Die

THE WITCHES' BREW MYSTERIES

Steeped to Death

Death By a Thousand Sips

The Grim Steeper

Earl Grave Tea